Catherine Deveney is an award-winning features writer and reporter for the *Observer* and other newspapers. She lives in Rossshire, Scotland, with her family.

Dead Secret is her third novel.

ALSO BY CATHERINE DEVENEY

Ties that Bind
Kiss the Bullet

DEAD SECRET

DEAD SECRET

Catherine Deveney

First published in Great Britain in 2013 by Old Street Publishing Ltd
Trebinshun House, Brecon LD3 7PX
www.oldstreetpublishing.co.uk

ISBN 978-1-908699-24-4

10 9 8 7 6 5 4 3 2 1

A CIP catalogue record for this title is available from the British Library.

Typeset by JaM Typesetting

For Peter Black Rafferty.
A daughter's song.

FRIDAY

CHAPTER ONE

Growing up wasn't a process; it was a moment. It was the moment I watched Daddy die. Everything began to unravel then. Not slowly, like rows of neat knitting pulled stitch by stitch, but quickly, in great big, uneven chunks that left ragged, unruly holes.

Even now, I prefer to say that up until he died, we all lived a life full of secrets rather than a life full of lies. "Lie" is such an ugly word. And so deliberate. It wasn't like that.

I didn't want him to die, but I particularly didn't want him to die in that dingy little upstairs hall of his. You'd think it would be irrelevant, that only the dying would matter. But it was so enormous that all of it was important. It mattered that he was lying on that grubby, beige-coloured carpet; that there was a seeping stain on the wallpaper above his head. It mattered that the white paintwork was chipped and flaking, that it was pockmarked with spots of primrose yellow from a past life. It wasn't a good enough place for anyone to die, and certainly not Daddy, but then you don't get to choose, do you? None of us gets to choose. All he could do was die and all we could do was watch.

I used to think life was about options. Brown bread or white? Coffee or tea? Rent or buy; bus or car; sink or bloody swim. The minute he died I knew choice was just an illusion. All of it. Endless options making you feel in control and none of them worth

3

a damn. You can choose white walls over primrose yellow if you want. But you can't choose between living or dying. Once you know that – I mean *really* know it – you can't ever be a child again. And when Daddy died, for the first time I really knew.

Strange the way I keep calling him 'Daddy'. Like one of those upper-crust girls who has a father with a fat cheque book. But we never had any money and I never called him that when he was alive. I called him Da mostly, though I jokingly called him Pa for a bit after we watched an old episode of *The Waltons*. We hooted at the sickly, saccharine nonsense of it all. But I, who hooted loudest and with most derision, loved that family. I never stopped to work out why.

It was only after he died that I sometimes called him Daddy. Just in my head. Just in private. When he went, I grew up in the way I saw the world. But I became a little girl again in the way I saw him. Right from the start, I knew for certain that even when the funeral was over, even when things seemed to be normal again, they never, ever would be. You have to understand. He... it... this... all of it... was that important.

He was all Sarah and I had. My sister Sarah is four years younger than me and was only a few weeks old when Mother died. Sometimes, I think she's lucky that she never knew her at all. For me, trying to remember Mother is like a puzzle that never stops nagging. Sarah doesn't have to bother. Over the years I've tried and tried to bring the fuzzy images in my mind into sharper focus. I remember she had a coat with a fur collar that she wore in winter, and I remember being carried in her arms once and laying my cheek, stinging with cold, against the soft fur and falling asleep. The scent she wore was trapped in the fur and in later years I identified it as the scent of roses. Maybe

4

that's because I went into a chemist shop once and sniffed every perfume bottle in the shop, and when I sniffed one of those old-fashioned bottles of Yardley's English Roses, my stomach lurched. But that's all that's left of her. A vague scent. I can't remember her face and I can't remember her voice. There has to be a reason for that.

Mother had remarkable power for a dead woman. She was the source of all secrets in our house, the well from which they all sprang. Da never spoke willingly about her to Sarah or me. We knew better than to ask. But I couldn't help wondering whether he thought of her in his dying moments. Whether, as he lay there in a silent carousel of summer heat and pain and chipped-paint squalor, he remembered something else, a time when the carousel had spun to music. He loved her once. I know he loved her. Even knowing what I know now, I don't think he ever stopped.

❧

At first neither Sarah nor I realised that Da was suffering heart failure. He was weak and shivering with cold, despite the sticky heat of the warmest June in years, and there was sweat on his brow. He gripped the wall to get to the toilet to be sick, and on the way back, he lay down in the hall. Sarah and I tried to coax him back to bed, but though he wasn't a big man, he was solid. There was no way we could move him without help.

I don't think he knew where he was or what he was saying. There were a few words that didn't make sense, then he seemed to focus on us. "Love," he said, but his eyes said more. When I re-run that scene in my mind now, I always reply. I say, "I love you too, Da." But I didn't then. I was too busy trying to pretend it wasn't the end.

He retched weakly. I took off his pyjama top to sponge the thin sickness that trickled from the corners of his mouth; little rivulets that ran into the folds of his neck. I only minded because I knew he would. He was such a private man. So very, very private. But by then he was already slipping in and out of consciousness. The journey had started, or maybe ended, and he was past caring.

At first there had been all that panic. Get the sponge, feel his pulse, call the doctor. Stop it happening. *Take control.* I always feel compelled to push myself forward as the strong one. But I'm a bit of a fraud, as you'll find out. I may be the eldest, but Sarah is the natural coper in our family, not me. I dialled 999 but Sarah was shouting to me from the hall that he was getting worse and I ended up crying down the line in panic, unable to speak. "It's okay," said the operator, "just tell me where you are," and I sobbed the address into the mouthpiece. She didn't know what I was saying. Such a kind voice she had. Patient. Asking me to take my time, to repeat it slowly.

It was worse afterwards when the terrible stillness came, when we knew there was nothing else to do but watch. His chest was like a slowly deflating balloon, sinking lower and lower with each breath. His skin became paler, almost translucent, as his breathing dropped. My heart began to thump, beating faster and faster as his slowed, and for a moment I had the strangest sensation that his heartbeat was transferring into my body. Neither Sarah nor I spoke. I sat and cradled Da's head in my lap and listened as a distant siren came closer and closer.

Sarah let them in. Their feet thumped on the wooden stairs as they ran up and I could feel the vibration running through the floor. They were quite gentle as they moved me away from him, but firm too. While they worked on Da, Sarah and I sat on the stairs like two strangers in our own family's house. Like it was nothing to do with us, really.

I watched them through the bars of the banister and I wanted to ask them why they were bothering with all that equipment, why they were rushing and pushing and pulling. He was gone already. They might make his heart work like a mechanical pump but we knew he was gone. Well, I did. I seldom know what Sarah really thinks.

I could see the barrel shape of his chest and the little hairs inside his nostrils and the slackness under his chin. It looked like Da from the outside but whatever had been inside, whatever spark had fuelled the engine room of Joseph Connaghan, was gone. There seemed no point in all that commotion. It was only later that it felt important they had fought for him and shown that he mattered, that he wasn't just some random old man. That we hadn't given him up willingly.

They wouldn't let us travel in the ambulance. I kept asking why they wouldn't let me be with him but they said it was better not to. Maybe they thought I'd go crazy if I suddenly realised I was shut in the back with a corpse. A couple of women from further up the street had come out onto the pavement and were standing in their slippers, looking down the road at the ambulance. And Mr Curtis from next door, of course. Mr Curtis watches everything in Rosebank Street.

Mr Curtis shrinks when people talk to him. He looked like he wanted to run back inside and peep from behind his curtains when one of the ambulance men shouted to him to ask if he could drive Sarah and me to the hospital. Normally I'd have been angry. I don't like people organising me. But I didn't say a word. Neither Sarah nor I could have got behind the wheel. We did the whole journey in silence. "I hope..." he began, as he drew up outside the hospital, and then he looked at me and trailed off. I banged the door shut and ran inside, leaving Sarah to mumble thanks.

A nurse showed us into a waiting room at the hospital. Sarah stood silently. I walked up and down. The walls were pale yellow, the curtains lemon with streaks of lime green. They made me think of a soft drink we used to order on holiday abroad, a lemon soda that was served with rocks of ice and twists of lime in the glass. Funny what your mind thinks of in a crisis. Sarah's eyes followed me everywhere I went in that room.

The nurse came in, closing the door gently, precisely, behind her before speaking. The doctors were still working on Da but he wasn't responding. Did we want them to continue? Bloody stupid question. There was no point in saying yes because he was gone. If he wasn't, they wouldn't have asked. I suppose it was her way of giving us a decision, letting us take control of the goodbye, but by then I already knew there was no such thing as control.

I looked at Sarah. What exactly were we meant to say? No, it's all right nurse. It's only my old dad rasping out his last. Tell them to go and have their lunch break. I know I shouldn't have taken it out on her. She was nice, really. But who would want to say no to a question like that? And what was the point of saying yes? "How can we answer that?" I snapped at her. Sarah apologised for me. I hate it when she does that. She can be so bloody prissy sometimes, Sarah. "It's okay," said the nurse, and she touched my shoulder as she left.

8

He was laid on a white sheet when they finally took us to see him. There was another sheet over him but his chest was still bare and I wanted to pull the sheet up to keep him warm, protect him from the chill of death that rippled through the 85° heat. I could scarcely breathe in that heat, but I still looked at him and felt cold. Grey stone, snow dusted; ice-cracked earth and lichen stiff with frost. Extra socks. I wanted extra socks for my dead father's feet.

I think maybe the nurse had combed his hair because it was slicked down neatly where usually it had a mind of its own and sprouted in unruly bushes in different directions. His hair was white and without the animation of life he suddenly looked so old. He was sixty-eight but he could have been more. I wanted to tell the nurse that wasn't how he looked. It was only a month since I had left for a summer season in Brighton. He could have passed for ten years younger then. But nothing stays still for long. Everything in life shifts beneath your feet like moving grains of sand.

I don't know why it mattered to me that the nurse should know he didn't usually look that old. Except that as soon as he was gone, I felt the need to make him exist in people's minds, make them understand the real Da, make them love him as I loved him.

But then I looked at his face as I bent and kissed him one last time, a face so familiar and yet now so unfamiliar, and I felt the solid base of my life suddenly shift and tilt.

The real Da. I ran a finger gently down his cheek, still soft with the leftovers of life. There had been so many mysteries in our young lives, and while Da was alive it hadn't really mattered. Or so I'd thought. We had him. It was only now he was dead that

I began to wonder if I had ever known who the real Da was, if I had ever really known him at all.

Secrets. Secrets. Sss... secrets. They have lapped back and forth inside my brain for five years now, ever since Da died, constant as the tides. My understanding has ebbed and flowed steadily too; sometimes it reaches a peak, like the spring tide, when the water is high and deep and complete. I try to hold onto it, the completeness of that understanding, but somehow it always drifts away from me again, receding far out into the distance as if it will never return.

All I know for certain is that in the week from Da's death to his funeral, from kissing him in that hospital bed to laying him in the ground, everything changed. One week, yet it forced me to face a lifetime's denial. I had always known the secrets were there. Da's death just forced me to face them.

Growing up, Sarah and I were affected differently by the mysteries of our family life. For me, they produced a kind of emotional restlessness, an inability to stay still and relate to people. Maybe I was frightened that if I stopped, I'd have to think. Sarah was frightened to do anything *other* than think. I got itchy feet and my sister became trapped in a padded cage, craving safety and security. Sarah and I were always opposites.

It was only after Da died that I came to understand the wasted years. The flitting from job to job. The lack of direction. The men. I think I always wanted to know about Mother. On some subconscious level, perhaps I *did* know. Perhaps the awfulness of what happened was locked somewhere inside me, a kind of suppressed, intuitive knowledge. Either way – knowing or not knowing – I was always going to be rootless. If I wasn't certain where I came from, how could I know who I was? You can call it amateur psychology if you like, but these things matter. Of course they matter.

It wasn't until the truth came out that I finally learned how to stand still. And maybe how to stop being mouthy and lashing out at people I care about. So many milestones since then, important things that Da has missed. With him gone, nothing is ever complete now; nothing is ever truly whole. At the age of thirty-three I'm finally going to graduate and Da won't be there. And Sarah is about to have her first baby, the grandchild he'll never see. I miss him. We miss him. We've never stopped missing him.

It's five years this summer since he died. It's not his anniversary that has made me relive everything so intensely these last few weeks, made me write it all down. I am not a great one for anniversaries; it is the everyday absence that is most painful. No, it's hearing Shameena Khan's new recording of Puccini's arias. She sent it to me in the post with a note, explaining what I already knew: that the roots of this recording went back to Da's funeral. Every time I listen to it, I feel inspired to to write down a little more of what happened that summer.

It was so beautiful when she sang for Da. I think of rain after drought when I hear those opening notes, of water pattering gently on scorched earth. There is nothing quite like music for making part of your life come alive again and re-run like a movie reel in your head. The record you danced to the summer you were sixteen. The song you got married to, or made love to by candlelight. Or in the case of Puccini, the music you buried your father to.

Shameena Khan was – is – my best friend. We've known each other since we were schoolgirls. Nowadays everyone has heard of Shameena. But she was only just breaking through on the opera scene five years ago when she flew up from London to sing at Da's funeral. There can be few of us who were in the church who didn't guess what a career Shameena had before her. For me, nothing could ever compare to the way she sang that day. It was music to live for; music to die to; music to make the carousel turn.

Her singing fused with something in me that day, something that is gone now and will never come back in quite the same way. It was a moment where love, and pain, and insight, and beauty, suddenly melted into one another and bubbled up as something new, a brief, transient glimpse of infinity. Such a voice. The recording is wonderful too, really wonderful. I am listening to it now, as I write. It is as much my tool as the keyboard I type with.

The power of the music is pumping up the room, taking every inch of space and making it swell, the way a sponge swells in water. It fills me too, until there is nothing left of the present, nothing left of now. There is only yesterday. In every note I can see the summer Da died, and smell it, and touch it. More importantly, I can feel it. At times I even find myself slipping back into those strange, one-sided conversations I had with him in the week after he died.

I am right back there, caught in the strange, stifling heat of that June, while the music washes over me, a warm, rhythmic, rolling wave of memories.

CHAPTER TWO

Tinned chicken soup is death food. We eat it the day Da dies. I watch the pallid, glutinous mass of it slide reluctantly from the tin in a solid lump and squelch into the pot. Aunt Peggy is shaking the tin hysterically, like it's someone's shoulders. No soup for me, I tell her, but she carries on shaking. Peggy never takes no for an answer.

"Best to eat," she says briskly.

Christ.

Peggy is Da's younger sister, the closest Sarah and I ever got to a mother. I'll never forget the way she looked this morning as she walked with Uncle Charlie down that peppermint-green hospital corridor towards me. It made me think of a miniature doll Da gave me once. It was free on the cover of a magazine I had nagged him to buy me, a little Japanese doll with a white porcelain face, but when I unwrapped the cellophane, the doll's arm had fallen off. Peggy looked like that: face like chalk and broken.

I put my arms round her and neither of us said anything but I could feel the tremor that was invading her thin body as she clung to me in the corridor. She's the only one of Da's family left now. "Oh Becca..." she whispered finally. "To come home for this..." She moved out of my arms and grasped my hand. "At least you were here." I suppose it was just guilt that made me wonder if there was a reproach hidden somewhere in there. Home for Da's death, if not his life.

All those years away, working in one lousy hotel after another. I'd only got back again two days ago. Brighton this time. I'd lasted a month. It was supposed to be a receptionist's job but I'd ended up working the bar and cleaning rooms and waitressing. The day they told me the breakfast chef hadn't turned up, I told them Superwoman hadn't flown in either and left. I told Da I was coming home to see him before taking something else, probably in Bournemouth. We had talked about going for a holiday together in the autumn, maybe Italy. The brochures are still tucked down the side of my unpacked case. The case is lying open on the floor of my bedroom, the clothes strewn over the lid, straggling remnants of a life that no longer exists.

Peggy is fussing now. I watch her opening tins, and cutting bread, and clattering pots in the cupboard. She pulls out a battered old milk pan with a twisted lip that has a strip of congealed milk down one side where the pan once boiled over. She shakes her head. "Ah, Joseph Connaghan," she says tearfully, picking up a scourer from the sink and scrubbing vigorously. Charlie touches her shoulder and she momentarily lays her cheek on his arm. Peggy never lets Charlie do anything in the kitchen and I doubt he's ever ironed a shirt in his life. But she doesn't shoo him out today as she would normally. He stands beside her at the sink, buttering bread clumsily on a board. It's his way of talking.

He never says much, Charlie. He just seems to spend his life serenely absorbing all Peggy's high voltage. She generates all this crackling electricity that blasts out heat and Charlie simply sucks it all up and transforms it into light. He's Peggy's light bulb. Or maybe her fuse. She'd combust without Charlie.

I think Peggy would have liked children but it never happened. She had three surrogate kids instead: me, Sarah and Charlie. She helped Da bring Sarah and me up, and when we weren't around, she channelled everything into Charlie. She made him dinners that would feed a ravenous navvy and when he sat down to one of her mounded plates, we'd tease him and ask if it had been a hard day in the trenches. Charlie would just smile that slow smile and sprinkle salt liberally over the heap without looking at us. Actually, he was a nine-to-five man who worked as a clerk in an accountant's office.

Sarah is sticking close to Peggy as always, organising bowls and spoons.

Dutiful Sarah. Without saying anything, I go up to Da's room to phone Shameena, conscious that I am being furtive, sneaking away. For some reason I always tend to do things as if they are a secret, even when they aren't. That's one thing about the Connaghan family that you really need to know. We are a family who operates on secrets. We understand them. We are comfortable in their silence...

෨෯

The memories after he dies come unexpectedly, like sudden little puffs of smoke from the chimney of my brain. The first comes when I am halfway up the stairs. I am seven. It's late in the year because the fire is full blast and the wind is rattling the loose casement in the sitting room. I am sitting on Da's knee after my bath and the cheap, rough weave of his work trousers scratches against the skin of my bare legs as I wriggle in his lap. Sarah is playing with a bucket of bricks across the room.

Tentatively, I put my hands on his face. For a moment, my curiosity makes me see only his features, not my Da. Eyes. Nose. Mouth. I trace the contours, my soft fingers running down the stubble of his cheeks like velvet down an emery board. It feels

15

strange, rough. Where do they come from, those dark hairs? I wonder, prodding them, trying to push them back into the pores.

It is like the exploration of a blind person: the fingertips run over the mound of Da's cheeks, up over the bridge of his nose, halting at the hard, knobbly, uneven ridge in the middle. I press hard.

"Ouch!" says Da.

Startled out of my own little world, my eyes dart up to his. He is suddenly Da again and not just a series of features.

"Ouch," he repeats, rolling his eyes in mock agony.

I giggle and press again.

"OUCH!" he yells, and I laugh uproariously.

Sarah drops her bricks at the noise. She pads across the room and leans on Da's knee, trying unsuccessfully to swing her leg up.

"Up!" she demands, her soft blonde curls falling across her face. "Up!"

Da lifts her with one arm, moving me onto one knee and her onto the other, tucking each of us into the crook of an arm. We look at each other across the divide of his chest. In our house, there is always one between two. Always a half instead of a whole. Da kisses the tops of both our heads. Daddy's girls. He is all we have. Neither of us wants to share…

༺༻

His room feels cold with absence. Such stillness. The conversations in my head begin almost immediately. *Where are you, Da?* I find myself talking to him as if he will answer, searching as if it is impossible that he really is gone. I keep walking from room to room in his house. He is in every one of them and yet in none. In here, he is in the indentation of the pillow, where his head lay only this morning. He is in the discarded washing and the slippers that peep from under the bedclothes. His body lies in the hospital morgue now. But where has the rest of him gone?

"Rebecca!"

The voice startles me.

"Rebecca!"

It is Peggy.

"The soup's ready," she calls.

I look around the room before closing the door. It is dusty, stuffy, the air stale with trapped heat. But still it makes me shiver with his absence.

In the kitchen, Aunt Peggy pours the soup into the bowls with a ladle while the rest of us watch silently. My body and mind are in disagreement. My stomach is churningly empty, and yet I don't want to eat. It doesn't seem right. It's so cruel the way the world simply keeps on turning no matter what. On the way home from the hospital, the car had stopped at lights and there was a young couple standing on the pavement, framed in the car window. She was laughing, her arms wrapped around his waist, her eyes raised to his face teasingly. He bent down and kissed her lightly on the lips. It was bewildering this happiness, this intimacy. I wanted to bang on the window and tell them. Don't you know? Don't you understand? Da's DEAD.

I can see the steam rising from the soup bowls. Sarah catches my eye, and for once I know for sure we are thinking the same. She picks up her spoon and dips it in, stirring the soup round and round before sipping it. My spoon clanks on the side of the bowl and I swallow the mouthful whole, feeling it scald my windpipe, burning right down to my gut. The pain helps. Tinned chicken soup. I'll never eat it again as long as I live.

CHAPTER THREE

Shameena's voice on the recording pushes then pulls me, thrusting me back into the past as the music takes hold, yanking me forward again into the present at the end of each track. I yo-yo back and forward at first, until the spells in the past become longer, drawing me deeper and deeper into the memories and I am no longer conscious of one track ending and another beginning. Figures from the past make cameo appearances in my head, events and conversations, snatches of dialogue: disjointed, disparate, sometimes out of sequence…

Me… Shameena… that first time we spoke about my mother. Shameena was such an important part of my teenage years that she pops up in most of my memories of that time. We were at her house. No, that's not right. Mine. It was my house, in the bedroom Sarah and I shared. It was when we had those stupid pink floral duvet covers that Sarah insisted on. Shameena and I were lying flat on our backs on top of cabbage roses, one on each bed, giggling. Shameena often made me laugh. There was always a sense of mischief bubbling away beneath her demure façade. At times, her mischief bordered on recklessness and it was that quality that drew us together: we each recognised it in the other. I loved Shameena like a sister. And, if I'm honest, I loved her because of whose sister she was.

Shameena often came round after school because we had

the house to ourselves. I liked the company and she liked the freedom. That day, she was making me laugh with an impersonation of Sunday afternoon teas in the Khan household, when her mum and her mad aunties got together and did each other's hair, and criticised each other's dress sense, and tried to outdo one another with tales of their kids' sheer brilliance. The way Shameena switched between Urdu and her own Glaswegian accent was hilarious. When we finally stopped laughing and lay silently gazing up at the ceiling, she asked, "What did your mum die of, Becca?"

"Dunno."

Shameena stared at me.

"You don't know! How can you not know?"

"She died when I was four. Da never talks about her."

Shameena considered this for a moment.

"That's dead romantic, that," she said eventually.

"What, my mother snuffing it?"

"No! Of course not! Your dad not talking about it."

"Is it?"

"I bet he's got a broken heart and can't bring himself to talk about her."

"You reckon?"

"Yeah."

"So do I, actually," I said, so quietly that I'm not sure if she heard.

I remember watching Shameena as she sat up and took out a brush, dragging it through her thick, black, waist-length hair. Deftly, she twisted the hair into a rope, then piled it up on top of her head, looking at the result in the mirror.

"Haven't you ever asked about her?"

"Sometimes."

"And?"

I shrugged. "He doesn't say much."

Shameena twisted her head round to profile and sucked in her cheekbones, glancing sideways in the mirror. "Do you think it makes my face look thinner if I put my hair up like this?"

I considered her with ostentatious care, from every angle.

"Nope."

She laughed, let the rope fall, and threw a hair scrunchie at me.

"Why don't you go to the records office without him knowing and look up your mum?"

The suggestion had startled me.

"I couldn't do that," I said instinctively.

"Why not?"

"I just couldn't. It would be like… like… a betrayal." It was the first time I had articulated the subconscious feeling that to need a mother would be a slight to my father. It was almost as if I was adopted and felt a tug of loyalty between my birth parent and the person who brought me up. But both were my real parents, so why should Da and my mother be in competition? Why did there have to be a choice between them?

❧

Shameena was the first person I phoned the day my dad died. I still remember the sound of her voice when she heard mine: 'Oh *hi*, Rebecca!' I was unwilling to shatter the normality. How luxurious normality is. How underrated. I longed to be there with her, in a moment that was not filled with crisis. A moment that was not now.

You got back okay? Shameena said, and then rattled on without waiting for an answer. Why would she suspect anything was wrong? I had just spent two days with her on my way home from Brighton. Two more days I could have spent with Da if I'd known he was dying. The guilt after he goes is instant, insistent.

There was a strange hiatus before I said anything, before Shameena realised. It can only have lasted a minute… less… but for that short time, I simply surrendered to her voice, to the illusion of normality. She had been unlocking her front door when the phone rang and I could hear she was slightly breathless with running to pick up. My senses felt strangely heightened as I listened to her. I pictured her in the hall of her flat, kicking off her shoes, maybe putting her door keys down on the old mahogany wooden table she has. I could hear the clink of the keys, feel the honey smoothness of the polished wood beneath my fingers.

It was boiling in London, Shameena said. Still I said nothing. I imagined the scene outside her flat where I'd so recently been. A haze of heat and city dirt, the drone of London traffic and the steady flow of workers from local offices traipsing into the downstairs deli, leaving with paper bags and polystyrene cups, steam shooting through the lid vents. They would walk past the old man on the corner of Shameena's street, the one I had watched from her window as he stood with his cap out and his eyes down, leaning on a stick.

He is there every day and people don't see him any more. He is simply part of the landscape, to be negotiated like the seats of the pavement café, and the restaurant bins in the lane, and the metal grille which is awkward for stilettos. The man wears an old, torn overcoat, even in the heat. It hangs awkwardly on his scrawny frame, like a coat scrunched on a hook. His skin is grey, the colour of left-over porridge, and I looked at him two days ago and wondered how long he had left. Yet he outlived Da. How mysterious life is.

"Rebecca?"

She had realised. Stopped suddenly.

"Is everything okay?"

"No. No… Sorry."

"What's wrong? What's the matter? Is it my dad?"

I can hear the panic, her voice rising to a squeal. She thinks I am phoning to give her bad news about Khadim.

"No, Shameena, no," I say quickly. "No it's okay, it's not your dad." The tension lowers at the other end. "It's mine."

I was in Da's room as we talked, perched on the edge of his bed, and I looked at the bedside table with his book spread-eagled on it, open at the page he was never coming back to. Which was the very last word he had read? His reading glasses lay beside it, one leg flailing hopelessly in the air. A thin film of dust lined the concertina folds of the bedside lamp and I ran one finger through it.

There are not many people I have ever cried with, but Shameena is one. We have shared bereavement before. His name unmentioned, his presence towering between us.

Shameena offered to come to Glasgow straight away, but I told her to stay where she was until I knew the funeral arrangements. She had rehearsals to attend. I told her about that awful feeling I had when I looked at Da, the sudden fear that he had been essentially a stranger. The way his death flicked a switch. I wanted to know about him. I wanted to know about Mother. I wanted to know about me.

"Death steals people from you, Becca," Shameena said slowly.

"At least, you think it does at first. But gradually, they come back to you and you remember their living as well as their dying. And that will happen with your dad. He'll become himself again. He'll come back to you in time. "

"But I've lost my chance to find out the truth. He's gone."

"No, sometimes death is the catalyst… the start… It's amazing the things that come out when someone dies. Amazing," she repeated softly. "You wouldn't believe…" The line goes quiet. "There is one person," she continues eventually, "who will know almost as much as your dad did."

It took me a moment to understand. She meant Peggy.

"Rebecca," Shameena added hesitantly. "Your dad… he was lovely."

Her voice cracked and my eyes swelled up painfully with unshed tears until I felt they would burst. I nodded, as if she was in the room, as if she could see me.

"You'll sing at the funeral?" I asked.

"Of course."

Shameena has seen more of my dad than her own in recent years. She needs to sort it out. It is a long time since she and Khadim have spoken, a long, long time. But not as long as fo ever is going to be. For the first time, I understand what for ever really means.

CHAPTER FOUR

Da's body is to be moved from the hospital morgue to the funeral parlour.

"We need to make arrangements," says Sarah quietly. She gets up from her chair and fetches her handbag. In my handbag, everything lies in a heap at the bottom: loose coins; old bills; makeup in cracked containers; the scattered remains of a packet of chewing gum; a few shredded paper handkerchiefs. Sarah's bag is organised into neat compartments. Sarah is a lawyer.

She opens the flap and takes out a small notebook and a pen. Christ. I can't believe she is going to make a list for Da's funeral. Sarah catches my look and flushes slightly. Men always find that attractive about Sarah, that shy little blush. Cool efficiency on top but not too scary underneath. They don't like to be threatened, men, do they? Sarah is a very sweet person. I am not sweet.

We decide that Charlie and Sarah will go to the funeral parlour to speak to the undertaker, while Peggy and I ring round people to let them know. There aren't many. Da didn't socialise much and Peggy is the last of the immediate family, apart from one or two cousins. I will need to ring Khadim, Shameena's dad. Obviously, she won't be phoning home to tell him. When Sarah comes back, the two of us will go and speak to Father Riley, Pa's parish priest. I don't want to go. I have, as you will find out, a bit of a thing about priests.

❧

Another puff of smoke from the memory chimney. Smoke from a strange fire, this one, a fire that has slumbered for many years, neither fanning into flames nor quite dying into soot and ash. The childhood memory of a strange night when the police turned up here, on the doorstep of our council house in Govan. I had almost forgotten about it, but then it comes in my head so suddenly that I begin to wonder if I have made it up. Perhaps it is not real memory at all.

I cannot be more than five or six. It is a hot night, a bit like to-night. At least in my memory it is. Sarah is asleep in her cot and Da has insisted I go to bed too because I have school tomorrow. But I can't sleep. Earlier, we'd been out playing in Elder Park, and the evening sunshine is still streaming in the window, a river of light flowing steadily through a crack in the curtains.

There is steady breathing coming from Sarah's cot as I toss and turn, and eventually I get up to ask for a drink of water. I am hoping Da will sit me on his knee and tell me a story about his parents' home in Donegal. Like the one he told me about the tinkers who came to the door with a bundle in their arms and asked for a penny for the baby. Grandma said she had no pennies and they said they'd put a curse on her. She died young, so maybe they did.

But just as I come out of the bedroom, the doorbell rings. Da opens the door. I am watching from the upstairs hall, holding on to the banisters and peering through the slats. I think I remember the prickle of the carpet on my knees where I am kneeling, but how can I be sure? Did I really feel the prickle of the carpet, or have I just made that bit up? And if I made that little detail up, how do I know which other bits I made up? How much can we rely on memory?

Da has his back to me and doesn't spot me, but as the door swings open I see the two policemen in uniform standing on the mat. They seem alien, the door like a barrier between my world and theirs. I want Da to close it, to keep the policemen on their side, in their world.

"What do you want now?" he says, and I remember thinking that Daddy must feel as I do because he doesn't sound very friendly. He leans his head momentarily on the door. "When is this going to stop?" he asks, his voice low and fervent.

One of them murmurs something I can't hear and then the other says, "It would be better if we could come in." This second one looks at Da as if he doesn't like him. Da says nothing, but he stands back from the door and opens it wider, watching silently as they file past him. Then he follows them into the sitting room and shuts the door. The paint on the back of the door is beginning to peel, separating like the skin of a partially peeled orange.

I sit at the top of the landing, looking down the stairwell into the hall below. Why do the police want to talk to my daddy? They frighten me with their hats and their uniforms and their strangeness. I resolve to keep an eye on that door, watch for it opening. Perhaps if I stare hard enough, I will actually see the paint move as it peels. There must be a precise moment when it curls back from the door. Like the moment blades of grass push further through the earth as it grows. My forehead rests against the slats of the banisters until the sharp edges begin to hurt. It is when my eyes are closing that the door handle suddenly turns, making me start. I move back slightly. I can hear murmuring and then the door swings open.

"We'll say goodnight then, Mr Connaghan," one of the policemen says.

Da doesn't smile. "So I won't be hearing from you again?" he asks.

One of them – the surly one – shrugs, but the other says, "Highly unlikely, Mr Connaghan. Unless, of course, we get any new evidence."

Da nods and opens the door. He looks perfectly normal as he sees them off, but when he shuts the door, I see him lean back against it. His head tips back and it seems as if his knees are giving way under him. His shoulders heave as if he is crying. I have never seen him cry. It frightens me and I run back to bed.

He never mentions it in the morning, though when Auntie Peggy comes to take me to school the two of them have a whispered discussion that becomes quite heated. I don't hear most of it but at the end Peggy starts raising her voice and saying, "Look, just accept that's the end of it," and he says, "Peggy, there will never be an end to it." I ask Peggy what they were talking about when we walk to school but she just says, "Nothing for you to worry about," and we stop at the shop to buy crisps for playtime.

That day we have plasticine at school. Blue plasticine that we roll into big meaty sausages before singing, "Five fat sausages sizzling in a pan." Miss Stewart says the plasticine should be brown for sausages, but I prefer blue. I remember it is the day we have plasticine at school because that night, I really want to ask Da about the policemen, but I end up telling him about the blue sausages instead.

When I think back to those first years in Glasgow, I remember uneasiness. Not unhappiness, but uneasiness. Whispered conversations between Da and Peggy. An almost instinctive understanding as children that there are things we mustn't ask about, things we mustn't talk about. An awareness that the Connaghan family is a little different from other families. Maybe that's why, later, we got on so well with Shameena's family, the Khans. They were different too. Different for different reasons, but we pulled together in our shared sense of being outsiders.

In the days after Da died, my memory frustrated me. It sent out these puffs of smoke, like a series of signals that I could not interpret. What message was my subconscious trying to give me? Try as I might, I could not remember Mother dying. There was no trauma there to be discovered. Not like there was now for Da. I couldn't remember her being ill. I couldn't remember being told she was dead. I just remembered knowing that she was gone.

We moved to Glasgow from the Highlands after she died, and in my head, there is only our city home: the cramped two-bedroom maisonette in Rosebank Street. It's a street that never seems to house any adults, only rangy, mean-looking dogs, and packs of straggly-haired kids. Down one end there was an enclosure for the wheelie bins, and up the other, the street's status symbol: Mr Curtis's beige Skoda. In later years, Da's battered Fiesta sat alongside, and the drug dealer at number 56 got a white Ford Capri.

Nothing of the Highlands – no matter how hard I try. After Da dies, the memory chimney belches out smoke in its own shape, in its own time. However hard I try, I seem unable either to stoke the fires or dampen them down. The earliest memory I have is being lost in a huge department store in Argyle Street, not long after we arrived in the city. It was a few weeks before my fifth birthday and I had to start school soon. Da and I had gone for my uniform. I don't know where Sarah was. Peggy probably had her. Looking back, I don't know how Da would have managed without Peggy. Anyway, it was a rare treat because it was just me and Da.

I was standing next to him at a counter when I saw a whole display of Matey bubble bath close by. The bottles were like little sailors and I started to finger them, thinking how much I'd like one, but knowing without asking that there wouldn't be any money for it. I shifted them all on the display, arranging them by coloured tops, creating little groups of friends. Out of the corner of my eye, I kept watch on Da's black jacket. But when I looked up, I realised with a jolt of panic that his black jacket had been replaced; there was a woman in the black jacket I thought was his.

I ran then, through the store. There was a doorman in a white coat who tried to take my hand but I screamed and screamed for Da. That's how I know that I understood Mother was gone. I never screamed for her.

Da came running at the noise, cheeks pink with embarrassment, and I threw my arms round him and sobbed into his legs. He held me close, then, and said that I must never be afraid if I found myself alone. He would be somewhere close by because people don't just disappear. I knew that wasn't true but I was comforted by it anyway. "I'll never leave you," he had murmured, stroking my head. "I am always near."

Afterwards, when he'd calmed me, he took me to the sweetie shop and bought a whole bag just for me. Lemon toffee bonbons, dusted with pale yellow icing sugar that I sucked from my fingers. "Do I have to share with Sarah?" I asked immediately, but Da shook his head. The bag made my pocket bulge, and I kept one hand in Da's and one hand in the open bag, sniffing back the shuddering remnants of tears and then popping the sweets into my mouth.

In my whole life, I only remember Da mentioning Mother off his own bat once. It was the day we went to Charlie and Peggy's silver wedding anniversary party. I was nineteen. I wore a close-fitting green dress, with thin, delicate straps and an embroidered bodice. I bought it from a catalogue and paid it up over ten weeks at three pounds a week. I don't wear dresses much, but as soon as I saw that dress I knew it had my name on it. I have never been able to throw it out, though it has long gone out of style. When I slipped it on, it was like slipping on another personality. I felt more alive, more vibrant, more confident.

Da certainly thought I looked different. I remember coming in the room and seeing a look of shock that blew across his face and disappeared again like a passing breeze.

"You look so like her," he said, almost to himself. His face had turned pale.

I said, "Who?" and he said, "Your mother."

It was such a shock to even hear him use the word "mother" and my heart skipped a beat.

"What was she like?" I said quickly, so, so quickly before the moment got swallowed up.

"She was… she was…" he said, and for one awful second I thought he was going to cry because he gave a little gasp, like a stifled hiccup.

"Am I really like her?" I asked, and he said, "On the outside anyway." Then he turned so that I couldn't see his face, and he put his shoes on, and I knew that was the end.

"Come on," he said, before I could ask anything else. "You know what Peggy will be like if we're late."

Years later, when we were sitting the two of us with a bottle of wine between us, laughing about stuff me and Sarah had got up to, I brought Mother up and said I wondered what she would make of us now. Da didn't get angry exactly, but the atmosphere in the room changed.

"Why have you never spoken about her?" I asked, because I had drunk two thirds of the bottle to his one third. My heart beat a little faster even hearing the question out in the open. I'd waited all my life to ask it.

"Lets not talk about that, Becca," Da said, his smile fixed. "Let's not spoil tonight with sad memories."

I shrugged and got up to make coffee and by the time I came back, Da had switched on the television and we sat in silence, watching a late-night comedian who didn't make either of us laugh.

And now he's not here. In my head, I hear his voice in my ear, just as it was when I cried into his coat as a lost child. "People don't just disappear, Becca. I am always near." But he did, didn't he? He did disappear. Maybe that's why there was such a sense of betrayal, of abandonment. Parents spend their lives creating security for their children, reassuring them that the world is safe. Their death is the ultimate admission that they were lying all along.

CHAPTER FIVE

Shameena's CD has finished and gone right back to track one but I cannot move to change it. I don't want to be part of what's happening now in this room. When the CD arrived I was reluctant to listen and braced myself against the memories. But gradually I find myself wanting to go back to that time as deeply as I can and relive it. It's almost like finding an old coat from years ago, and trying it on and thinking, *yes*, that's what it was like. It is dangerous, I suppose, but I don't want just to 'remember'. It's not enough. I want to experience it again so that this time, I can make sense of it.

The thing about pain is that it's just too powerful; you have to anaesthetise yourself or how could you live with it? Five years on, what I am telling you has to be a diluted version: one part pain to two parts deliberate amnesia. Maybe if I had written this in the months after Da died, my memory would not have had as much time to protect me. But an account back then, when it was all so raw, would have lacked insight or overview. It's as if everything has been locked away in a box until I was strong enough to examine it. Until now. Until I heard that music again.

It's the conversations with Da in that first week after he died that take me back into the past, into my old 'present', most vividly. They play relentlessly in my head and I can either be an observer to them, listening in on my old self, or if I let go, I

32

slip back into them in as if I am having them all over again. Perhaps you will think that conversations with the dead are a sign of insanity; certainly those days and weeks seemed tinged with madness. But they don't scare me now because I see them for what they were. They were both holding on and letting go… trying to find a piece of him that still existed that would make it possible to give the rest of him up. I stood in his room, listening for a sound in the silence, a whispered answer to my questions, knowing that you can't instantly stop talking to someone just because they die…

☙

Da. Da where are you? I can smell you. Not the artificial smell of soap and aftershave, but the smell of you. The you-ness of you. It drifts beneath my nostrils, faint and hard to define, like a ghost smell. Is scent the last part of you to leave the world? Or are you actually here in the room with me?

The thought sends a sudden rush of blood through me, a rush of excitement, but of fear, too. I honestly don't know which is greater: my longing or my fear. The longing eats me greedily, like a cancer. But the terrifying thought of seeing a spirit makes me nauseous and shivery, even on a humid June night. The truth is, I am frightened of being in a dead man's room. Even your room. I want to see you again. But I want the old you, not the new you. Your old warmth is chilled by a new vocabulary. Ghost. Being. Soul. Spirit. I don't want your spirit. I want your humanity. I don't want to feel your presence. I want to feel the softness of your jumper on my face, the way I did when you hugged me to your chest. Great, crushing bear hugs. "Ah, love," you used to say when I came back home, wrapping your arms round me and almost swinging me off my feet.

33

Over there, where the light of the street lamps is streaming through the chink in the curtains, is the chair where you used to toss your clothes at night. I can see a shirt and a pair of trousers. They hang casually, as if you are coming back soon to wear them. You didn't know when you took those trousers off that you would never step in them again. I'm glad you didn't know. There's only one thing worse than your going, and that's the thought that you went in fear.

Your death has left me with so many questions.

I felt sorry for Peggy today as I watched her washing dishes, her thin frame and rounded shoulders stooped over the sink, the kink of a steel-wool perm curling up over her collar. I had the feeling she was crying into the washing-up bowl. I knew it wasn't the time to corner her but I couldn't help myself. I suppose I have a certain ruthlessness at times, but I prefer to think of it as focus. Determination.

I don't really know what I expected when I asked her if there was anyone on mother's side that I should contact about your funeral. But I didn't expect all that hostility. Not the burning anger that made her shout that since not one of mother's family had been in your house while you were alive, they were hardly likely to turn up now you were dead.

Why was she so angry? She kept shouting and I ended up yelling back. I am ashamed of that now. But all that stuff about grief pulling people together is rubbish. Grief makes people cut each other up.

"Didn't he love my mother?" I demanded. "Oh he loved her all right!" She spat those words out and they seemed to sizzle up at me like hot fat. I almost physically shrank back from her they were so ferocious. "He loved her like a man possessed. He was blind." Da,

34

what did that mean? I kept asking her, wouldn't let it drop. "Just leave it!" she kept shouting. But I couldn't. Did she not love him back? I kept asking. Charlie came to see what was going on, just as Peggy said, "Love him? She bloody well destroyed him."

I stared at her. She was pale with anger, and a deeper distress had eaten up the familiarity of the face I know so well. She untied the apron round her waist and walked past me, the small, dumpy heels of her brown court shoes clicking stickily on the linoleum floor. There was a damp patch beside the sink where the water had splashed over the edge. Charlie just looked at me and I lifted a cloth and wiped it mechanically.

When Sarah came back, she tried to persuade me to go with them and said I couldn't stay here on my own, that she would have to stay with me. In the end I had to say to her, "Look Sarah, will you just piss off!" She flushed that way Sarah does, and went and got her coat. I'm sorry I hurt her, but I had to be here on my own with you. I couldn't talk to you with anyone else around. You understand, don't you? You understand my need to know?

The strange thing is that when it got dark, I suddenly got frightened. I didn't want to come in here to your room. And yet, if you really will come back, then surely you will come here to this house and this room.

I wore one of your jumpers tonight. There was a pile of clean ones in your chest of drawers but I didn't want a clean one. I wanted one that still had you in it. I buried my face in it and inhaled, like an asthmatic inhaling oxygen. It drowned me, but I wanted to drown in you. Already I am frightened of forgetting. Your face is fading already. How many hours is it since you left? Fifteen maybe. Not even a day and already I find it hard to imagine the exact shade of your eyes. I have looked at them for nearly thirty years

*but already I am confused. Were they more grey than blue? Or
more blue than grey?*

*There are little bits of you being stolen all the time, as each hour
passes. Your exact eye colour has gone today, and maybe tomorrow it will be the exact shape of your nose. Perhaps it will be like
a picture where a little bit more gets rubbed out each day, until
there is nothing left but an imprint. I think it would be easier if it
was just the way you looked that was disappearing, but what was
inside you is disappearing too. Can I trust you? Can I believe in
you? I keep thinking of your promise to me as a child. Do not be
afraid, you said. I am always near you...*

No, as I say, you can't stop talking to someone just because
they die on you.

SATURDAY

CHAPTER ONE

Saturday, the day after Da dies, dawns warm and sticky: a hazy, pearly white June light that promises more heat as the day wears on. The night has been sultry and oppressive, the temperature never dropping, a stew of heat simmering at a steady bubble. I twist and turn restlessly all night and wake feeling drained, with the sheet kicked down at my feet. There is a second, a tiny brief second of hope, like a flaring match, when I open my eyes and think it is just another day. And then consciousness sweeps over me and I remember. The day dies instantly, the flame of hope a thin, useless, trail of smoke from a blackened, fizzled-out match-head.

It is that hopelessness rather than tiredness that makes my eyes close again; there is nothing left to wake for. For a while, I drift in a twilight world, where consciousness is heavy with the shadows of sleep. Not fully sleeping, not fully waking. Then, slowly, lured into dreams, the slow-motion fall from consciousness, like the fall from dusk to darkness.

Coloured dreams, ferocious dreams, monstrous in their vividness. Da is there, walking in the street ahead of me and I run to catch him. But though his pace never changes, I can't reach him, no matter how hard I run. When I am sweating and out of breath, the ground between us suddenly disappears and I run smack into his back, and he turns so that I am staring into his face. Or what is left of his face.

It is Da all right, but there are great chunks missing: gouged black holes in his cheek and a red, bloodied socket where his right eye should be. And then the face turns on his shoulders like a revolving door, metamorphosing into Tariq.

Da, Tariq. Da. Tariq.

Tariq is Shameena's brother. I got to know them both through Da when he worked on the buses beside their father, Khadim. Over the years, our families became so close that Shameena and I were like blood sisters, close in a way that Sarah and I were never able to be. But Tariq was not like a brother. No, Tariq was never like a brother.

There is a glaze of sweat on my back when I wake again. Thumping heart, a rush of noise in my head like a train in a tunnel. I jump from the bed in a panic, stumbling against the chest of drawers, smashing my hip bone painfully against the drawer handle. Tariq. Da.

Outside the open window, the squeal of kids now, banging sticks on the army of wheelie bins that stand sentinel at the top end of the road. A car engine cuts and dies. Sarah, I think, peeping round the edge of the curtain. Damn it. Des is with her. Pompous, pin-suited, lawyer Des, with his ice-cream-cone hair and shiny shoes.

Da and I had a bet on about Sarah and Des. Da said she'd marry him. He said Sarah needed looking after, that she craved someone solid and dependable like Des.

And minted, of course, I had said. Minted helps. Da had smiled at me, a wry, disapproving smile, and said it was just that Sarah needed security. Security?

Bloody imprisonment, I said. Sarah and I might not always see eye to eye, but I wouldn't wish Des on her. I wouldn't wish

Des on anyone. I said I hoped she got smart, cleaned what she could out of Des's fat bank account, before running off on a world tour with a long-haired rocker from a heavy metal band. It's the sort of flippant, immature, stupid stuff I used to come out with sometimes. It didn't mean anything, really. Da just rolled his eyes.

"When are you going to grow up?" he said.

Des has his own law practice, which is the kind of thing that impresses Sarah. "I suppose he's good looking enough in an almost-forty kind of way," I told her at the time, and Sarah said in her tight little voice, "He's thirty-four, Becca." "Split hairs if you want, I said, but he acts forty and you are only twenty-four, for God's sake." Des gives occasional lectures at the university and majors in them in his everyday conversation if you let him. Which I don't. When I was going off on another seasonal job once, he had the nerve to tell me Sarah was worried about me taking all these temporary posts and didn't I think a smart girl like me could do better for myself? I said considering how well a dumb boy like him had done, I probably could. Sarah didn't talk to me for two days.

She met Des at the university when he gave a guest lecture to her year and she stayed behind to ask 'Sir' some questions. After they had been seeing each other for a while, she came home once all sparkly-eyed and in love and said guess what, her Des was thinking of taking his PhD. She's a bit of an intellectual snob, Sarah. "What in?" I said. "Smugness?"

They are in the sitting room when I come downstairs. Des gets up and kisses me stiffly.

"I'm really sorry, Rebecca, about your dad."

"Yeah," I say. "Thanks."

I look at Sarah. Her eyes are red-rimmed and she looks tired. "Want a coffee?"

"I'll make it," she says and goes out, leaving me with Des and an awkward silence.

"It's good you got back home in time, Rebecca, you know, that you got the chance to be with him at the end," he says finally.

"Yeah."

"Lucky."

"Mmmm."

"Well, not lucky, but… well… you know what I mean… fate."

"Yeah."

We lapse into silence. Des crosses his legs.

"Job wasn't working out then?"

"Nah."

I stare out of the window at Mr Curtis next door, walking up the path with his little Yorkshire terrier. Mr Curtis doesn't look unlike his pet. Such a gallus walk.

Kind of mincing and a bit nebby. But he was kind when we came back from hospital, even knocked on the door and asked if there was anything he could get for us. Millie from number 38, on the other hand, who knows us much better, was embarrassed and pretended not to see me when I went round to Mohammed's for milk. People surprise you.

I can't be bothered being polite to Des. In the circumstances, I don't think I should be expected to try.

"I'll just give Sarah a hand," I say, and leave the room.

Sarah doesn't even look up when I come into the kitchen. I stand beside her as she pours the water into mugs. "I'm sorry about last night. About telling you to piss off. I didn't mean it. I was just… you know…"

She flushes.

"It's okay."

Her hand is trembling as she puts the sugar in and I reach out and steady her. The gesture makes her break. She puts the sugar bowl down and clings to me and the two of us sob like babies, more united in sorrow than we ever were in joy. Daddy's girls. I wipe the tears from her face with my hand.

"We'd better go see Father Riley today and tell him what we've organised with the undertaker," I say quietly. "Make sure he can do the mass."

She nods. "We'll go together?"

"Yes," I say, raising my eyes and making a face.

She smiles. She knows I am making an effort if I am willing to go talk hymns and flowers with Father Riley. "Do you want to get changed first?" she asks, looking at my tight, frayed jeans, and I feel the old, familiar flash of irritation. Sarah looks like she is going for a day at the office in a navy trouser suit and pale pink blouse. Just looking at her always makes me want to tousle my hair and put a rip in my shirt.

"It's okay," I say, more drily than I mean to. "You look prim enough for both of us."

CHAPTER TWO

The truth about Sarah. Sarah is my sister and I should tell you that I love her. And I do. But it is not quite that simple. The complications of our relationship drove what happened after Da died, affected how I reacted to events. I was never sure if that was because I wanted to protect her or destroy her. Even now, years later, there is a doubt in my mind.

The fact is that back then, I loved Sarah and I hated her, sometimes at the same time. I always felt hemmed in by her, maybe because I had to look after her when we were small. The thing about death is that it strips away veneers, makes you get right down to the base coat. But that summer, we hadn't removed all our layers of varnish yet, me and Sarah. It was too early to know the colour of the bottom layer.

We're not the first, of course. Not the first siblings to feel icy shards of resentment swirling round the warm blood of love in our veins. I suppose if we're being honest, I'd have to say that I'm more to blame than Sarah. When she was small, she was like one of those devoted little puppies, but I kicked her often enough for her to learn how to nip.

Da insisted we stick together. Everywhere I went, Sarah went. There was no escape. Sometimes after tea, I'd sneak to the door and open it, then shout quickly, "I'm just off to the park." I'd try and belt out the door, slamming it behind me before he could answer. Most times it didn't work.

"Take Sarah with you," he'd shout, and Sarah would come running to the hall, cheeks bulging with the last of her dinner.

"Hurry up and get your shoes on, stupid, or I'll belt you one," I'd hiss venomously.

She'd sit down on the bottom step in the hall and buckle her shoes silently, glancing up at me watchfully through a curtain of straw-coloured hair. She knew that I would walk far too quickly for her, that she would be hauled roughly all the way to the park, but it was enough to be with me.

Past Mohammed's Asian grocery shop on the corner of Rosebank Street, the stacks of wooden fruit boxes piled higgledy-piggledy on the pavement outside: a pile of speckled bananas; some loose mushrooms, dark earth still clinging to the milky stalks; a few wizened red peppers. Past the glossy black-painted exterior of the Blacksmith's Arms. "Come *on*, Sarah," and I'd yank her hand to pass the pub quickly, the whiff of stale beer lurching through the swing doors as customers walked in, or staggered out. Sarah would say nothing but her hair would fall over her face and her legs would work overtime to keep up. As the years went on, I think Sarah took a quiet satisfaction in being an ever-present thorn in my side. Sarah has always done everything, even vengeance, quietly.

The only time I was nice to her was when someone else wasn't. She was a pain in the butt but she was *my* pain in the butt. In the park once, Davie Richardson from number 42 was tormenting her. He had her pinned against the green iron railings of the swing-park and was getting his dog to jump up on her. It was a vicious looking Alsatian called Satan, which tells you everything you need to know about Davie. Sarah squealed with fear and

Satan got more and more overexcited. Every time Sarah tried to move from the railings, Davie would move forward and give the dog a bit more leash so that she had to jump back. She ended up screaming at the top of her voice, drumming her feet on the ground in a frantic dance of terror.

I could hear her screams from the other side of the park and came running. Davie and his pals were doubled up with laughter.

"Up!" shouted Davie, and the dog leapt.

I didn't bother warning Davie. I just drew back my foot and kicked him in the backside as hard as I could.

"Oi!" he shouted, dropping Satan's lead and pivoting round to grab my wrists. "Get your ugly mutt off her," I yelled.

A low growl rumbled from deep inside Satan and he crouched low, preparing to leap. One of Davie's friends grabbed the lead. Davie's hold was tightening round my arms as I struggled against him. I lifted my heel and stamped it so hard on his foot he howled. His pals jeered, a mixture of laughter and derision.

"Come on, Davie boy, for God's sake!"

"She's only a bloody girl!"

But Davie had dropped my arms with the pain and I followed through, elbowing him right in the stomach. I wasn't one for the Queensberry rules. As he doubled up, I grabbed Sarah's hand. Satan was growling, straining at the leash. "Mad bitch," Davie yelled as we walked away. "Bloody *lesbian*!" I didn't look back but stuck my two fingers up in the air above my head and walked on. Sarah caught the gesture and gasped.

"You tell Da and I'll batter you too," I warned.

She said nothing, but gripped my hand tight and wouldn't let go all the way home. For once I let her. Back past Blacksmith's, past Mohammed's, her small hand warm and sticky in mine.

46

"Want a couple of apples, Becca?" Mohammed shouted as we went past. He came and leant on the doorway.

"This year's or last's?" I shouted over my shoulder.

"Last's!"

"No ta."

But most of the time, it was like Sarah and I were fighting on opposite sides. If I had to single out the biggest sign that on some level Sarah and I missed having a mother, it was in the way we competed with each other for Da's love. A few weeks before my tenth birthday, Da told me he was making me a surprise present. He was always so clever with his hands. Our house was small, but he would take his tools into his bedroom and locked himself away for hours at a time. I stood outside and listened to the banging of hammers and nails, and the rhythmic grating of the saw, and the high-pitched screech of his electric drill, until I was feverish with the excitement of it all.

"What is it, Da?" I yelled, jumping furiously outside the door of his room. I had my outdoor shoes on and the floor vibrated ominously. "What is it, Da?"

He laughed then. I heard him behind the door and he shouted, "Wait and see! You'll know soon enough…"

But oh I was sick with the wait and the excitement. He would come home with mysterious packages and go straight to his room with them. And then the day itself came. I'll never forget it. He told me to wait outside his bedroom until he got it all ready, but Peggy had to keep stopping me trying to push the door open.

"Wait until he says, Becca," she laughed, hugging me while I waited.

"Okay," Da shouted, and I pushed the door open and gasped. A doll's house. A doll's house with a roof that lifted right up and

47

a front that opened out to reveal two storeys with a long attic room on top. It had metal doors and windows with the tiniest of fragile handles. I thought it was the poshest house in the world, a film star's house, because it had a balcony for sunbathing and a garage with a little car beneath the house.

"Happy birthday, Becca," Da said.

He couldn't afford much in the way of furniture because that was shop-bought, but it had a little miniature plastic table, a few chairs. It looked a bit empty, but God, I didn't care.

"We'll add to it," he said gruffly, motioning at the furniture, and I jumped on the spot and clapped my hands. He smiled then.

"Like it, Becca? Do you like it?" he said eagerly, and I didn't answer. I just ran to him and threw my arms round his waist. It was the best birthday of my life. There have been men who have given me expensive presents since, but no present has ever come close to that doll's house. Except maybe a little bracelet of cheap beads Tariq gave me when I was sixteen.

We bent down, the two of us, and Da pointed out the little flight of stairs I hadn't noticed, and I kept spotting other things I hadn't seen.

"Ooh look, Auntie Peggy," I shouted, and she came over while I pointed out the black-and-white diamond-patterned paper that Da had bought in the model shop in town and pasted to the bathroom floor.

"Your Da's clever, Becca, isn't he?" Peggy said.

It was then Da suddenly straightened up and said, "Where's Sarah?"

None of us had noticed in the excitement that she had left the room. She was in our bedroom lying face down on the bed, and Da went in and sat beside her and stroked her back.

48

"What's the matter with you, misery guts?" I shouted, secure in the knowledge that it was my birthday and I was the day's VIP.

Sarah sat up furiously at the contempt in my tone, and I saw her cheeks were red with temper.

"I hate you, Becca!" she yelled.

I just laughed. It was mine. The doll's house was mine. And there was a certain triumph in seeing perfect, composed little Sarah lose her cool.

"Now, now, now," Da said gently and lifted Sarah onto his knee. "What's the matter?"

"You never made anything for me when it was my birthday," whispered Sarah, trying not to let me hear as she put her arms round his neck.

"I know, but you haven't seen the other surprise," Da said. "I was looking for you to give you *your* surprise.

Sarah stilled, looked up hopefully at him and sniffed. I frowned. He took her hand, led her back through next door. I hadn't noticed it in all the excitement of the doll's house. But on the bedside table there was a little tiny wooden house, a money box with a slot in the roof for the pennies to drop. It was roughly made compared to the doll's house, but it was bright and attractive, a little pixie house that had a wooden toadstool on its path, painted red with white spots.

Sarah didn't swoop on it as I had swooped on mine. Her eyes just brightened and she fingered it gently and then she looked at him and smiled.

"Here," Da said, handing her a coin, "put the penny in."

There was a tune when the penny dropped. We thought it was magic but Da opened it up and showed us it was just a little musical device with a small lever.

49

When the penny dropped on the lever, the music played. He said the model shop had imported them from Switzerland, which we knew was a long way from Glasgow. Of course, there wasn't nearly the craftsmanship in the little money box that there was in the doll's house, but I was still a bit mad with Da.

"It's not her birthday," I complained. "Why is she getting that when it's not even her birthday!?"

But Da said it was a *late* birthday present for Sarah because hers had been shop bought and he wanted to make her something too. It is only now, as an adult, that I recognise what that says about him, how hard he worked to treat us equally.

He was so proud when Sarah graduated from her law degree. To tell the truth, it gave me a pang that I had never made him that proud, that all these years I'd bummed around from job to job. And yet, I always sensed that what he felt for me was something slightly different from what he felt for Sarah. But people say that, don't they, that parents love their children in different, special ways. He was soft around Sarah, gentle. But he laughed more around me. Sometimes I thought Sarah was his pride and I was his joy.

CHAPTER THREE

Father Riley is out when we phone. His housekeeper says he's away visiting family but he'll be back for this evening's vigil mass at 6pm if we want to come to that and catch him after the service. I don't, frankly. I don't want to go to mass. I arrange to meet Sarah there but I'll probably be accidentally-on-purpose late so that I can skulk outside like I always did. I have plans for this afternoon.

Da's bureau is made of dark mahogany, rich and brown and shiny as a conker. A lid that lifts down to make a writing desk. Three drawers. Stumpy little feet. A lovely thing in its way, though I would never have chosen it for myself. It is from a bygone age, just like Da really. Sarah and I were always aware that Da was older than everyone else's dad. I used to complain that the house was too dark and heavy and old-fashioned with its solid old wardrobes and bookcases and autumnal patterned carpets. Da just said you didn't get craftsmanship like the old days and he was probably right. He loved that bureau. He never locked it but there was an unspoken rule that Sarah and I didn't go into it, and we never did. It would have been like reading Da's diary.

But it is time now. I run my hand over the lid of it. It is polished, smooth as a mirror, but the surface has tiny, fine-line scratches that show its age. Scratches that tell of its history and give it character, like laughter lines around the eyes. The hinges squeak as it opens and small packages and envelopes tumble from the inner shelves as the lid swings down. Whenever Da had opened it, things had fallen out. I used to tease him and say him I was going to sort it out one of these days, and he would tell me with mock sternness to keep my nose out.

Boxes of screws, silver new and shiny. Twists of paper with old rusty nails, pulled from God knows what and kept for a good thing. Just in case. The inner working of a broken radio. A burned-out television valve. God, he was eccentric. A broken handle from the old electric cooker. A length of electric cable. And paper clips and pencils tied with string, and multi-coloured elastic bands, and pencil sharpeners with shavings still attached, and bottled ink, and string and staples and tacks.

In the middle drawer there are some photographs, a couple of formal ones in cardboard frames and a few more recent insta-matics in a plastic wallet. The framed one has a cover and inside, a leaf of thin, rustling paper that covers the photograph. I have seen this photograph before. It is of Da's parents. Grandma Con-naghan is small and neat with dark dreamy eyes and the vaguest smile but Grandpa gazes suspiciously, almost belligerently, into the camera lens. He is small and squat like Da, his shirt sleeves rolled neatly to his elbows to reveal powerful, muscular fore-arms. Forearms carved from years of outside work on the tiny strip of land they called a farm.

Da told me Grandpa had used those muscles to cut the turf of his own wife's grave and I thought it was the saddest thing I'd ever heard. Da was only ten when his mother died but he talked so vividly about those days after she'd gone, about the house be-ing full and the kettle always on, the sound of cups chinking in saucers, and the chatter of the mourners in the front room, and

52

the procession in to see his mammy where she lay. There was wailing then, and tears, and the chant of prayers; decades of the rosary being said over the body. And then there was nothing. Just nothing.

Da had an older brother, John, who was fifteen. He was supposed to inherit the farm but he said sure, he wasn't wasting his whole life in Donegal. He was off to America for a better life. So he sailed off and none of them saw him again. His better life was dying of TB out there.

Grandpa said everyone was getting on with their lives now and they had better all get on with theirs. He packed up a small case for all of them and set out for the Derry boat that came to Scotland. We never compared notes on what it was like growing up without a mother, Da and I, but I do remember that he once said Grandpa was a good man, a good, good man but hard, and losing his mammy had been a bit like losing the feathers in his pillow and sleeping with a pillowcase of stones under his head instead. I never felt that. Da was the feathers in my pillow.

I place the crinkled paper back over the photo and empty out the snapshots from the plastic wallet. Most of them are of me and Sarah. First Communion, and Christmas, and some from the year we went on the family holiday to Ireland. That was the year Da kept going on about our roots, and how important it was that we knew where we came from. He said that he would take us on holiday to show us our family history.

Sarah and I were ecstatic about that holiday. We didn't ask why it was that if family was so important, he never told us about Mother. We didn't give a brass monkey where our family came from but we did want to be able to say in school that the

Connaghan girls were going on holiday, same as everyone else. It wasn't Majorca, but still. It was a holiday.

Da took us back to the little patch of barren land, a bracken-strewn stretch of rocky turf and hillside where they kept a few sheep. We walked the field and he showed us the stone outline of the croft where they lived. And there, in the field, with the silence broken only by the wind, he cried at the smallness of it, and the way his parents tried to hew a life out of granite for all of them. It was so much smaller, so much more barren, than he remembered. He walked away then, so we wouldn't see his tears, and Sarah and I hung around at a loss, shivering, and not just with the cold, knowing neither what to say nor what to do.

After a minute I ran across the field to him and slipped my hand in his and he smiled at me as we walked in silence together, while Sarah hung back across the other side. He tucked my hand into his coat pocket. "Ah, Rebecca," he said, "What would I do without you?" He always made me feel important. He told me about John and America then. And about him and Peggy, and then about the baby girl who died and took Grandma with her. Sian, he said Grandpa called her, though she was born dead.

He said nothing then for a minute. He was lost in thought and I shivered a little in the wind.

"Are you sad, Da?" I asked him.

"A little bit, darlin'."

I was worried then. I thought maybe he wanted to come back here to live, but he shook his head and said no, there was no living to be had in Donegal. There was only beauty here, he said, and you couldn't eat beauty. That's why they had all come away in the first place. I think they also came because Grandpa was running away from the ghosts, though Da never put it quite like that.

He was ten when they left and Peggy was five. It was nearly Liverpool they went to, but then a letter arrived from an old neighbour in Donegal who had come to Glasgow and he said there was work to be had in Scotland on the roads. I'd get him to tell me over and over the story of Grandpa docking in Glasgow with four pounds in his pocket and two addresses, one for digs and one for work. It was my favourite bedtime story and I would bury my head in the pillow as he told it.

"Are you cryin', darlin'?" he'd ask.

"Naw!" I'd spit scornfully. "I'm sleepin'!"

But I wouldn't pull my head from the damp pillow and Da would sit for a minute, stroking my hair until I really did fall asleep.

It is a full hour before I find it, in an old tattered envelope in the bottom drawer. I have gone through all the loose papers, the old school reports, and a parchment, yellow and withering with age, that turns out to be a report of Da's days in National Service. "Character: excellent," it says, as if character can be examined and diagnosed like flat feet. I am putting it back when I see the large brown envelope right on the bottom. It is falling apart; the flap is no longer there and the sides are beginning to separate.

I pull out the sheets of paper inside and a number of photographs fall out. Da leaning on a gate in his naval uniform, his foot resting on the top bar, hands clasped in front of him. And Da again, with a young woman looking laughingly into his eyes. Jesus. I stare at her, those teasing, haunting eyes. She… can it be…? Mother?

CHAPTER FOUR

Even I can see we look alike. Same coppery highlights in shoulder-length brown hair. Same colour and shape of eyes. Here she is again, her arm looped through Da's. And here, on her own, making kissing gestures at the camera. Kath, Lochglas Bay, it says on the back. And here, leaning against a wall with a sultry smile. Look at her, the way she pouts so provocatively, so aware of her own power.

I suppose it sounds strange to say I had never seen a photo of Mother until now. But anything is normal when you don't know any different. There is no point trying to relate what I tell you to your life. Unless you are an outsider too.

There are letters too, still in their own, smaller, original envelopes. On some of them, I recognise Da's distinctive, old-fashioned, looped hand. For a moment, I finger them hesitantly, uncertain whether to read them. It's not just about privacy. If I read a dead man's letters, I run a risk. Whatever picture they give me of Da, it will be unalterable. He won't be here to explain or to expand. Whatever they tell me will be fixed in time; fixed in stone.

The letter slips from the envelope. There is still time to put it back. I can walk away, keep everything intact. But I know I won't. I need more than I have, and I have to be willing to lose everything to get it. I unfold the paper. Basildon Bond; azure not white.

56

Da always used azure. It is dated 1966 and there is a Glasgow address at the top, an address in the west end. My eyes scan over the page quickly but I know before I even look that it is to my mother. I can scarcely breathe. The voice of a dead man talks.

Dear Kath,

Friday night, another weekend alone. I called earlier. Kirstin said you were out with Jackie, that there was a dance in the village. I feel pretty low tonight and a bit confused. Part of me is glad to think of you out having a good time and another part is just insane with jealousy. I'm not proud of it. But the thought of other men talking to you, dancing with you, laughing with you when I can't, is hard for me take.

I went for a pint with a few of the others from work but I didn't stay long. I didn't have the patience for the conversation somehow. I just wanted to get back to phone you. You've taken over my head a bit, Kath. There's not much room for anything else in there.

But then you were out, and standing in that draughty old phone box at the end of the road, I wondered why I had bothered to rush back. It's a pretty cold, dreich night here tonight, which I suppose isn't helping my mood much. The rain is pelting at the windows. At least I don't have to get up early tomorrow, thank God. I said I'd go over to Peggy's and help Charlie paint their kitchen. Peg was going to make dinner in the evening but we'll see how the painting goes. We'll probably end up with fish suppers from the chippie.

I'm desperate to come and see you again in the next few weeks but I can't really afford it until after pay day. We need to talk seriously, make plans. I wish you'd tell me how you really feel. Sometimes it seems like every time I get close to you, you fly off. Like some gorgeous butterfly opening her wings and saying come and get me, but never quite letting me. You don't need to tease me, Kath. There's no need to make me jealous. I'm jealous anyway. I'm so scared I'm going to lose you.

I'm sorry. Maybe this letter isn't helping either of us very much. I just miss you. I suppose that's all I'm trying to say, really. I'm sore with missing you. I may not be the most exciting guy in the world, Kath, but I'll always love you. You won't ever have to doubt it.

Yours always,
Joe.

I fold the letter, put it back into the envelope, a feeling of guilty unease rising inside me. It feels vaguely distasteful, like rifling through someone's underwear drawer. But I swallow it down like bile, that unease, unwilling to let scruple supersede gut need. I need to know... everything, anything. I take another letter out of an envelope, and then another, and another, opening them, reading them, folding them again almost mechanically. Da's tone undulates through the letters, shifting and reforming like shapes in a kaleidoscope; bright as shooting stars in one, dark and sombre the next. Even back then, when they were alive, she didn't make him happy.

The letters cover a six-month period and towards the end, in May 1967, they had obviously decided to get married. A summer wedding. Da talks of an old house they are to buy together in Lochglas that is dirt cheap but needs renovation. In one, he talks poignantly of an aunt dying; in another about a trip to the cinema. Banal talk nestling up close to serious talk of living and dying and loving.

And through it all, an unfamiliar voice: the voice of the lover from my father's lips. '*When I held you, down on that shore at Lochglas,*' he writes in one, '*I sensed for the first time in my life that there was some purpose, that there was something eternal as the rock on which we stood. I'm no poet, Kath, I don't know a clever way to say this. But I just felt certain in that moment that though I'll die some day, nothing can ever take away what I feel for you. It will be somewhere out there in the atmosphere, always.*'

I keep that letter in my hands for several minutes, staring at it. Reading, then rereading the words. *Somewhere out there in the atmosphere, always.* The voice of other people's love is a foreign language, one you can't understand unless you share the same country. It's a language that lovers use to exclude the rest of us from the intimacy of their own private world. This I hear in my father's voice as I read, and somehow, hearing a part of him that I never knew makes me feel estranged, creates a barrier even more brutal than death.

And then, at the back of the bundle, letters in another hand, a bold, careless scrawl scratching untidily across the envelopes. Only a few, far fewer than in Da's writing. I take the first one out: black ink on rose-coloured paper. The paper is creased in four, as if it has been folded and unfolded several times. It is only a page of a letter; the rest is missing.

My God, but you were in a funny mood in your last letter! What brought that on? You are so different from me, Joe, so intense and serious. I love that fierce heart of yours but you know, sometimes, in my most honest moments, even I am not sure I deserve you. I am going to do my best to love you for ever. But 'for ever' scares me a bit. Doesn't just a little part of you think, who can ever know about for ever?

Someone – Da, presumably – has doodled at the side of the page in blue ink, as if they have been reading the letter and become lost in thought. There's a little hat on the page, like one he used to draw on the side of newspapers when he was doing the crossword. I refold the page, take out another letter in mother's scrawl. I don't recognise the address. Bayview, Lochglas. There is no date. The voice is so different from Da's. Not burning and intense but flippant, playful – maybe even a little heartless.

Dear Joe,

A note – in haste! Dad was at a golf-club dinner last night so I asked him to try and corner David Carruthers about the job. (Makes me laugh to think of my dear old Presbyterian dad speaking up for his Papish son-in law-to-be amongst the Masonic mafia!) Anyway, turns out David Carruthers was very impressed with you at the interview and Dad thinks he's going to offer you the job, which obviously would solve everything. Thought you'd like to know.

Now listen. I have a special request. But first, before I ask, you must picture the scene. I am sitting at the bay win-dow overlooking the loch, wearing a black mini skirt. (Dad HATES it – that's how much you'll love it.) The thing is...

my dearest love! ... I need more money for the living-room carpet. No, no, Joe! Don't think wallet... think LEGS! So, any chance of any more? You know you accountants are loaded.

Love, Kath. xx
PS Jackie said to send her love.

I stare at the letter. What is she talking about? An accountant? Da wasn't an accountant. He was a bus driver. He had always been a bus driver. My eyes keep darting back and re-reading the sentence. *You know you accountants are loaded.* Whose life is this unfolding in front of me? Who is this stranger I called Da?

CHAPTER FIVE

The letter sits discarded on my lap as a memory suddenly puffs from the chimney. One of my earliest. Me, trying to climb up the steps of Da's bus. I must have been about three. Da was sitting at the wheel in the depot in Larkfield in Glasgow when Peggy and I called in. Peggy was behind me and put her hands under my armpits to lift me up the step, but I screamed and twisted and waved my legs in the air.

"Self!" I'd shouted furiously at her. "Self!" I remember getting even crosser then, because Dad and Peggy had laughed.

I always hated being laughed at. I had run to the front bus seat and buried my face in the cool leather, sobbing angrily. Da came to me then, lifting me up gently and sinking his face into my hair, whispering soothing words as he held me. Then he'd blown raspberries in my chest and thrown me in the air, and I had giggled and shouted "more", until I finally put my arms around his neck and nestled in.

He worked on the number 34 route that passed close to our house and sometimes, on the way home from high school, I'd let other buses go past until I caught Da's. But sometimes, I'd get Khadim's bus. Before one-man operation came in, Khadim used to be Da's conductor but then he had to retrain as a driver. He used to tell me he had arrived at Central Station in Glasgow one freezing November day with five pounds in his pocket and big dreams. Not so different from Grandpa Connaghan. The five pounds, anyway. I used to look at Khadim dishing out bus tickets and wonder what happened to his dreams.

When I got on his bus, Khadim would wink at me and let me off the bus fare. Sometimes, he and Da would give each other lifts home if they were changing over shifts, and if he was on Da's bus when I got on, he would come and ask me about school. He had a sailor's legs for a swaying sea, Khadim, standing firm against every lurch and jolt of movement.

He used to joke that I shouldn't be carrying French books home, that I should learn a proper, useful language. Here, he said one day, and took out a pen from his pocket and tore a little page from the notebook he always kept in his pocket. He wrote carefully and handed me the paper. 'Teach Yourself Urdu'.

"Good book," he said, and nodded his head. I told him saucily that I'd think about it if I ever wanted to go and live in downtown Calcutta like him. And Khadim had shaken his head and said Calcutta was in India, not Pakistan, and didn't Western schoolgirls know anything? But his inky dark eyes had danced as he turned away, and he went and said something to Da at the front of the bus that I couldn't hear, and they had both laughed. I liked Khadim.

Da did too. It was funny really, because Da didn't have much experience of "coloured fellows" as he called them before he met Khadim. He never saw a black man till he came to Glasgow from Donegal. I think, if he was honest, Da was a bit wary of cultures other than his own, but he had a natural sense of justice that cut through all of that.

The day Da's friendship with Khadim was really sealed was the day a couple of young guys got on and started messing about

63

with Khadim. You could see they were trouble from the start with their Doc Marten boots and their hard, slitty eyes. Da had just taken over the shift and was dropping Khadim off in Pollokshields. Khadim was standing at the front talking to him, still with his uniform on. I was reading a book on the bus that day so I don't know how it started. But all of a sudden I heard one of them say that black bastards like him were taking jobs from white men, and why couldn't he go back to his own fucking country, and in the end Khadim said he was going to have to ask them to get off the bus if they didn't stop.

"Get aff the bus?" said one of them, getting up and digging his finger into Khadim's shoulder. "Who's gonna make me get aff?"

The bus suddenly jolted as Da slammed on the brakes. He jumped out of his cab and said quietly, "I am." A current ran through the bus, all eyes swivelling to the front. My heart hammered. I wanted Da to get safely back behind his wheel. The two of them looked at Da in surprise. But Da wasn't a big man, and after the momentary surprise, they turned to one another and sniggered. Da said the bus wasn't going anywhere until they got off, and for a minute it looked like it might get nasty. A toddler began crying loudly at the back of the bus and an old woman with a shopping bag on her knee stuck her oar in.

"Yous are a disgrace," she said. "Jist get aff and gie's a' peace. That wean's screaming because of yous."

"Fuck off, grandma," one of them said, but then this big guy appeared from upstairs. He was enormous.

"The driver's tellt yous two to get aff, now get aff," he said. "Because see if yous don't, ahm gonnae put you aff maself. Now move it, ya wee shite bags."

They weren't going to argue. But on the way off, one of them went up and stuck his face right into Khadim's, and for a minute I thought he was going to headbutt him. But then I saw his lips move and the next minute a great gob of spit had landed on Khadim's cheek. They jumped off the bus and ran.

For a second nobody moved. Then Da jumped up angrily like he was going to give chase, but Khadim put out his hand and grabbed the sleeve of his jacket. Da looked at him and Khadim shook his head and muttered something, and Da climbed back into his cab and the engine started up again. I saw the spit on Khadim's face begin to trickle down and felt my stomach heave. I took out a tissue and handed it to him. He accepted it without a word and wiped the slime from his face, and everyone on the bus looked out of the window in embarrassed silence until the old woman with the shopping bag said, "Y'alright son?" though Khadim was in his forties.

It was the day after that Khadim invited us all to his house for the first time. Da and Khadim seemed like a definite partnership after that, thought they made an odd combination. The wee, square, dark-haired man with the faint Irish burr that had never quite left him, and the big Pakistani with a long white beard and a round, curry gut.

I always wondered why someone as smart as Da ended up driving buses but I assumed Grandpa had never had enough money for him to stay on at school and needed him out working. He never liked his job much, but whenever I suggested he do something else he just said what else was he going to do at his time of life, as if he didn't have a choice. But why would you drive buses if you were an accountant?

It always pained him that I went from one temp post to another. He wanted me to go to university, make something of myself, and I always assumed it was because he never had the chance. I wasn't interested. I was smart enough, but though I never knew why, I just didn't feel settled enough to have ambition. I didn't know what I wanted from life enough to go out and get the qualifications to do it.

Qualifications. If Da really had been an accountant, he would have to have had qualifications. I lift out every drawer of the bureau, sifting quickly through the school reports and the photographs, the bills and accounts, and finally come to a large brown envelope on the bottom. I lift out the single sheet of parchment inside and my eyes dance down the page as the key words leap out. My heart skips a beat. Glasgow University. Joseph Connaghan.

The date suggests Da would have been twenty-eight, a mature student. National Service accounted for some of the time after he left school. But had he worked after that to pay his way through university? And how had he and Mother met? I stare at the parchment and then slip it back into the envelope, feeling sick and confused and vaguely betrayed.

CHAPTER SIX

Can you imagine how hard it was to quell all those emotions and go out to meet Sarah at the church? It helped that I felt proprietorial about the knowledge I had gathered from the bureau; it was mine. It also helped that it was incomplete. I told myself there was no point in saying anything to Sarah until I knew the whole story. I picked up my bag and left the house, walking slowly in the heat but with my mind racing.

I hear Father Riley before I see him.

I am standing over at the trees in the church grounds and his voice booms out as the doors open, hard as hellfire, roasted with an Irish brogue and years of Capstan full strength.

"Yous'll all be wanting home for the football on the telly tonight. Starts in five minutes, so the Lord will forgive us if we sing only one verse of the final hymn and let's hope He gives us the right result tonight."

There is a little ripple of laughter; Father Riley is a wag, so he is. So human as well as holy. That's what everyone says. Voice like thunder and a heart the size of a pea, if you ask me. The pews empty and the crowd flows through the doors and I catch a flash of Sarah's blonde hair somewhere at the top of the steps. She comes down to stand with me and we wait for the priest.

"Father Riley," says Sarah tentatively, as he goes to sweep by us. She touches his arm. I suspect he would have pretended not to hear otherwise.

"Ah, girls," he says briskly, putting his arm on Sarah's shoulder and propelling her with him. "Yous are lovely but can it wait? I've got a lovely steak pie on low in the oven and the footie is about to start. Are your souls in danger or can it wait?"

"Our dad died yesterday, Father."

"Ah dear, dear, dear," says Father Riley. He sighs. I think the sigh is more for his steak pie than for Da, but Sarah says I don't give priests the proper respect and maybe she's right. There's a reason for that, as you'll find out later. There are too many secrets to give them all at once.

"You'd better come in now," he says.

He turns the key in the lock of the church house and leads us through into a sitting room. It isn't a room he uses himself, I am sure. More a births, weddings and funerals kind of room. I suppose even priests have to keep a part of themselves for themselves.

It has been a grand house once, the kind of place that a housekeeper fussed over. But it is too big and draughty to heat properly nowadays. The place smells vaguely fusty, like the holiday cottage in Ireland we once went to with Da. It is a room too long shut up, with only stillness and dust for company and no warmth in its chilled veins. A grandfather clock ticks loudly in the corner.

"Sit down girls, sit down," says Father Riley. "I'm sorry for your trouble, surely I am. Now I know your faces, and I know your daddy, but your name again is…?"

"Connaghan," says Sarah. "I'm Sarah and this is Rebecca."

"Ah yis, yis. Your father will be James."

"Joseph," I correct.

"Ah yis, yis, Joseph. Of course. And what happened to poor Joseph now?"

"He had a heart attack, Father," Sarah begins levelly, and then her eyes fill with tears. "He hadn't been ill… he just… just…" Her voice falters.

"Ah dear," says Father Riley, shaking his head softly. "You never know the minute. Were yous with him?"

"Yes, Father."

"Well now, that's a comfort anyway, isn't it? Sure, he didn't die alone."

I suppose he's being kind in his own inadequate way. I look around the room, cold and functional: devoid of flowers or wedding photos; of hideous china dogs won at fairs; of crayon-drawn posters smeared with chocolate; of graduation portraits. It's everything that's NOT here that tells you about Father Riley's life. I'd lay money that the room he uses himself isn't any different, except it will have a television and a well-stocked drinks cabinet. You could rattle around in there, keel over with a heart attack, and the only human voice would be from the box in the corner. I said that once to a young priest I knew. You'll die alone to the tune of *Coronation Street*, I warned him.

"Yes, Father, we've been to the undertakers," I hear Sarah say. "And we are hoping the funeral will be Friday morning if you can say the mass for us."

"Yis, yis, Friday," he says. "Ten a.m. now, will that be all right for yous?"

"Ten," repeats Sarah, looking at me. I return her stare blankly. I feel completely detached. None of this seems real. We could be organising a coffee morning instead of Da's funeral.

"We'll have the service the night before when the remains are brought into the church... say six-thirty?" says Father Riley.

The remains. The word makes me flinch.

"That will be fine," says Sarah. "I'm sorry... I don't know, really... we haven't got any experience... I'm not sure what we..."

"Ah, don't worry now," says Father Riley, going over to a desk by the window. "I'll give you a book of readings suitable for funerals and maybe you could have a wee look through and see which you think would be nice."

"Now," he says, reaching for a notebook and pen, "hymns. Have you thought yet about hymns?" His pen hovers over the page.

Aye, here's a list I prepared earlier, I think. Da's Funeral Hymns Should He Snuff It Unexpectedly... Aloud, I say I'd also like some secular music to be played. Father Riley isn't keen. Some priests might allow pop music at funerals but he's not one of them. None of this, 'My Way' carry on. And wouldn't a good Christian man like James want things to be done right? His name was Joseph. Oh yis, yis, sorry.

Anyway, I say, it's opera I'm thinking of, not pop music. An aria from Puccini's *Gianni Schicchi*. Is that a requiem? No, a comedy. Sarah, thinking I'm being facetious, looks warningly at me. Father Riley says tightly if it's not a hymn, it'll have to be at the end. Not part of the liturgy. I look at him resentfully but silently. Yeah, like the football chat, I think.

Father Riley wants to know who the singer will be.

"I have a friend, Shameena. A family friend."

The little flicker, the blink of the eyelids, when I say her name might have gone unnoticed if I hadn't been staring at him.

"Is she a Catholic?" he says.

70

"Catholic Muslim."

I don't think he likes me. Which is fine because I don't like him either with his hard little raisin eyes and his soft, doughy belly and his florid skin. I hate men with florid skin. Sarah always protests when I say that and says you can't hate someone just because their skin is a bit red but I can. I hate men with florid skin and right now I hate Father Riley.

"Perhaps we could have a quick look through a hymn book if you have one, Father," says Sarah quickly. "I think we'll be able to pick some out that Dad would have liked."

I sit back. Sarah can choose the holy stuff.

"'Soul of my Saviour'?" suggests Father Riley.

"Oh God."

They both look at me.

"A lot of people like it," says Father Riley, the colour rising in his neck, staining it purple.

"Aye, well I'm sure it's Top of the Funeral Pops, but I hate it."

You know, I can almost laugh writing that sentence all these years later, though the laugh is a little shamefaced. It was so typical of me back then: mouthy, snappy, rude. But I have to stop short of apologising for the old me. Sarah did enough of that. I look back now and I see so clearly how much I was hurting. And how scared I was. I needed Father Riley to offer me something and he couldn't. Nothing that meant anything to me. Given half a chance, he'd no doubt give me that old line about my Father in heaven looking after me. The best way he could do that, I would have told him, was to leave me one on earth.

Two faces staring at me in the silence. Sarah is wearing her horrified, 'what-do-you-think-you-are-playing-at-Rebecca?' expression. Father Riley stares stonily. "Let's have a little respect, shall we?" he says with wounded dignity. "I can see you are not a believer, Rebecca, but you are asking the Church to bury your father and I think that's what we should focus on."

"I'm sorry," Sarah says. There she bloody goes again. "It's been such a hard couple of days. 'Soul Of My Saviour' will be fine. I'm sure Dad would have liked that."

What is she talking about? Sometimes I think Sarah knew a different Da from me. He'd have hated it. 'Soul of My Saviour' is old-time Ireland. A hard Ireland, where his mother died when he was just a boy. 'Soul of my Saviour' is childhood, with his toes sticking through rough woollen stockings, and beatings in school, and lots of God but no mammy.

Sarah looks exhausted all of a sudden. Her elbow is resting on the arm of the chair and she leans her head against it, eyes cast downwards. Father Riley looks at her sympathetically. He is warmer towards Sarah than he is towards me, but priests sniff out their own, don't they?

"Ah dear, dear," he says. "You've had a hard couple of days right enough, Sarah, so you have, but you just remember that your daddy's with God now. He'll look after him for you, so He will."

Oh here we go. I knew it was coming.

Sarah nods tearfully, gratefully, and scrambles in her bag for a tissue. I fix my eyes on the grandfather clock in the corner. Tick, tock. I don't feel at all grateful. Tick. Tock. I look up at a picture of the Sacred Heart on the wall. The compassion of Christ. It makes me feel angry. Inexplicably, furiously angry.

"We were supposed to all be looking at holiday brochures this morning," says Sarah. "Becca and Dad were going on holiday together and I was going to go if I could get time off. We'd thought

72

maybe Italy… or even Spain. Dad would have liked it so much, all that sunshine…"

"Well Sarah, you just remember that the sunshine in heaven is brighter and warmer and altogether sweeter than the sunshine in Italy." Father Riley sits back, a little smugly, I think. He is pleased with that line.

Sarah tries to smile through her tears, presses her tissue to her eyes. "That's a really comforting thought, Father."

She means it. She bloody means it.

I can smell the rich scent of steak pie wafting from the kitchen at the back of the house. It makes me feel vaguely nauseous. I just want out of here. I look through the window at the last small group of parishioners still talking in the grounds after mass, at the sunshine dappling through the trees and casting shadows below.

I stand up and they both look at me expectantly.

"I'm not feeling too well," I say. "I think I'll just step outside for a moment in the fresh air…"

CHAPTER SEVEN

The church is cool inside, and the scent of summer flowers and incense from the evening service lingers in the air. I sit down on the back pew. It is less committed.

On the back seat I am just visiting, not really part of anything.

The wood feels hard against my backbone. Da always said I hadn't enough flesh on me. Like a sparrow, he said. "You need a good steak in you, girl," he used to say when I came home. But I like the austerity of the hard wood right now, and the warm golden glow of it, and the round carved edges of the rows. And the stillness. I wish I understood about that stillness. I wish I could tell if it is the stillness of peace or just the stillness of a vacuum.

I stare straight ahead at the massive crucifix above the altar and the trickle of plaster blood and paint on the hands and feet. Blood of my saviour, bathe me in your wounds. At the side altar to the Virgin Mary, the candlelight flickers and dances. As a child, I used to think the Virgin's eyes followed me, that they actually changed expression. Sometimes I imagined they were reproving, and sometimes I thought they were imbued with a kind of tenderness for me, her child. Right now they seem neutral, staring without judgement.

A metal coin clinks into the iron box as an elderly lady in a headscarf lights a candle in front of the altar. She kneels before the statue and I hear her whispered prayers, a little sibilant hiss in the silence. It is always old ladies who light candles. Old ladies in patterned headscarves. I wonder what she wants at her age that makes her pray so fervently. Salvation? And what about me… what do I want in a church that is empty save for evening shadows? To look for Da, I suppose.

Father Riley's words keep running through my head. The sunshine in heaven is brighter, warmer, sweeter than here on earth. Religious people don't half talk shite. You can keep your sunshine heaven. I want sunshine that blisters your skin and sun milk that soothes it. No need for sun milk in heaven. We had a teacher at school once, Miss Edwards, who used to talk about heaven. She told one of her classes that she had been away to be a nun but had come back. I don't know why she bothered. She might just has well have worn a habit as those frumpy tweed skirts and jumpers.

Some of the girls made up stories about why she left the convent, most of them involving great spiritual crises. But I said I reckoned she'd left because she'd fallen madly in love with the man who came to clean the convent windows and had been caught kissing him by the Mother Superior. Everyone had looked at me wide eyed and then we had all snorted with laughter at the thought of Miss Edwards ever kissing a man, which was as far as our chaste imaginations went.

Miss Edwards talked a lot about heaven. She was into guitars and tambourines and listened to hymns like that ghastly 'Go Tell It on the Mountain' thing on her car tape deck and she had never even heard of Oasis. I know that because she gave me and Maria Toretti a lift to a fourth-year retreat once. We had to listen for 30 whole minutes to a tape called 'Hymns of Praise' and when it finished she said she thought it was terrific that me and Maria were developing our faith by going to the retreat like this. Maria and I looked at one another slyly in the back seat and tried not to giggle. We were only going because we fancied Father Douglas.

Father Douglas was young and intense and beautiful, and almost enough to keep you a Catholic. He preached a lot about purity, his dark hair falling over his face so that he had to keep shoving it back. We quivered while we listened to him, not entirely from religious fervour. It's just a pity he ran off with Maureen from the café round the corner from the school. Good ice cream, I suppose, and she was a voluptuous blonde, but Maria and I still thought he'd have been better off with one of us because we'd have understood him, while Maureen was a Proddy. I'll bet *she* never knew all the words to 'Sweet Sacrament Divine'.

Father Douglas, we were told gravely at a school assembly, had risked his immortal soul and his place in heaven, but after what Miss Edwards said about heaven in RE classes I thought he would probably have a better time with Maureen anyway. Heaven, Miss Edwards said, wasn't a place at all. That was just childish and we had to grow up now and think as adults. Heaven was a state of consciousness. A state of being. After that I stopped going to church at all. What kind of incentive was a state of bloody consciousness?

I want a place. A place where you still wear short skirts and lipstick. Where you still drown in heavy, musky perfume and fancy the guy in the corner shop, and put six boxes of baubles and two packets of tinsel on the Christmas tree till the branches droop and it looks like it belongs in a tart's boudoir. Where dinner is sizzled prawns in spicy sauce and there is always, always, the possibility of falling in love with the waiter who brings it. A peaceful state of mind? No, thanks. I want the rest of me there too. I want heaven to be a place I walk around, not somewhere you float about on puffs of cotton-wool consciousness. I want heaven to be earth without the duff bits.

I was never sure exactly what Da thought. He told tales sometimes about the Christian Brothers who taught him in Ireland and how they beat the devil out of you with a switch if you stumbled over the Lord's Prayer. And how the priest would lift the latch on your door and walk in as if he owned the place, and how Mammy always said the priest took the place of God and you must therefore do everything he said. Da said he lived in terror of the priest because he took Mammy's words literally and thought if the priest told him to jump from the top of the Post Office roof in Donegal town, sure he'd have to do it.

He still went to church of course. He was enough of an old Irish Catholic for that. I can picture him still kneeling in these very pews, his chin resting on his hands. Sometimes you would see his mouth move in silent prayer, but mostly he was just still, staring at the altar. He made Sarah and I go, though I think as far as I was concerned, he knew the writing was on the wall.

He took to going to the Saturday-night vigil but I always used the excuse I was washing my hair and doing my makeup for going out and that I would go at twelve on Sunday. I'd leave the house at quarter to twelve and then go and drink coffee and read the papers in Roberto's, the Italian café that was a short walk from the church. Sarah knew, of course. I don't think she ever missed mass in her life. She was always so prim and disapproving, but I used to tell her to keep her mouth shut or I'd tear her Ronan Keating poster into a hundred pieces and feed it to one of Mr Curtis's yappy little dogs.

77

Later, when I was in my twenties, and Da and I had our nights with a bottle of wine between us, I knew he wasn't sure about God. He wanted to believe all right. But whether he ever did, really deep down inside himself, I don't know. I think he had his moments, usually sentimental ones at midnight mass, when his heart and his eyes filled up with it all, and for that moment he believed. But he said God was a civilising force on people whether He existed or not. He was very conservative Da, really, in some ways.

"You'll come back to the church Becca," he used to say. "You'll come back to it when you're older."

Is this the moment? I try making a little bargain with God. I'll come back, if You just make everything all right again. Not bringing Da back, because I know he can't come back, not now. But maybe a sign. Let me feel a presence. Not my heavenly Father's, just my earthly one's, because right now I have no sense whatsoever of his existence and the emptiness terrifies me. I close my eyes, trying to pray. I close them so tight the blackness explodes into grey patches of shooting light. I open them again. I don't know what to say. I try again. "Please," I begin. "Please God… Da," and I stop. Please. God. Da. Three words that get as close as I can to a prayer.

The old lady in the headscarf is having trouble getting up from the side altar. She sways as she stands, waddling up the aisle on heavy, bowed legs, her shopping bag over her arm.

"All right, hen?" she says as she passes, not waiting for the answer.

I can't wait for an answer either. The heavy wooden door bangs shut behind me and the evening sunlight nips my eyes after the gloom. Maybe Da is in there somewhere among the flowers and the melted candle wax. But if he is, I can't find him.

Des is waiting in the car for me and Sarah, but I walk right past him and out the gates and back along the tree-lined avenue to the main road. I head to Da's house without stopping. Somewhere in the recesses of my brain I can hear Des shouting to me but I keep on going. It is only a ten-minute walk but by the time I turn the key in the lock, I am sweating slightly with the heat and the exertion and a new sense of purpose.

Half an hour later, the phone rings. I sigh, expecting it to be Sarah. It's Peggy.

"Sarah is very upset," she says, her voice thin and tight.

Bloody typical of Peggy. I'm never upset, of course.

"Yeah, well we're all upset, Peggy."

"How do you think she felt being left in that room with Father Riley? She sat for half an hour with him before she realised you weren't coming back. And she said you were rude to him. Honestly Becca, you're so *selfish* sometimes. You just go your own way and to hell with everyone else. It's always been the same…"

On she witters. On and on. God, I could write the script. I've been hearing it long enough.

"Becca!" she says sharply.

"What?"

"Are you listening? I said I think you should come over here tonight."

"I'm tired, Peggy. I'll sort a few things out here and then go to bed. I'll come over tomorrow."

"You're being ridiculous, Rebecca. Why are you staying there on your own? And whatever are you thinking of, trying to sort things already? There's no need for that. You're only going to upset yourself. Charlie and I will take care of that. Come on now," she says, beginning to wheedle, "there's no need for you to be in that house alone right now."

It is the way it was throughout our childhood. Peggy being bossy and knowing what was best; Sarah being reasonable and compliant and doing what she was told; and me being pushed to the outside for daring not to. Peggy always wanted her little brood round her where she could see them and count them, whereas I was forever wanting to wander off and examine the secrets of the reeds in the hidden end of the duck pond.

"Sarah wants you to come over," she adds. "Though God knows she has reason enough not to want to set eyes on you tonight. We're all here. Des too."

Christ, that settles it then. Peggy knows from the silence she is losing.

"Haven't you made your point now, staying there last night by yourself?"

"What point?"

"Charlie!" says Peggy sharply. "Charlie, come and talk some sense into this girl."

I can hear Charlie mumbling some protest in the background.

"Just talk to her Charlie, for heaven's sake!"

I hear him take the phone. He clears his throat.

"Becca?"

"Charlie."

"Peggy thinks you should come over."

Dear old Charlie.

"I know Charlie and I would, but I'm just so tired I think I'll have an early night and come over tomorrow if you don't mind."

"She's just worried about you," he says, almost apologetically.

"I know."

"You're all right now, Becca?"

"I'm fine, Charlie."

"Rightoh. I'll put your Aunt Peggy back on."

"Brilliant, Charlie," I hear Peggy say sarcastically, as she takes the phone.

I'm not entertaining Peggy any more. She'll keep chipping away if I let her.

"Peggy, I'll see you tomorrow," I say firmly.

"Right," she says, hard and clipped, and I raise my eyes. I love Peggy. I do, really. Beneath that brittle exterior, she has a soft heart. Her heart is warm and squishy, like half-melted chocolate. But she has a tendency to punish emotionally when you don't do exactly as she wants. Always has had. When Sarah and I were in trouble as children, Peggy just had to turn the frozen mitt on and Sarah would crumble. She'd run to Peggy with big unspilled tears in her eyes and bury her face in her lap and Peggy would relent and take her 'special girl' on her knees, and then look from the corner of her eye to see how I was reacting. It was water off a duck's back to me.

There is a bottle of wine in the kitchen cupboard. I open it and pour a glass. After Peggy's call I think I need it. I think about putting some music on but I don't think I can handle it, hearing music from Da's sound system and him not here.

❧

The memory of that moment jolts me back into the present. Shameena's music blares out around me still. I wish Da could have heard her sing at his funeral. But perhaps he did.

81

CHAPTER EIGHT

I took the bottle and headed for bed, another nocturnal conversation with Da running in my head.

Why didn't you tell me Da? I can't believe you didn't tell me. My head is hurting trying to work it out. I hoped tonight would be cool but it's hot and murky and I keep thinking that this room smells of death. I don't know how to describe what death smells like but it smells of this, whatever is in here. Heat and dust and sadness. With the door open, I can lie in bed and see the spot in the hall where you died. I keep looking at it. My eyes won't leave it alone.

I am talking to a dead man. Best kind, I'd have joked, once. The only kind that doesn't answer back. Now I'd give anything for an answer. But you're not here, are you? I am left talking to you in my head, and the only answer is the dust falling through the air in the beam of light from the lamp.

Did you lie to me? Or was it that you did not tell me the whole truth? Did you tell me you had always been a bus driver... or did I assume? I keep asking myself why it matters so much but it DOES matter. Being an accountant, well, it's a sign of a whole other life that I knew nothing about. It means I never really knew you. I've lost my future with you. Now I feel the past is slipping through my fingers too. Soon there will be nothing left.

I still don't get it. Why would you earn your living as a bus driver if you were qualified to be an accountant? Of course, I knew you were smart. You had books on astronomy and books on physics and books on ancient Greece... books and books and books. You even started learning Italian when we said we fancied a holiday in Italy. But I always thought you were one of those working-class men who was slightly in awe of formal education. One who had never had a chance to turn his natural intelligence into qualifications, and who thought people who did were much cleverer. How could I be so wrong about someone I loved so much?

Tonight, after looking in the bureau, I started trying to go right back to childhood. Remember everything in order. See if there are clues about you. About Mother. About why there were so many secrets. I keep thinking there must be things I know that I don't even realise I know. But the memory-fires refuse to ignite. Early memories are so elusive, fragile wisps that disappear or change shape when you try to grab them. I'll remember something, then think, did it really happen that way? Or do I just think it happened that way?

When I looked in that bureau tonight, I thought all the surprises would be about mother. But there was little about her, not even a death certificate. I still don't know what my own mother died of. I always wondered if it was something like cancer that took her slowly. Maybe you had to watch the light fading and when the darkness finally fell you couldn't bear to talk of what once had been. But wouldn't I have remembered that, even as a tot? A mother whose hair was falling out, who was disappearing slowly from me, eaten up by pain and sickness?

There is one clue that might lead me to more answers. A simple but crucial clue. You always said, Da, that the simple things in life were the most important. It is the address on Mother's letter: Bayview, Lochglas. She was preparing that house for the two of you.

Was it where we lived? I looked Lochglas up on the map. On the rare occasions we talked about living in the Highlands, you always just said we lived near Inverness. Lochglas is only ten miles north of Inverness.

You see the way my mind is working, don't you, Da? You know what I am thinking? I suggested a trip to Inverness once and you said no so savagely, I never suggested it again. I felt guilty for being so thoughtless. Too many memories, I thought. But what would I find now? Are mother's family still in that area? I suppose her parents would be dead now, though I suppose it's possible they could be in their eighties or nineties. I don't know whether she had a big family or a small one, but there must surely be someone up there who at least knew her. It's twenty-five years but it's not a lifetime. It's not impossible. She must have left a mark somewhere. A life doesn't just get erased, does it, Da?

Questions... Peggy refuses to answer any. And you... well you don't seem able to. Unless this is your answer. Did you lead me to the bureau? Are you telling me to go? To find answers for myself? I NEED answers. I keep thinking about the funeral, about being forced to finally say goodbye to you. But say goodbye to whom? I want to know who you really were. Once you are in that coffin with the lid closed, I'm so worried I will never know the truth. I have to know more than the name on the brass when we place your coffin in the ground, when we cover it with the cold, black earth.

SUNDAY

CHAPTER ONE

Silent midnight. Alone, with only the steady pulse of thought like a mental heartbeat inside my head. Already I have begun to hate Da's house. There is only emptiness now: a house without substance; a house of dreams and shadows and memories. Loved but loathed. I am trapped inside it, like a crab trapped in its own shell, the housing on my back both my protection and my burden. Inside the shell there is only space, and inside the space the midnight thought grows and grows until it explodes into reality: Lochglas.

I start out not believing I will really go. Finding the map, measuring the distance, packing a small case: they are all simply actions to test the idea. Trying the thought on, wearing it like a shoe, seeing how it fits. Lochglas. The door clicking behind me, my own footsteps on the stairs, the start of the engine… they are not irrevocable. A short drive to the all-night garage. Some chocolate perhaps. A bag of ground coffee. The first edition of tomorrow's paper.

But I drive past the garage. Ironic that Da's car should have a full tank of petrol. The journeys he never went on; the milometer finally stuck. Left. Down to the roundabout leading to the motorway. M8 Stirling. Still it is not irrevocable. A few miles on the motorway, foot to the floor, a release of tension. That's all. Perhaps no further. Faster. Faster. Perhaps not Lochglas. Peggy and Sarah, after all. Peggy and Sarah.

Lochglas. Walk about in the shoe; look carefully at the reflection in the mirror. See it; feel it. Stirling? Already? I barely noticed the miles I walked. The soft leather fits snugly round my foot. And then, near Perth, the moment where the shoe has been worn too long to take back. The decision is made before it is made. Go on going on. Only the price left to pay. Expensive shoes, a high price: Peggy and Sarah.

Midsummer midnight, a seductive darkness that never quite blackens. Ahead, only white lines and headlights. But through the side window, glimpses of a world flashing by: a full, round moon that sparkles silver on the black water; and a dragon's-breath puff of mist drifting free across the loch; and a solid wedge of inky shadow reflecting from the army of trees standing sentinel at the water's edge. Da would have loved this: the surreal magic of it; the spontaneity of the journey; and knowing that, the beauty becomes a kind of ache.

The car speeds through the night, eating up the miles. The mental pulse beats steadily, from memory to memory, year to year. The year we went to Ireland. The year Sarah broke her leg. The year Da won fifty pounds on a fifty-to-one outsider in the Derby and took us all, Sarah and Charlie and Peggy and me, out to eat in a restaurant. Peggy said he should save it but Da wouldn't hear of it and I loved that about him, the way somewhere inside him, he knew how to live.

The first stab of tiredness cuts into me. I open the car window and switch on the radio. It crackles and hisses, the reception blocked by the hills. I turn it off again. Tomorrow, I think, I will phone Shameena. Let her know the arrangements for Friday. Maybe I'll tell her where I am. Maybe not. I love Shameena but right now I am in a world that is shrinking. There is only me and

Da, and a shadow of mother standing behind us. And Tariq, of course. Tariq is always on my shoulder.

It is time to talk about Tariq. It will not surprise me if you find what I say childish. I don't expect anyone to understand. I don't really care if you do or you don't. You may think it was unimportant because I was only sixteen. But you would be wrong. Tariq is ageless, timeless. He simply is.

It was those boys spitting at Khadim on the bus that led me to Tariq, albeit in a very indirect kind of way. The next evening, Da came home from day shift and said we had been invited to Khadim's house for a meal. Sarah and I looked at one another in surprise. We never went to anyone's house. Da was friendly to people but he kept his distance; he wasn't a sociable man. He never went to parties, or to the pub, or even out to the pictures, though Peggy and Charlie would have looked after us any time he wanted.

I screwed up my face.

"Do we have to?" I said. I was fifteen and didn't want to go anywhere that involved adults.

"Of course we have to," said Da. "We've been invited."

"Why?"

Da shrugged.

"He wanted to say thank you. About what happened on the bus yesterday."

"What happened?" said Sarah.

"Couldn't he just say it?" I asked.

Da sighed.

"Couldn't you just go without having to have your tuppence-worth all the time?"

"Excuse me for living."

"Is nobody going to tell me?" demanded Sarah.

"What's your problem anyway, Rebecca?" said Da, dishing out shepherd's pie onto three plates. "Get the cutlery, will you?"

"It will be embarrassing," I said, sighing heavily and throwing open the drawer. I brought the cutlery over to the table where Da was trying to shake off a wedge of grey, lumpy mashed potato from a spoon. "Still," I muttered, watching it fall like a rock down a hillside, "at least we'll eat."

Da had few alternatives when it came to cooking and most of them involved mince. Sarah and I took a culinary interest at a remarkably young age. Sarah even took cookery books out of the library and we'd drool over the pictures and then leave them lying around the sitting room, open at the pages of some dish or other we fancied most. Da never took the hint. So Sarah and I started cooking. It wasn't so much interest as self preservation.

"I mean, I like Khadim, but we don't know his family, do we?" I said as we sat down.

"Well, we won't if we don't go," said Sarah.

"Oh shut up, Sarah!" I banged a knife and fork down in her place.

"Rebecca!" said Da sharply. "Don't talk like that." Da found my teenage years the most trying. The moods and the stroppiness. He got Peggy to do all the women's stuff, of course. The day he arranged for our little "chat", he could hardly look me in the eye.

"As far as you are concerned everything's embarrassing," Da continued crossly. "Even going to Peggy's is embarrassing. Being asked to go the corner shop is embarrassing. Being picked up from parties is embarrassing."

"Well it is," I said. "My friends all get the bus home."

Da shoved a plate across to me. "We're going."

"When?"

"Friday."

"Amy said I could maybe go to hers on Friday."

"Too bad."

I scowled and took a mouthful of shepherd's pie, crunching into a half-cooked carrot.

"Any pickle?"

"Khadim has a girl about your age," said Da, opening the fridge door. "And a boy a year older. Doesn't keep too well." He handed me a jar of Branston with a gummed-up lid and dried pickle down the side.

"Who?"

"The boy."

"What's the matter with him?"

"Heart trouble."

Shit, I thought. A Friday night stuck with a girl I've never met and her sickly brother.

"This pickle bottle's disgusting," I complained. "It's all sticky."

❧

Shameena and I hit it off immediately. She was a stroppy cow, like me. She had been made to dress up in her best clothes and she sat mutinously on the sofa when we arrived, kicking her heels against her seat.

"Hi," she said, scarcely looking up when we were introduced.

"Shameena!" said Khadim sharply, and Shameena struggled to her feet to shake hands with Da and Sarah and me.

I thought she looked like a bit of a goddess actually. A glorious, sulky goddess. She had on a bright red salwar kameez and a scarf edged in gold that hung down over her plump, golden arms. Her eyes were outlined with thick, jet-black kohl and two huge gold earrings dangled from her lobes. Best of all was the diamond stud through her nose.

"Like your stud," I said, and she suddenly grinned.

Khadim's wife Nazima inclined her head in welcome and avoided looking us directly in the eye. She was like a tiny, colourful bird in her blue salwar kameez, with sharp, precise little movements as she turned this way and that. Her dark, expressive eyes stole glances in the way a bird steals crumbs and darts away with them again. Khadim looked like a giant next to her. Nazima communicated in smiles so that she didn't have to talk. She had a few words of English but Khadim had to keep translating into Urdu for her.

"She's never bothered learning English," Shameena explained to me. "Twenty years here and she can scarcely speak a word. She understands quite a lot though."

I felt a bit honoured. Didn't look like they had many white visitors. Nazima's life was her family: her husband and son and daughter; the cousins who lived nearby; and Khadim's brother who lived in Edinburgh. She didn't go out to work and I could see why she had so little English.

We were only in a few minutes when Nazima called Shameena and the two of them disappeared into the kitchen before reappearing with bowl after colourful bowl of food, enough for a maharaja's feast. Pakoras and samosas and bowls of rich, dark, curry. Indian vegetables and naan breads and popadums. Brightly coloured sweets, rolled in coconut and coloured yellow and pink and green like the tail feathers of an exotic bird.

Nazima motioned us with swift little hand movements and smiled into the carpet. Her son, Tariq, had been delayed and we would start the meal without him. This could be tricky. Da was a stew and mince and tatties man. But he surprised me the way he not only ate, but enjoyed, the feast that was put before us. Da always did like colour. He loved the richness of the clothes Nazima and Shameena wore, the intensity of the colours and the sparkling threads of gold and silver that ran through them. He loved the exotic sweetness of the sliced mango on the table, and what, to him, was the fire of the curries. Specially mild dishes, Khadim said, for his new friend Joseph. I felt a bit touched by that; I had never known Da to have a friend.

Da laughed and said he'd never tasted anything as delicious as this Kashmiri chicken with its mouth-watering mixture of spices and bananas and pineapples. He was in such good humour that night. Halfway through eating, Tariq arrived home. When the door opened and he walked in, I nearly dropped my fork. Sarah was sitting opposite me with her back to the door and she clocked my stare before she turned to see who had come in. When she turned back to the table she gave me a little grin of amusement, and I flushed with annoyance and glared at her, kicking her lightly under the table.

He was gorgeous. Tariq would have been about eighteen or nineteen then. His eyes drew me, great dark pools that seemed older, deeper, wiser, than the rest of him. He wasn't that much older than me and Shameena really, but there was something about his eyes that put him in a different league from us and the spotty youths we hung around with. Despite his slenderness, Tariq seemed like a man rather than a boy, and that was irresistible to an almost-sixteen-year-old girl.

I found him deeply attractive but underneath the warm, golden tones of his skin it was obvious that he was not well. He moved slowly and seemed breathless with the least exertion. Nazima fussed the minute he came through the door, and sat him down and laid bowls before him like he was an honoured guest, and he smiled a slow, warm smile at her and told her not to fuss. He sat next to me and turned those huge dark eyes on me and nodded.

Tariq had been born with a congenital heart defect. Doctors told Khadim and Nazima that he would be in a wheelchair when he was a teenager, but see, they said, he was not in a wheelchair. Allah was good. They thought he got better all the time. But he needed an operation soon. They prayed all the time for their son, said Khadim, and Nazima closed her eyes and clasped her hands as if in prayer.

"They're not kidding either," said Shameena, under her breath to me. "All the bloody time."

Tariq heard her and grinned lazily at his sister. I glanced up quickly to see if Khadim had heard too, but he was too busy encouraging Nazima to spoon more Kashmiri chicken onto Da's plate.

"We go to church every week too," I said.

"Just once? You're lucky. We pray five times a day and go to the mosque at least once a week."

"God!" I said

"No, Allah," grinned Shameena and we both giggled. "The only time I don't have to go is you know… that time of the month," she whispered to me behind her hand, so that nobody else could hear.

"What?"

She shrugged.

"That's the custom. Don't ask me. I don't complain. I had two last month."

I laughed, choking on a chunk of naan bread.

"Pass Rebecca some water, Shameena, " called Khadim from the other end of the table, and then turned back to some involved conversation with Da.

"Didn't they notice?" I asked.

She shook her head, pouring water from a jug into my glass.

"Mum did, but she just went along with it because she didn't want any more arguments. Me and Dad are always fighting."

After dinner Shameena and I went up to her room, though to be honest, I was a bit reluctant to take my eyes off Tariq for one second more than I had to. Entering Shameena's room was like walking into the very core of a jewel and being enveloped by the colour of it, the sparkle of it. It was warm and rich and intense, the walls a deep terracotta red, the bedspread purple with terracotta elephants marching round the edge. On the walls were gilt-framed pictures: a family photograph; an illustrated verse from the Koran… and a picture of Johnny Depp. Long gold chains and jewelled necklaces hung over the mirror on her dressing table. A purple salwar kameez etched with silver flowers hung on the outside door of the wardrobe, half-covering the mirror, and on the floor below, a discarded pair of Levi's lay in a heap.

It was the mix of cultures that made the room so exotic, though it didn't occur to me at the time that Shameena's life might be a clash rather than a fusion of influences. It took time for me to understand how difficult things were for her, how much of an outsider she was too. I do remember a glimpse of it that night as I rifled through her music collection and stared in amazement at the amount of opera in it. It was then Shameena first confided her dreams of being a singer. She wanted to audition for the opera school in London but Khadim wouldn't hear of it. He wanted her to be a lawyer or a doctor. Or an accountant like Tariq.

"He says it's just a silly dream," she said, and something in her voice upset me. Even back then I knew that dreams weren't silly. Perhaps especially back then.

"I don't suppose there are many Pakistani opera singers…" I said hesitantly. How did a Pakistani girl get to like opera? But of course she wasn't a Pakistani girl. She was as Glaswegian as me. There wasn't any reason why she shouldn't like opera as much as me. Except I hated it. All that bloody fa la la stuff.

"There was this woman, right," said Shameena, rolling onto her stomach and facing me, her feet banging off her headboard, "called Noor Jehan and she was a Pakistani singer and she was so good they called her the Melody Queen. That's what I want to be. The new Melody Queen."

"What happened to her?"

"She made all these films but in her very first film the young director fell madly in love with her and they eloped."

"Did they live happily ever after?"

"Nah. They did what everyone who gets married does. Made each other miserable."

We both laughed, and Shameena jumped off the bed then and took the purple salwar kameez off the back of the door and told me to just shove it on over my jeans and top. I was so skinny I'd need some bulk anyway, she said. She took out a kohl pencil and outlined my eyes carefully.

"You suit that," she said, and then picked up the purple scarf that had slipped onto the floor from the hanger. "The dopatta," she said, and threw it round my shoulders. Da was always asking why I didn't wear dresses more, but this felt amazing. I felt regal and mysterious and exotic.

"I feel like an Indian queen," I told Shameena.

"Aye right," she said. "A Pakistani queen, if you don't mind."

The purple was so intense that I felt richer and more alive, as if life had a colour switch like a television and someone had just turned it up full. I swivelled and twirled in front of the mirror and laughed self-consciously, and just then we heard Tariq calling us through the door to come for some tea.

"Tariq," called Shameena through the closed door. "Come here a minute!"

"No!" I whispered vehemently, but the door opened and Tariq stood there in the doorway, slightly breathless just with the effort of walking up the hallway.

"What do you think?" said Shameena, gesturing to me with a malicious little grin, and I later wondered how she had known so quickly, and if it was me or Tariq who gave it away. Tariq's eyes flickered briefly with surprise when he glanced at me, then quickly the veil came down on them again. But he smiled, that sweet, slow smile that has never left me.

"Nice," he said, and softly closed the door.

CHAPTER TWO

The memories kept me awake on the long road, as the dark shadows loomed towards me then disappeared into the rear view mirror. I turned the memories over in my mind, like the pages of a photograph album. The forgotten images. The treasured ones you turn back to again and again. Da and Sarah and Charlie and Peggy. Shameena. Tariq. Nazima and Khadim. Our lives all touching and intertwining.

At first, Da thought it was Shameena who made me so keen to visit Khadim's house again after that first visit. And partly it was. But it was Tariq too. It was so hard to talk to him because we were never alone. The first time was a night in August, a perfect night when we all sat out in their postage-stamp garden till nearly ten o'clock, Da and Khadim and Nazima on chairs at the back door, me and Sarah and Shameena and Tariq further up on the grass.

Shameena knew, though we never spoke about it. This night, we were all talking amongst ourselves, the adults and the young ones, and then Shameena winked at me and said to Sarah to come into her room and she'd show her these new earrings she'd bought. And dumb Sarah said, "Coming, Rebecca?" I wanted to hit her. But Shameena said, "Oh, Rebecca's seen them; we'll only be a minute." She was at least twenty. I glanced up at her window while Tariq and I were talking and saw her looking out. She gave me a furtive thumbs-up sign.

Tariq was still in his first year of accountancy at university then. His health hadn't yet deteriorated so badly that he had to give up. But he did have a date for his next operation, a month down the line.

"Do you mind hospital?" I asked him, picking the daisies round me carelessly and throwing them into a pile. I used my thumbnail to slice through a stem, feeling the juice on my finger, then threaded another flower through to make the beginnings of a chain. My self-consciousness around Tariq made me need something to focus on. He made me feel clumsy, ungainly.

Tariq shrugged at the question and plucked at a blade of grass. "I'm used to it. My whole life has been spent in and out of hospital."

"Must have been hard watching your friends do things you couldn't do."

"I had to find quiet things to interest me. Music. Reading. Computers."

The daisies were becoming limp and difficult to thread. It was getting late.

"Did you want to be like the others?" I asked.

"Of course I did. Every kid wants to be like the others. I wanted football boots. I wanted my dad to watch me play for the school team. I wanted to join in on the school sponsored walk and run at sports day. I wanted to be free. And I wasn't free."

"Maybe this operation will make you free."

He shook his head. "Nothing can do that. It might buy me more time, that's all. I'll need a transplant to be free, and even then I would need medication for the rest of my life. I'll never be free, not like you are."

"That would be weird, having someone else's heart," I said, and instantly regretted it.

"Yeah." He rolled onto his front and looked at me. "People are funny about the heart, like it's more than just a heart. Like it's the core of you."

"I know. You know the composer, Chopin? Da says he died in Paris, but though his body was buried there, he asked for his heart to be taken back to Warsaw, where he was born."

"Really?" said Tariq. The evening sun was casting shadows on his face as he looked at me. "I don't know why there's so much romance about the heart. People seem to think if you get someone else's heart, you kind of... I don't know, *become* them or something. But my specialist says it's just a pump. A mechanical pump."

"I suppose it's because it's supposed to be the feeling bit of you, the bit that loves," I said, and then blushed. But I knew Tariq was right about reading too much into the heart. I had one that worked; I could afford to be sentimental. Tariq didn't and he couldn't. I threaded another daisy through my chain.

"I would probably get a white man's heart if I got a transplant," said Tariq, and looked to see my reaction. "Or a white woman's."

"Does that bother you?"

"No. It might bother them, though. Did you read the story in the paper about the man who didn't want his son's heart going to 'a Paki'?"

I shook my head, studying my chain to avoid looking at him.

"He's just ignorant," I muttered, because I couldn't think of anything else to say.

"His son had died in a motorcycle accident," said Tariq. "I saw him interviewed on television. He was crying. He said he and his wife had been asked if his son's heart could be used for

100

transplantation and he said no at first. He was too upset. Then doctors told him he could help prevent other parents feeling the way he was feeling right now. There was a young man waiting for transplant. So he said yes. It hurt, he said, knowing that his boy had to die for someone else but he wanted to help. He wasn't a bad man. I watched him and I thought he was just like my dad. He loved his son."

My glance up to Tariq's face is instinctive. "So what happened?"

"He found out the recipient was to be an Asian. The interviewer asked him how he felt when he heard and he said, "I told doctors I didn't want my Shane's heart going to no Paki."

"Don't think about it. Most people wouldn't think that way. The guy's just…"

"Just a dad who lost his boy," finished Tariq. "He wasn't evil. He didn't seem it, anyway. He wanted to do something good. But then he wanted me excluded from the good. I don't really understand… Part of me hated him and part of me felt sorry for him, you know?"

I didn't know what to say to Tariq. Then I remembered something I had heard Da say and I said, "Good and bad aren't as black and white as people think." Now that I think about it, I wonder what he was thinking about when he said that.

"No," Tariq had replied. "I suppose not."

He lay back on the grass and closed his eyes and I looked at the shadows underneath his eyes and the fine line of his mouth. His lips had a faint purplish-blueish tinge, as if they were bruised.

"Why aren't they doing a transplant for you now?" I asked.

"They want me to be stronger. They think doing this operation will help in the meantime, buy me time to get stronger."

"I think you're very brave," I said. "I'd be frightened."

Tariq said nothing.

"How long will you be in for?"

"A week maybe. Or maybe this time I won't come back," he said.

I looked up quickly at him but his eyes remained closed.

"Of course you'll come back. What are you talking about?"

"It's a big operation." He opened his eyes and turned to me. "I said I don't mind about hospital and usually that's true. I always feel better when I come back from hospital. For a while. But this time…"

"What?"

"I… I feel… a kind of bad… I don't know… like this time it won't make me better. That maybe this is it…"

I put my hand on his where it lay on the grass and then quickly withdrew it and looked down to where Da and Khadim and Nazima were sitting. Nobody had noticed, except maybe Da. He looked away so quickly I wasn't sure.

"I can't say to anyone in the family," continued Tariq. "It would upset them too much." He looked down at Nazima and smiled faintly. "You see the way my mother is."

It would be impossible not to see. Nazima adored Tariq. It was Tariq who kept her breathing. She flew round him like a sparrow round an eagle, flittering and fluttering and paying homage.

I wanted to throw my arms round Tariq but I didn't know what to say to him and I felt a lump in my throat in case what he was saying was true. It was difficult to swallow. I was hopelessly out of my depth.

"I think," I said, "that everything will be fine."

It sounded trite, even to an almost sixteen-year-old.

"Why?" said Tariq. "Why will it be fine?"

"Because I want it to be." I threaded another flower through a loop and didn't look at him. "And I'm a madam. I get what I want."

I was aware Tariq was looking at me and when I finally dared glance up, he was smiling.

"I'll bet you are," he said, and I grinned at him.

I heard Shameena and Sarah's voices at the back door. Tariq glanced up at them, and then at me, as if he was considering. Then he whispered to me.

"You know Roberto's, the café on Paisley Road West?"

I nodded. It was the café I hid in when I should have been at mass.

"Meet me there. Thursday. 4.30?"

I didn't have time to reply. I felt my stomach lurch. Sarah threw herself down on the grass beside me.

"Shameena's earrings are gorgeous, aren't they?" she said.

"Yeah," I replied, as convincingly as I could. "Gorgeous." I'd never seen them.

CHAPTER THREE

I could barely wait till Thursday. The best thing about being in a single-parent family was the freedom. Peggy helped a lot when we were wee of course, but by the time I was fifteen and Sarah eleven, we were in that no man's land between needing watched and being allowed a little freedom. Da thought it reasonable for me to look after Sarah for a few hours after school. But she'd be fine while I met Tariq. There was no way I was missing that.

"Where are you going?" Sarah asked me that Thursday.

"Out," I said importantly. "With a boyfriend," I added, purely for effect and it worked, because her eyes widened. "So keep your trap shut."

If it had been me, I'd have extracted some gain for me in keeping my trap shut but Sarah, she was such an innocent.

"Don't do anything stupid while I'm out," I warned her, "or I'll get found out."

I was five minutes late for Tariq that Thursday because of going home to change. There was no way I could meet him in my school uniform. I ran and ran, till my heart thumped and I could hardly breathe. My legs felt shaky. Near the café I slowed down, took huge deep breaths. I fished out a baby-pink lipstick, peered into a shop window to apply it. Took hooped earrings from my purse, ran a comb through my hair. Scooshed the last of my perfume Peggy had given me last year for my birthday. Never mind.

It was my sixteenth in a week. Somebody would give me more.

Tariq was already there when I arrived, sitting with a fresh orange juice at the back table of the café and watching the door.

"I didn't know if you'd come," he said. "You never said."

Not come? Was he mad?

"You smell nice," he said.

"Thanks."

It seemed an intimate thing for a boy like Tariq to say, somehow. I reached out and touched his hand briefly as it rested on the table and then glanced up. The waitress had caught the gesture and was staring at me. She turned and said something under her breath to the owner behind the counter. He looked over when she spoke, saw me looking and shrugged, looked away again. I went up to the counter and ordered a coffee from the man but it was the waitress who brought it back and she slopped it down carelessly on the table without a word, so that the coffee spilled into the saucer and then splashed onto the table. I glanced up at her and she looked hard at me and then at Tariq. "Anything else?" she said, looking back at me.

"Yeah," I said dryly. "A cloth."

Tariq looked uncomfortable.

That first afternoon set a pattern. We met most days, spinning out one drink each to last a couple of hours. By the end of the first week, the waitress hardly glanced at us any more, but there was a deterioration in Tariq. He was getting weaker, I could tell. He hadn't a puff, and he was even thinner, his shirt hanging loosely round a neck that was slender as a lily stem. He had deep shadows under his eyes and his cheeks were sunken. The doctor was trying to get his operation brought forward.

I remember the last day we met in the café. He was quiet and

105

subdued and he said, "Rebecca, what do you think happens when you die?"

"Dunno," I said. I was using my finger to sweep a trail of sugar on the table top into a little pile.

"It frightens me to think about it," said Tariq. "I think about hell sometimes."

"Do Muslims have hell too?" I was surprised. Wasn't it only Catholics that had hell? I always thought we understood hell better than heaven.

"There's a description of it in the Koran."

He began quoting, without hesitation, his voice soft.

"Garments of fire shall be cut, and there shall be poured over their heads boiling water, whereby whatsoever is in their bellies and their skin shall be melted…"

"That's a bit gory, isn't it?"

"I can't stop thinking about it. What if it's true?"

"You haven't done anything bad."

"I'm here, aren't I?"

"Is that bad?"

"Yes… no. I like being here but… but I know my parents wouldn't approve of me being alone with a girl."

"There's at least ten other people in here."

"You know what I mean."

We lapsed into silence.

"I'm supposed to marry my cousin in Pakistan. When I get better."

It was a shock. "What, someone you don't know?"

"I've got a picture." He brought out a snap from his wallet and put it on the table in front of me. I didn't want to see it. I hated her, whoever she was. I glanced at it cursorily, aware only

106

of huge dark eyes set deep into a fragile, fine-boned face.

"Do you like the look of her?"

I didn't look at him but my heart pounded. Tariq ignored the question. Or maybe he didn't. "The thing is," he said slowly, "I don't feel Pakistani." He said it as if he should be ashamed.

"Why should you? You weren't born there. Do you feel Glaswegian?"

"Yes... no... well, a bit. I don't really feel I belong anywhere, to be honest. It's like... I'm really, really proud of my Pakistani background but I don't feel completely part of it. But I don't feel completely part of here, either. I am not Pakistani and I'm not Glaswegian. I'm a Glaswegian Pakistani, and that's different, separate.

I glanced down at the snap on the table.

"Will your parents make you marry her?"

"Not make me, no. If I don't like her..."

I said nothing.

"I try to do the right thing," he said, looking at me, his voice almost pleading for understanding. "To please my parents and please Allah."

"You believe in Allah?"

He hesitated. "I try."

I hate docile people. But Tariq was not docile. There was something almost noble about his quiet restraint. Maybe I admired it because I am not restrained, couldn't possibly be. I couldn't help thinking how much more like Sarah he was than he was like me. But there was no chemistry between Sarah and Tariq. You cannot dispute chemistry.

I tore the discarded sugar packet from my coffee into strips.

"What... no, who... *is* Allah?" I asked Tariq.

"Allah is the supreme being who has power over the universe."

Tariq answered automatically, the way we used to answer our Catholic Catechism in primary school. Who made you? *God made me.* Why did God make you? *God made me to know him, to love him, and to serve him in this world, so that I may be happy with him forever in heaven.* Same idea, whatever the creed.

"Mmm. God or Allah?" I said to Tariq. "Maybe they are both the same. Maybe we'll find out we're worshipping the same God."

"I'll find out before you."

"Don't talk like that."

"I'm scared," he said.

The words are so stark.

"Oh Tariq." I took his hand. I could feel tears burning at the back of my eyes for the rawness of those words, for the cost to him of saying them out loud. Shit. I couldn't, mustn't, cry.

"Don't be frightened," I said, digging the nails on my left hand into my palm in a vain attempt to stop the tears that were welling in my eyes from spilling over.

Tariq's hand brushed the tear lightly from my cheek, and I resisted the urge to grab his hand and hold tight.

"We'd better go," he said.

I feel ashamed when I think of that conversation now. It was Tariq who brushed my tear away, not me who brushed his.

Outside the café, a gang of white boys were hanging around, lolling against doorways, fags in hand. I came through the door first and saw their eyes swivel to me. There was one boy whose eyes looked the meanest. He was dressed in dark jeans and a black t-shirt with a narrow stripe across the chest, and he looked at me in that thin, predatory way teenage boys do when they first discover sex. Like foxes foraging through dustbins for a bone to gnaw. Like they're permanently hungry, and will eat, no matter the meal.

Tariq followed me out and I felt, rather than saw, the gang stiffen. The one with the striped t-shirt stepped right in front of Tariq, blocking his way. Tariq moved to the right. The boy stepped with him, blocking him still. Tariq moved to the left. The boy moved too, like their bodies were locked in some macabre, magnetic dance. Tariq simply stood still then and looked at him, not in defiance, not in fear. He simply looked. Slowly, slowly, the boy moved aside, never taking his eyes from Tariq. "Black bastard," he muttered.

Tariq never even flinched. His body did not stiffen. His face remained neutral. For a moment I thought of Davie Richardson in the park when we were kids, and I had the same desire to lash out. But I knew the consequences for Tariq if I did. "You want to watch the company you keep, darlin'," one of them sneered at me as Tariq and I walked slowly past. I thought of Tariq's words in the café. Not Pakistani. Not Glaswegian. A Glaswegian Pakistani.

I suppose there would have been a lot of stuff like that ahead. I never got the chance to find out. Tariq was too ill to meet after that. He never went back to university. We visited the Khans as a family the night after my sixteenth birthday, which was the night before he went into hospital. Everyone was there so we couldn't talk alone. But when I came out of the toilet, Tariq came out of the sitting room. He must have been waiting, listening for the flush, trying to time it. He pressed one of those friendship bracelets into my hand, the kind you get in Indian shops. It had pink beads on it, with tiny little red flowers painted on them.

"Happy birthday," he said.

We'd never kissed before. Never done anything other than

hold hands across a table. But Tariq kissed me then, in the hall of his house, and maybe the danger of discovery added to the thrill of it. It wasn't a deep, passionate kiss. It was over in seconds. He held my face in his hands and his poor blue lips caressed my top lip, then my bottom lip, light and swift as a butterfly. And never, never in all the years that followed, did any one of that succession who followed Tariq in my life, not Mr Mad or Mr Bad or Mr Dangerous, ever touch me the way he touched me, ever come close to the sweetness of that moment…

CHAPTER FOUR

Shit. The car swerves as a lorry thunders past. That was bloody close. Last thing I remember my eyes were glued to the white line, but I must have drifted, silently, dangerously. My hands shake on the wheel. The photograph album in my mind kept me awake at first, then slowly, seductively, it lulled me too deeply into its pages. The indicators tick-tock rhythmically as I stop the car in the next layby, close my eyes. Just for a moment. Just a rest.

Mr Mad… best forgotten. Mr Bad… well there were a few of him. I threw myself away on Mr Bads, deliberately I think now. Useless, disposable Becca who came from nowhere and was going nowhere. What did it matter?

And then there was Mr Dangerous, the only one I came close to loving. That's why he was Mr Dangerous. He wasn't free, of course. I see now that I never chose anyone who was free. Not after Tariq. Not *even* Tariq.

Maybe I thought I wasn't worth it. And I learned that if you think you aren't worth it, men don't think you're worth it either. If that sounds self-pitying, forget it. I am not a victim. I don't want anyone's pity, not yours and not even my own. Certainly not now. It's just that after Tariq, nothing was worth it. Love, sex, lies, games… it was all the same to me. Tariq was my one shot at purity. After that, I didn't believe in purity any more.

I see Mr Dangerous as I drift into a short, intense sleep in the car; see him standing naked in the half-light of the hotel bedroom, the smooth line of his back skimming into neat, muscular buttocks. He always stood by the window afterwards, drowning in the choppy waters of his own despair, while I lay watching him from the bed. He would lean his arm against the wall and lay his head on it, then he'd lift the curtain just a fraction with his free hand and peer through the crack into the world, like he couldn't make up his mind whether to join it or not.

In my memory, it is always half light, constantly falling shadows. It was winter and he was never free except in the afternoon. By the time we drove well out of town where he could be sure he wouldn't be recognised, darkness was already closing in.

He'd stand there with his back to me as the last of the light melted into darkness, like ice melting into water, until there was nothing left to illuminate the room but the insipid, dusty glow from the desk lamp.

The first time I ever saw him he had his back to me. I thought he looked like Tariq from behind: the same wiry, black hair that kicked out at the collar when it needed a cut; the same ascetic thinness. I fell for him then. People say women always fall for men they know they shouldn't. It's the challenge. If they can make the ones who mustn't fall in love with them want them, how powerful is that?

It became a corrupt kind of power, a power I wielded lethally, like a weapon.

A samurai sword that I used to slice through every sinew of conscience. "I have responsibilities," he'd murmur against my lips, and I'd use my tongue to lick the words into silence. I mistook that power for something else, as I so often have.

His desire was predictable; there was no cunning needed. A shorter skirt. A higher heel. The deeper plunge of my neckline; the moist, pearly lustre of lip sheen, glistening like the juice of blood oranges on my lips. I thought I was in control, didn't realise until it was too late that I was playing with my own emotions as well as his. I could have loved him. He wasn't worthy of it, but who said love was worthy?

He couldn't contain his desire to get into bed but he couldn't wait to get out of it. Before he had even withdrawn from inside me he was cutting the emotional ties that might have bound us, till all that was left was a sad, tattered heap of lost possibilities.

He never held me afterwards. His first instinct was always to move away from me. I cried the first time he stood at the hotel window, two sharp bitter tears of humiliation. He stood there so long he never knew. And I never cried again. I learned to watch him coolly, dispassionately, waiting for him to turn towards me. As he always did. He'd come over to the bed finally and lie for a few minutes, against my shoulder, wrapped in a blanket of his own self-pity.

"I can't do this," he said once, murmuring against my shoulder, waiting for me to comfort him, absolve him. Absolution, that's the thing. Confession. And after confession, familiar temptation. "I think you just did," I said. This time, I did not lift my arm to hold him. He half sat, twisting onto his elbow. "My God, Rebecca, you're hard," he said bitterly.

Why couldn't I understand? Things were so complicated. He had another life, a life quite separate from me that couldn't include me. So choose, I said, with a carelessness I didn't feel. He looked at me then like he hated me. He probably did.

I don't think he ever took responsibility for what happened; he wouldn't admit it but he blamed me. I was a woman and I was strong and I should have been strong for him. He despised himself for wanting me, but he despised me more for making him. And I despised myself for being with a man like him.

So many broken promises, he said once. Broken vows. I had to help him.

Leave him. Move away. And when he called, I asked? What then? Should I refuse to talk to him? Because he *would* call. Even he knew he would.

Sometimes he called my mobile late at night. He liked to call when I was in bed.

Sometimes, he didn't say anything for a full minute but I always knew it was him. I couldn't go to his house, obviously. And he couldn't come to mine. So he had to make do with connecting to me by a telephone line. It suited him best, engagement at a distance.

Whatever the pattern of his remorse – the cold shame of his head against the wall, or the pleading need for understanding – there were always tears. He would sit by the desk with his head in his hands, or he'd come over to the bed and turn into the firm curve of my upper arm and sob, the warm drip of bitter tears running down my breast and ribcage onto the sheets. I would hold him loosely then, stroking his hair lightly, or circling my thumb gently over his arm.

"I'm sorry," he would sob. "I'm sorry, I'm sorry, I'm sorry…" Sorry for who, I would think, looking up at a small patch of damp spreading from the light rose.

Sometimes I would look down on the dark hair and try to pretend he was Tariq, imagine what it would have been like to be with Tariq. It's the biggest betrayal I can think of, to make love to someone while pretending they are someone else. Somehow,

114

I could never feel guilty. There was so much pretence between us that a little extra didn't seem important. Every lover I have ever had, I've imagined was Tariq.

It must end, he would say. I would kiss his tears then, but in a half-hearted, desultory kind of way. Even as I tasted them, I knew we would be back here next week, back in this room with the magnolia woodchip walls, and the desk with the dusty globed lamp, and the fusty smell of a shower sprouting mould in the grout between the tiles. We were caught in a cycle of guilt and recrimination and desire, and the most powerful of those was desire. Even at the very height of his protests about how this must never happen again, I knew for certain it would. There would be confession in between, of course.

That's the way it is with Catholic priests.

☙

As I write this all down so many years later, I can see how bad it sounds. Secrets rarely make pretty reading. I think I felt a vague shame even back then, when it all tumbled around inside my head on that lonely car journey north. That's my memory. A sense of embarrassment that if Da did still exist in some way, he might now know what I had been up to. It was a strange turning of the tables. First I read his love letters to my mother, then he found out about my affair.

I did not need to ask if he disapproved. I knew the answer too well to even consider asking the question. But I wanted him not to think too badly of me. I am not a bad person. A priest, yes, but *he* was the priest, not me. His collar, his cloth, his promises to a God I couldn't share.

The convent schoolgirl in me thought it was the worst thing I could do, but another part of me took a perverse satisfaction in that. Perhaps it was just another sign of my instinct for self-destruction. This God Father Dangerous had devoted his life to had taken Tariq, so I took him. One of mine for one of His. Maybe part of me was prepared to burn to have even a second's revenge.

CHAPTER FIVE

The miles flashed by. Newtonmore. Kingussie. Miles eaten by memories. I don't know which of us used the other more. Father Dangerous was screwed up about sex because of his vocation; I was screwed up about love because of Tariq. Sometimes you make do with one and pretend it's the other. But in my heart, I know the difference. I never had sex with Tariq but he taught me the difference.

And the others, well, there were not so many. A few. A few who for a week, a day, an hour, made me feel there was something in me that was worth having. I think, deep down, I felt that if I had been worth anything, Tariq would have lived. Those who came after were nothing, nothing at all. It didn't make me a bad person. There were worse things, I told myself as I drove into the night. It wasn't unforgivable, was it? It's wasn't like I killed anybody.

❦

It was Da who introduced me to him, the new, dynamic young parish priest. I think maybe he thought he'd lead me back to the Church. As I suppose he did, just not in the way Da thought.

I'd go to mass with Da sometimes that winter. I was old enough not to have to rebel any more. I kept him company, though later, for obvious reasons, I wouldn't go near the place.

The first time I saw him, he was down the bottom of the church steps as I came out. He was saying goodbye to someone and he turned and walked up the steps, meeting us halfway. I wasn't aware of much of a frisson on his part; perhaps his eyes held mine a little longer than necessary, but nothing more. But later he would say it was instant. I saw him a few times after that before I started dropping into morning mass. I don't know what I was hoping for. It was deliberate but not calculating.

I came in late once. The door slipped from my hand when I opened it, swinging back noisily. He said he would have seen me anyway, that the moment he walked on the altar he knew if I was there or not. His eyes would pick me out at the back from the sea of old biddies and young mums with noisy toddlers. If I wasn't there, he would feel the cut of disappointment. And if I was there, he was on fire. That's what he said. On fire.

Even I was shocked by that. You think when a man puts on his priest's robes, he transcends his humanity. No masculinity. No troublesome sexuality. But it doesn't work like that. In the end, I saw through those vestments. I saw his nakedness. The more fervent his sermon on that altar, the more anguished his prayer, the more I knew he burned.

He was disappointed that day I was late, began the mass with sullen heaviness. Then the door banged and it was like a match hitting petrol. I felt, rather than saw, the effect, the connection blazing silently between us from him on the altar to me at the door. It wasn't that he faltered; there was no hesitation, no stumble in his words. But I saw the awareness ripple through his body. Every tiny movement, every gesture, every almost imperceptible glance, became like a series of dots and dashes in our own personal Morse code. He knew I was there. And I knew that he knew.

We died together slowly. It took a year all in, from start to finish, though it was only after six months that we started renting the hotel room. In those early months when he needed to be held, I held him purely. Wanting more but expecting nothing. Sometimes, I thought he almost enjoyed the anguish of it, the torture. Suffering was grace.

We ended up in bed together for the first time only when he came back from Peter Gallacher's house, after Peter's wife Eva passed away. She was thirty-five. She left four kids under ten and Peter just sat there looking bewildered while the youngest screamed for a bottle. Father Dangerous said it was only when he got up to go that Peter had looked at him properly for the first time since he came into the house. "Will you pray with me, Father?" he said.

It touched him that, the simple faith of it. His own faith wasn't simple; it was a tangled web of love and devotion and doubt and insecurity. He'd come back from Peter's changed somehow. He saw how fragile life was. I think that night he was frightened he would die without knowing what it was like to be with a woman. He phoned me and asked me to meet him in a pub in town. It was the first time he had ever turned up not wearing his collar. His collar was his guard; I knew immediately the significance of its absence.

He greeted me with a kiss, held me close. Reckless he was that night, and it was I who burned then. His lack of caution made his desire for me seem so intense that I mistook it for love. I had imagined this relationship so often that when it finally happened, it seemed more important than it really was. To be that wanted, that needed, that important; it was everything. But it never lasted. The heat of his recklessness was always followed by a cold shower of guilt and remorse. Even that first night.

I told him in the end to choose, because I knew he never would unless I made him. It took me a while to make the ultimatum because inside I always knew what the choice would be. I had to make him say it. But he never could. Not even at the end. I gave him a date and told him he had until midnight to phone.

I lay in bed that night, my phone lying on the bedside table and switched to vibrate. At two minutes to midnight, the phone began to buzz, moving slightly on the cabinet top with the vibration. I picked it up and said nothing. The caller said nothing. We sat in silence for a while.

"Rebecca," he whispered finally, and then his voice broke.

I looked at the phone in the palm of my hand for a moment before gently pressing 'end call'. I switched the phone off so that it couldn't ring again, then flicked the bedside light, and lay staring into the darkness until my eyes adjusted to the lack of light, and I saw things the way they really were.

CHAPTER SIX

Aviemore. Only thirty miles to go to Inverness, and then the search for Lochglas. It is a fast stretch of road from Aviemore, takes little over half an hour to Inverness. Almost a hundred and eighty miles I have travelled. Miles and miles and miles of memories, laid like a motorway from Glasgow to Inverness. I had saved the most painful to the last but I didn't feel strong enough to examine it. It would have to wait.

I can see a pinky-orange glow of lights in the sky above Inverness before I reach the top of the hill, as if there is a space ship hovering somewhere behind the bank of cloud. On the outskirts of town, the lights from the Kessock Bridge shoot into the sky like red antennae and I stop the car at a lay-by before crossing, and look again at Pa's map. Not far. Twenty minutes maybe. Fatigue has seeped from my body right through to my brain. My eyes are stinging, partly with hayfever and partly with tiredness. I look at my watch. Ten to four.

Lochglas when I reach it is a one-street town, spread out in a meandering main street lined with hanging baskets. I slow right down and peer out. A Spar shop, a chemist, a Post Office and, up the far end, a butcher. The village is built on a slight incline and there is a lay-by at the top end, overlooking a bay. I park the car with relief and open the window. The air is warm and sweetly perfumed with the flowers from the hanging baskets.

It is too late to get a room anywhere and anyway, I don't have much money and it will be one less night to pay for. I pull the lever of my seat back and close my eyes.

I doze fitfully for an hour and then wake with my head lolling off the edge of my chair, my neck stiff and sore to move. I clamber sleepily into the back seat, stretching out as best I can, and don't wake again until shortly after seven. My leg is in cramp, and I open the door and jump out. There is a garage across the road that I hadn't noticed in the darkness. I am desperate for a shower and a change of clothes but it is too early to book in anywhere. I lock up the car and walk down to see if I can see Bayview anywhere, the address on mother's letter. I walk through the whole village before returning to the car and realising that there is a path leading down from the lay-by towards the loch below, and that a house sits in against the hillside just under me.

I scramble down the gorse-lined path towards it. The dawn has long disappeared into morning but the sky is still pristine with the promise of a new day, the horizon streaked pink above the loch. A small boat sits unmoving on the surface, the water clear blue, still and glassy beneath. It is going to be another scorcher. I reach the house and look at the wooden gate, a faded sign hanging by a single rusty nail. Bayview.

It is clearly abandoned; whoever owns it now has left it to rot. The house stands at an angle, as if deliberately turning its shoulders from the village to look out over the bay. It is half hidden, trees and bushes grown tall on neglect straggling across the gate, scratching across the window panes and down over the peeling façade of the painted porch. Only the upstairs windows are clearly visible through the greenery, like two watchful eyes peering through a curtain of unkempt hair.

The air is warm and thick with the heavy sweetness of honeysuckle, pale creamy flowers falling against my knees as the gate pushes a pathway through. The paint on the porch is faded green and flaking, washed almost colourless with the rain and hail of many winters, and seared by the summer heat. Shards of glass lie splintered on the narrow windowsills, and above, there are gaping holes in the window panes with jagged, crocodile's-teeth edges where stones have been lobbed through the glass.

I can feel my heart hammering as I walk up the path, the shattered glass crunching beneath my feet. For the first few years of my life I must have lived here. I want desperately to dredge something out of my memory bank. There must be a whole page of the mental photograph album devoted to this place, but I cannot find it. Did I play once in this overgrown garden? Were the lawns neatly cut and the bushes trimmed? Perhaps there was a swing over by that bush there. Perhaps I stood at that window with the faded green curtain and waved to Da as he dug in the garden.

Through the window I can see an old three-piece suite, the sofa toppled over on its back like a beetle turned on its shell and unable to get back onto its legs. It looks like one of those large floral prints from the 1960s and although years of sunshine have seeped the colour from its cushions, there are still flashes of yellow and orange visible. Yellow and orange. Did my sticky, chocolate-covered toddler hands grab hold of that sofa to haul me to my feet when I was taking my first steps? I remember nothing.

The door handle turns easily, the lock broken. To the left of the front door is the room with the suite, a light and spacious room with an open fireplace and a bay window. That must be where mother wrote her letter to Da all those years ago. The kitchen, with its yellow Formica-topped table and a rag of striped, washed-out curtain still hanging at the window, is at the back of the house. Broken bits of crockery lie on the work tops and the sink; half a saucer, a cup handle, a chunk of plate. White with yellow spring flowers. I have a vague feeling I have seen those cups before, a half-memory, the closest I come to recognition in the whole house.

The kitchen is the strangest room of all to go into. There is even a rusting old kettle still lying on top of the cooker, as if someone has just made tea. It reminds me of Flannan Isle, the story of the three lighthouse keepers who just disappeared without trace leaving a half-finished meal and an overturned chair. There is no meal on the table here but there is certainly a feeling of interruption, of a life that suddenly stopped mid-flow and simply never resumed.

At first, I am frightened of climbing the stairs in case the wood of the steps and the bannister is rotten and gives way beneath me. Carefully, I stand on every second step, testing gingerly before putting my full weight down. It seems solid enough. Upstairs there are only two bedrooms. There is an old bed with an iron bed head and a slashed mattress, half on, half off the frame. Up here, I am above the line of the overgrown bushes and trees in the garden and the view across the water is breathtaking. Why did Da move us from here to a cramped two-bedroom council house in Glasgow after mother died? Who would ever leave this place voluntarily? But I suppose if you love someone, memories can weigh heavily in the place where you loved them.

Memories can follow you around too. I always felt with Da that there were times he carried a load with him. It was strange the

124

way his mood swung sometimes. There would be nights when we would be sitting late at night, yawning, winding down before bed, when he would suddenly say, "Becca, let's go out somewhere," and we'd take the car and drive to the airport and have a coffee and watch the late-night planes. Or we'd go to the twenty-four-hour supermarket where Da would buy an exotic fruit he'd never tried before, or a packet of continental biscuits, or a new cheese. He loved spur-of-the-moment, unexpected trips.

Da would wonder around the supermarket aisles smiling, saying there was never this kind of choice when he was a boy. Sure, there was just the village shop in Donegal and fresh produce meant a battered old box with some apples. Apples that were more leathery and wrinkled than Grandpa's old farmer skin, Da joked.

"Is that not marvellous, Becca?" he would say, holding up a star fruit or a lychee that we didn't even know how to peel, or a piece of French Brie. Then he'd shake his head and pop it in his basket. "Marvellous."

He enjoyed the fact that he could go into a supermarket at one in the morning. He enjoyed the lights and the brightness and the people and the buzz. He enjoyed being alive.

And then there were the other nights, the nights when Da seemed haunted, invaded by some presence that he couldn't shake off. People talk about depression being black, but Da's depression wasn't black. It was grey; drained and colourless like a spectre that sat on his shoulder and sucked the life from him. Those were the nights when he would stare at the television screen and you knew he wasn't watching. When there was nothing, simply nothing, that you could say that would elicit more than a couple of words. Sometimes, he would go to bed at eight o'clock on those nights. His door was ajar one night and I saw him from the landing, lying on the bed fully clothed just staring at the wall. But I didn't go in.

He moved differently at those times. He looked older and he kind of shuffled, like there were boulders in his shoes that stopped him lifting his feet. His skin looked dull and pallid. Sarah and I dreaded the arrival of the grey visitor who descended without warning like an uninvited guest and locked Da away from us where we couldn't reach him. It wasn't that Da lost his temper with us; maybe it wouldn't have been so bad if he had. It was just that he withdrew from us and went somewhere else, leaving this impostor behind, a man who looked a bit like Da but wasn't really. It was like he had gone away for a while and I missed him when he left. There was just a shell left behind. A bit like death, really.

On the nights in the airport café or in the supermarket aisles, he was alive and he was free. But on his haunted days, he was like a man who had switched off the light and was stumbling around in the dark. Sometimes the switch would flick so quickly. Once, on one of our night excursions, he got me to drive all the way to Largs at eleven o'clock at night with a flask of coffee. Neither of us had work the next day and we giggled like schoolkids tripping over rocks on the beach. We were happy. Then we sat in the car with the coffee and we looked up at the stars.

"You know, sometimes it make me feel physically sick looking at the stars," he said suddenly. "The vastness of it all. It unnerves me."

I sipped my coffee, just thinking about what he'd said.

"What's the point?" he said suddenly.

"What?"

126

"Of any of it. What are we doing in Largs; what are we doing anywhere?"

I tried being flippant. "If you'd wanted to go to Gourock, you should have said."

But he didn't laugh as he would usually have done, as he would have done five minutes before. He opened the door and drained his cup into the road and said, "Let's go home darlin', eh?"

I put the cups in the bag and we drove back in silence. Half-way home he closed his eyes but I knew it was just to avoid talking. I knew he was wide awake.

He kissed me goodnight when we got home, and said thank you for a nice drive, and then he climbed the stairs to bed as if he had a hundredweight of coal on his back.

He didn't come down the next day till one o'clock in the afternoon. I kept going upstairs to check if he was up, but his door remained fully closed.

Looking out over the bay in Lochglas, I try to imagine Da in this house. But I can't. It is a million miles away from Rosebank Street, and the fumes of the buses in the depot, and the crowds in the city-centre shops. It is like a holiday home; beautiful but not part of you. When you go there on holiday, you say how wonderful it would be to live there all year round, but inside you know it is not your life really. It is someone else's.

I sit on the hillside and watch the day come to. The ground is baked dry as straw with the heat of the last week and the grass stubble prickles through even the thick material of my jeans. The Spar shop opens at eight o'clock and I go in to buy something for breakfast and to ask about a B & B for tonight. There is a woman serving, maybe in her mid forties, plump and cheerful and wearing a pink check overall.

127

"Right, love," she says taking my morning roll, a miniature cheese and a raspberry yoghurt. The electronic till beeps as she passes them through.

"That house," I say as she packs the things into a bag. "Bayview. Who owns it?"

The woman smiles.

"Taken a fancy to it, love?" she asks. "A lot of people do. Do you know, we have at least half-a-dozen people a year in asking about it. It's a lovely position of course, but it's gone to rack and ruin now. It's a Glasgow man owns it but he never comes near."

Even when she says, 'Glasgow man', it still doesn't click.

"A guy called Connaghan," she continues.

My heart skips a beat.

"Connaghan?" I say. "That can't be right. Didn't he move a long time ago?"

"That's right," she says, looking surprised. "But he never sold it. Not as far as we know, anyway. He just left it and never came back." She hands me the shopping bag.

It doesn't make sense. I give her a five pound note in silence. We had never had any money all our lives. Why would Da just let a house crumble when he could have sold it? Why didn't we ever use it?

"Why did he leave?" I ask, as casually as I can.

"Long story. There was a lot of trouble round that house," says the woman, and the till drawer slams shut.

"What happened?"

"Well, this fellow Connaghan and his wife lived there – oh, well over twenty years ago, maybe twenty-five. I was just a young lassie at the time so I didn't know much about either of them but I heard he was well thought of. At first, anyway. But the wife died and the husband moved away and never came back into the house. Just left it with furniture and everything, though over the years the house got vandalised and the stuff was thrown into the loch and chopped up for firewood. There's not much left."

"Did the wife get ill?" I can feel my heart hammering and a wave of nausea sweeps up inside me, even as I ask the question. I knew already that I am not going to like the answer. The woman hands me change. I notice the name tag on her apron. Marion.

"No, she didn't get ill," Marion says. "It was a huge scandal at the time, the biggest thing to ever happen in this place. It was all over the national news too but you'd be too young to remember that. Mrs Connaghan was murdered. They never found her body."

I grab hold of the bag, fight to keep my voice steady.

"Murdered? Who…?"

Marion frowns at me, suddenly registering the level of my response. She has no emotional investment in this story; there is nothing secret about it for her. Just a story she has occasionally told interested visitors. I can tell she is unnerved by my intensity.

"They never got anyone for it. Some folk thought it was Mrs Connaghan's lover – he's some kind of a big-shot businessman in Inverness. But others were convinced her husband must have done it in a jealous rage." She stops. "The man I mentioned who owns the house," she explains, mistaking my frozen expression for lack of comprehension. "Joseph Connaghan."

༺༻

My finger shakes as I try to dial the number. I need to talk; I cannot carry this alone. I can't call Sarah. Shameena. I start to punch in her number. It can only be Shameena. Three. Six. My finger hesitates, trembling, out of control. But what can I say? My finger hovers over the buttons. Shameena, remember you wanted to know how my mother died? Well, I think she was murdered. Maybe by my father, because why else would he have kept everything secret all these years?

Shameena will know what to do. My stomach begins to heave. I think I am going to be sick in this box. Two. Four. But what will she think, says the voice in my head. But what will she *think*? There is no one in the world I trust more than Shameena. But to tell her, to tell anyone, would be the greatest imaginable betrayal of Da. It's not who I tell; it's saying it out loud. It's doubting. I want Shameena to reassure me that Da could not have killed my mother. But I would be relying on someone else to tell me what I should tell myself.

I rest the phone back on the cradle, the last digits undialled. It would be like Da dying all over again. I leave the box, feeling more alone than I have ever felt in my life. I go into a shop and buy ten cigarettes because I don't have the money for twenty. I don't even smoke.

CHAPTER SEVEN

My mind races all through the night, the new information going round and round relentlessly in my mind until it became a whirling blur that makes no sense at all. But however complex the detail might be, the bottom line is inescapable. My mother was murdered and my father was at least somewhere within the frame. I was alone and the only person who could answer the endless questions was Da. I constantly asked questions of him inside my own head in those early days after his death. But no answer ever seemed to come.

ॐ

Did you kill her? Did you? Did you squeeze the life from her with your bare hands? I have to ask. There is only you left to talk to now, isn't there? Only you, a dead man. So let's talk, dead man. Love and murder, that's what we need to discuss. Come to an understanding. I want to understand. I really do. If I don't, who will?

I've heard it said that if you squeeze a person's neck hard enough, their eyes begin to bleed. Did mother's eyes bleed? Her neck would have been bruised if you did it that way, her eyes bloodshot and bulging. But maybe she wasn't strangled.

Maybe she was shot. Or poisoned. Would that be cleaner? Would that be your murder of choice?

And then there's the disposal of the body. The police never found it. Even if you had enough anger to kill her, is it possible the man I knew had enough composure, enough sang-froid to dispose of her? I cannot imagine it. Rowing out in the middle of the loch in the night, throwing her weighted body in a sack over the edge. Or driving into the woods and digging and digging, deep into the earth, your spade clanking when it hit stone. How you would sweat, digging a grave. Did you sweat, Da?

I'm sweating. I'm sweating just thinking about it. I've been digging too, digging down into layers I don't understand. This strange journey I set out on, it was to try and find you. To find the man you were, the woman she was. And now I'm terrified of what I have found. If you didn't answer me at home I don't suppose you'll answer me here, in this quaint little B & B room with its frills and chintz. Except that this is the Highlands, where you were with her, and maybe you've come back here. Maybe your spirit is made to come back here. Maybe that's what hell is, being confronted by the past.

What is your past? If you killed her, it would make sense of the years of silence. Except they weren't just years of silence, were they? That is too passive a description. They were years of secrets. But then, what father would want to tell his children their mother was murdered even if he hadn't done it? What father would want to tell his children their mother was murdered by her lover?

I am trying to imagine if you could have had that much hate inside you. Or maybe that much love. Sometimes I think love makes you even crazier than hate. I know about love, Da, though you may think I don't. That kind of love. I think you guessed about Tariq, about the way I felt. Probably you dismissed it. We were only teenagers. Nothing happened. Maybe that's why it was so powerful. It was unfulfilled. It didn't have time to corrupt.

Maybe that first love, before you get cynical, is the strongest of all.

I don't care what anyone says. I know about love making you crazy. When I allow myself to think about him, even all these years later, Tariq can make me crazy still. What I am trying to say, Da, is that I understand. About the depth of love, about the things it can make you do.

ॐ

The heat. The memories. The *memory*. The one I kept pushing down. I knew, I knew so well how crazy love makes you. And knowing that, the idea that my father could have done something crazy did not seem so inconceivable. When it stopped being inconceivable, it started being frightening.

You know already, of course. About Tariq. That it did not end well. The day after his operation, Da came home from work and went straight into the sitting room. He sat on the easy chair with his head in his hands. I saw him when I passed upstairs. He just sat there without the television on.

"Okay, Da?" I called, stopping halfway up the stairs. He asked me to come down then, and he moved over and sat beside me on the sofa. I think I knew immediately. I can still remember his words, still hear them clearly, as if it were yesterday. The strange, strangled quality to his voice as he struggled to contain his emotions.

"Rebecca," he said. "It's Tariq."

I don't think at any point he said Tariq was dead because he didn't need to say. I could feel a draining inside me, like someone had pulled a plug under me and my blood was pouring down from my head and out through my feet.

"When?"

"Two hours ago."

It had happened suddenly. Tariq seemed to have come through the operation well the day before. Khadim was back at work in good spirits and was going to the hospital on his way home. But he got the call before he left. There was no time for Khadim to reach him.

Two hours. What had I been doing for the last two hours? I had put a load in the washing machine. I had cleaned the sink in the bathroom. And I had written a Get Well Soon card for a boy who was already dead.

I didn't cry right away. It was days before I cried properly. I went and lay on my bed and listened to the sound of Da and Sarah moving around, to the phone ringing and the muffled conversations that followed, and the sound of the television news floating up the stairwell from downstairs. I listened to it all as if it was in a different world, somewhere far removed from me. Sarah came up around ten o'clock to go to bed. She was only twelve and her eyes were red but I knew she hurt more for me than for herself. She didn't say anything at all but when the light went out I heard her creep round my bed and her arms came round me in the dark. She lay there for a minute and neither of us said a word but I stroked her hair. Sometimes, when I'm really, really mad with Sarah, I think of that night and I can't stay angry.

Tariq was right all along. He knew he was going to die. I wonder, does the body tell the mind about death, or the mind tell the body? Is it a warning, a preparation, or a self-fulfilling prophecy? Did Da know the morning he died? Even the night before? Shameena said later that Tariq had tidied everything in his room before he left for hospital. His drawers, under his bed. He laid out his wallet and his prayer book neatly beside the bed, like he was emptying his pockets before he left.

It is Muslim tradition to bury the body within twenty-four hours. There would be no coffin. Tariq would be wrapped in a shroud, and placed directly into the earth. I could hardly bear to think of things crawling over him. Beautiful Tariq. Shameena said he was lovely, even dead. She said her mother kept stroking him, and kissing him and combing his hair, that she scarcely left him alone for a moment. She even sang to him. Shameena broke her heart telling me how she watched Nazima put her hand on his forehead and stroke him and hum an old lullaby she had sung to them as children. Like Tariq was her baby again and she was soothing him to sleep. A sleep he would never wake up from.

I knew I wouldn't be allowed to see his body again. But I gave Shameena the friendship bracelet and she promised that she would try to slip it on his wrist, or put it in his pocket, so that he would be buried with it. It hurt to give it away. It was all I had of him. But it hurt more to think of him going into the earth without something we shared going with him.

It was a few days later that we went to pay our respects at Khadim's house. We went round to Pollokshields, past the halal butcher and the late-night grocer and Ayesha's Asian fabric shop, which even when it was closed had a spotlight on the displays of rich satins and silks that flowed like jewelled rivers in the window. My heart always lifted when we reached it because I knew that I was about to see Tariq. But not that night. It was passing Ayesha's that made me really understand that Tariq wasn't coming back.

◈

135

Strange how many things go wrong when you are in the middle of grief. Like one thing topples and everything else begins falling towards it. Feelings go wrong, and relationships go wrong, and inside you want things to be different but you can't make them different. Every time you try to rebuild just one little part, something else goes crashing down round you, until you give up and simply sit amongst the rubble.

That's the way it was after Tariq. I went a bit crazy inside. Got in a lot of trouble, both in school and out. I didn't know how to handle my feelings, and I certainly couldn't talk about them because I wasn't supposed to be feeling that way, anyway. He was a good Muslim boy who was one day going to marry his good Muslim cousin, and I was a rubbish Catholic girl who lied about going to church and swore and drank.

I never meant to give Da the fright I did over the booze. It was all on the sly until one night he was on late shift and I asked some friends from school round. We clubbed together to buy some drink, but before they even arrived, I'd downed the best part of the bottle of vodka Da kept in the cupboard. Afterwards, I filled it up with water. He kept it for Peggy, really. Peggy liked a Bloody Mary now and then. I never saw Da drink, other than the occasional glass of wine and, very rarely, a whisky. He was always very controlled that way. I understand now. He couldn't afford to let go, could he? Could never risk saying something he shouldn't.

I had more when my school pals came. I meant to have them all out by the time Da came back. I'd be in bed. He'd never know until Peggy next had a Bloody Mary, and maybe I could have replaced the vodka by then. But I got so drunk I didn't care any more. Once I started drinking, I just couldn't think of anything

I cared enough about to make me stop. Certainly not myself. I didn't care if I got in trouble. Didn't care about the consequences.

Sarah was frantic; I remember that before I lost it. She'd wanted nothing to do with it all from the start. She hated the people I was mixing with. Later, she told me I was gabbling and crying uncontrollably and then I started being sick. She was trying to get me to be sick into the living-room waste basket but I was too drunk to have much of an aim. Then I passed out completely and she thought I was going to die because my skin became blue and my breathing slowed so dramatically she thought it had stopped altogether. When she started screaming that I needed an ambulance, everyone disappeared, terrified of being caught up in the stink.

What a sight I must have been by the time Da got home. Not that I remember much. The first I remember is waking up in hospital and finding Da, pale and grim, at my bedside. My head thumped. I had never felt so ill in my life. He took my hand but I closed my eyes tight shut again, too ashamed to look at him. I tried to turn away from him but couldn't. I didn't have the strength. I felt his hand on my arm.

"Okay, Becca," he murmured, "okay."

A nurse bustled in shortly afterwards and started taking my pulse and temperature and recording it. I still didn't open my eyes.

"You've been a silly girl," she said, "haven't you?"

Even feeling as ill as I did, I wanted to punch her lights out. But I was in no position to be bolshie. The hospital social worker came round to see me before I went home, and I listened meekly as she told me I must realise that as many deaths occurred from alcohol overdoses as other drug overdoses. She asked how much

I drank normally, and if I felt I had a problem, and if there was a reason why I had drunk so much this time. I listened to it all and answered meekly, without my usual sarcasm, because I just wanted home and to be left alone. I thought of Tariq outside the café, the way he refused to respond, the way his body and his mind stayed in his own control. It was a skill to take your mind out of gear and leave it in neutral. I could do it if I thought of Tariq. I'd learned my lesson, I told the social worker soberly, like an AA zealot who had seen the light. A good girl now.

They probably thought we were a typical one-parent family with a dad who was struggling to cope. We were never a typical anything, though. And Da wasn't an inadequate father. He said almost nothing about that whole incident, but that was nothing to do with inadequacy, or with not knowing what to say. I think he just knew when there was no need for words.

We never spoke on the way home when I finally left hospital but I didn't see that as a punishment. It wasn't the silent treatment that Peggy went in for.

"Never again," he said, looking at me when we pulled up outside the house in the car. I nodded. "You frightened the life out of Sarah," he continued, unfastening his seat belt. And that was that. We never mentioned it again.

I wasn't the only one to go a little mad after Tariq died. Khadim and Nazima... well, they were never the same afterwards. That night we went round after Tariq died was awful, truly awful. Sarah had made the tea that night before we left, a meal that was eaten in almost total silence as we contemplated the ordeal ahead. A stew with doughballs you could have fired from canons. Bloody inedible. I was glad to have an excuse not to eat. Da's stomach wasn't great at the best of times and he had to eat Rennies all night. I remember the little white chalky marks at the corner of his mouth. His heart must have sunk when Nazima brought out the pakora. I couldn't believe that even in the circumstances she made food, but we were honoured friends and honoured friends were always served food.

It was Nazima who shocked me most. Everyone was devastated, of course, but Nazima was destroyed. Her grief was woven over her, intricate and delicate, like a cobweb woven over a stone statue. Her face was frozen in a permanent frown of despair, her forehead wrinkled, as if in the middle of some terrible trauma she had suddenly been turned to stone and could no longer change her expression. The bird-like movements, the pecks and flurries, were gone. She moved slowly, heavily, as if she scarcely had the energy to lift her feet.

But it was the wailing I remember most. She was usually so quiet, Nazima, but now she kept talking in Urdu and crying and rocking on her chair, and Khadim had to translate. I had never seen her talk so much. Her children, she said, they were her life. One made her heart beat, one made her blood flow. Without one, how could she keep breathing, keep living? It was like trying to live without a vital organ. And then the wailing started and while she wailed, Khadim began to talk very fast in Urdu so that none of us knew what he was saying. The volume rocketed, and the emotional temperature rocketed, and it was frightening the way it felt, like things could easily get out of control.

I remember Da touching Khadim, and talking softly to him, until he eventually stilled. He simply stared ahead, his mouth quivering, a single unshed tear threatening to spill from his lower lid. Shameena sat miserably beside her mother and reached for her hand and spoke gently in Urdu, and Nazima wiped her dopatta across her eyes, mopping up tears.

I felt as if I would suffocate in the grief. I longed to get out. Da was lost for words, lost for what to do. Small talk didn't come easily to him. But even in his stillness I remember feeling that somehow he was very, very… what's the word? … 'present'. He was very present. Very 'there'. I think Khadim felt it. Nazima was past noticing anything external, anything anyone else did.

It was such a relief to get out into the air that night. It was like the three of us breathed a collective sigh of relief when the door closed behind us. But the three remaining Khans were trapped in there, trapped inside something from which there was no escape and I felt awful leaving Shameena.

Khadim didn't cope well with Nazima's devastation. She became locked inside a glass case of her own grief where she could see and be seen, but couldn't connect with anything outside her box. Grief didn't bind Khadim and Nazima together. It forced them apart. Somehow, they just couldn't help one another.

Da was there for Khadim but Khadim needed a woman, somehow. He wanted a female chat, not a male chat. He wanted sympathy, not solutions. The kind of sympathy women give men where they hold their head and listen, and cry with them, and indulge them, and make them feel that the most important thing in the world is the way they feel right now. The way they do with their children. And Nazima just wasn't able to do that.

I never had the nerve to ask Da about Khadim and Rita, one of the women who worked in the depot. I wish I had. I don't know how far it went between them. Probably not very. I quite liked Rita but she made an odd combination with Khadim. I saw them sitting in the staff canteen one day when I had to meet Da for the dentist.

I suppose Rita must have been roughly Khadim's age but I always thought she looked like one of those ladies from the cosmetic counters in town. Dyed blonde hair, and glamorous in a painted, made-up kind of way. Lots of heavy gold jewellery. At first I couldn't think what the attraction was for either of them, and then I realised what a powerful thing ears are. Listening. Rita walked into doors a lot. Bruised cheeks, black eyes, sore arms. Lots of accidents. Her husband was a bastard. I think she and Khadim listened to each other's problems.

I know Da worried about Khadim because when Rita left that day, he brought him over to a table and sat him down. It was a long refectory table and I was sitting a few seats away from the end where the two of them sat. I was reading a magazine but I could hear them both talking in low voices. I don't think either noticed that I never once turned the page of that magazine. I was surprised at Da, because he always refused to get involved in other people's private lives. But he was involved that day.

"Nazima is a good woman," I heard him say.

"I can't talk to Nazima," Khadim hissed back.

There was some low murmuring that I strained to hear but couldn't. Then I heard Da say something about being a Muslim and how he couldn't believe the change in him, and Khadim looked like he was going to cry and said where had being a good Muslim got him, because wasn't Tariq dead? Had God listened to him?

Khadim had put his elbows on the table and leant his head on his hands in despair. He missed Tariq. He missed him, he said. His shoulders had begun to shake. Where was the future now? What was the point?

My eyes were glued to the magazine page, to a sentence in an article about summer make-up. 'Lustrously pink with evening shimmer....' I read over and over while listening. 'Lustrously pink with evening shimmer...'

"There is always a future," I heard Da tell him. "Whether you want it or not, Khadim, the future just sweeps towards you in a wave. You can either surf the wave or drown in it but it will keep coming anyway. Sink or swim, Khadim. Tariq would want you to swim."

I thought about that advice often afterwards, and I wonder now about the place inside himself from which Da must have pulled it. Khadim's head remained bowed. 'Lustrously pink with evening shimmer...'

"Rita's a nice woman," Da continued, "but she's not the answer to anything. It'll just make things worse. And worse for her too. If it goes any further and her man finds out..."

The possibilities remained unspoken, but Khadim's head seemed to sink even lower towards the table. I felt sorry for him, so sorry for him. Da told him we had to go because he had to take me to the dentist and he touched his shoulder as he passed. Khadim remained seated.

"Rebecca," Da called, and I glanced up as if I'd been absorbed in my magazine all along.

"Bye, Khadim," I said and followed Da out.

Khadim arrived at our house late one night, maybe a week after that. The doorbell rang at 10.30 and we all looked at one another. I got up to answer.

"I'll get it, Becca," Da said, getting out of his chair, because he didn't want me answering at that time of night. I heard Khadim's voice, high and urgent in the hall. He was in a state. I heard Rita's name mentioned but couldn't make anything else out.

Da came in and looked at me and Sarah. "Girls," he said and left the rest of the talking to his solemn grey-blue eyes, the way he so often did. We got up immediately. "Hi Khadim," we said uneasily, walking past him and out of the room, but Khadim was too distraught to do more than grunt a response. Sarah and I looked sideways at each other on the stairs. We got ready for bed and then sat and chatted softly, but we left the bedroom door wide open in case we could hear anything from downstairs.

It was near midnight when Khadim left.

"Go home, Khadim. Go home to Nazima and sleep well," we heard Da say softly in the hall. I looked down from the top landing and saw them quaintly shaking hands.

"What was that all about?" I called to Da when the door closed.

"Nothing." I could see he was distracted when he looked up at me. "Someone from work has had an accident and is in hospital."

"Who?"

"Rita."

"Is she seriously hurt?"

"Head injuries. She'll be okay."

"How did that happen?"

I saw his mouth tighten.

"She walked into a lamppost in the dark."

And then he went in and closed the sitting-room door.

"Why is Khadim coming at midnight to tell Da about Rita being in hospital?" asked Sarah, puzzled. I shrugged my shoulders.

I still think Rita's man got the wrong end of the stick. I don't think anything happened. I can't see it, Khadim and Rita. But what I can see is that grief challenges your beliefs if you have any, like Khadim; and it challenges your lack of them if you have none, like me. I think Khadim was pushing things, testing them. Grief makes you a little mad and love makes you a little mad. The question is, just how mad did that make Da?

MONDAY

CHAPTER ONE

The trouble with talking to the dead is that they don't answer back. Not in a voice that you can hear, anyway. Not in a voice you can understand. It's like one of those one-sided conversations down a telephone line when you can hear the other person talking, but they can't hear you. "Hello?" the disembodied voice says. "Hello?" And down your end you're screaming, "It's *me*!" But it doesn't make any difference. No matter how loudly you shout, no matter how angry you get, there can be no communication. It's as if you are on two different networks.

Maybe it's like that between the living and the dead. How do you interpret silence? For a while, you strain to hear anything that might confirm a listener: the whispered tune of steady exhalations; the percussion crash of a sudden cough. But when all you hear is silence, it's hard to know if it's a living silence or a dead silence.

❧

Restless sleep interrupts the bursts of listening. I wake with a headache, nose miserably blocked with pollen, eyes gummy. Turn my face into the pillow. Three days without Da. Four till we bury him. Running out of time. I pad sleepily into the bathroom, the tiles sticky beneath the warmth of my feet, and splash cold water into my eyes, trying to wash out the pollen and ease

147

the burning. I have to get to the library today, find the truth of the story I was told by Marion, the assistant in the Lochglas shop. Look up old newspaper cuttings. Yesterday was a lost day. The library would have been shut on a Sunday, but then I probably wouldn't have made sense of any newspaper articles anyway. I wasn't making sense of anything yesterday.

I couldn't stay in Lochglas as I'd planned. I drove from the village like a madwoman, careering along the twisting single-track road to the bridge that would take me back to Inverness. Running away, I suppose. Over and over in my head I could see Marion in her pink overall, saying, "Joseph Connaghan," and looking at me curiously. It was like I had pressed some rewind button, and the scene just kept playing and replaying. Joseph Connaghan. And again. Joseph Connaghan. Her hand lifting the bag with my morning roll up towards me and then rewinding back down to her side. And forward and back. Joseph Connaghan. Joseph Connaghan.

My B & B is a small chintzy guest house down by the river. Floral sofas and polished sideboards, a piano with open music waiting to be played in the residents' lounge. It's not expensive, just a nice house rather than a hotel, but it's still more than I can afford. I wasn't in a mood for thrift yesterday. This place had a credit-card symbol in the window and I didn't care what it cost. I had other things on my mind.

I ask my landlady for directions to the library, but there is one other thing I have to do first. I have put it off too long. I need to make a call, but the mobile reception is hit and miss and this conversation is going to be difficult enough as it is. Round the corner from the guest house is a phone box. The heat is suffocating as the door closes behind me and it stinks, but the traffic noise from the road makes it impossible to keep the door open. As I dial, a picture of the house in Glasgow slots into place in my head, pulled from a mental filing cabinet. I see the empty room, the phone ringing out and shattering the silence.

"Hello?"

Her voice sounds dead.

"Sarah? It's me."

There is a silence and I look out at the street, watch a fair-haired girl in lime-green shorts and a white t-shirt pass by licking ice cream. My mouth feels hot and dry.

"Where the hell are you?"

"Inverness."

"Inverness! What the fuck are you doing in Inverness!"

I've never heard Sarah swear before. It's surprisingly shocking, like Santa telling a child to piss off.

"Sarah, I'm sorry. I couldn't… I just had to get away."

"You always have to bloody get away, Rebecca. You spend your entire life 'getting away'. And why Inverness, for God's sake?"

Sarah sounds angrier than I've ever heard her.

"You know why. We used to live up here."

"So?"

"So."

She doesn't wait.

"You just take off without a word, leaving me in that house with Father Riley on my own. It was so bloody embarrassing. It took me half an hour to realise you weren't coming back. I didn't even want to speak to you that night when I finally left. Des said you went shooting past him. By the time I got round next morning you'd taken off for God knows where. Charlie and Peggy and I have been frantic."

"I'm sorry." Now Da's gone, it's everyone else on one side, me on the other.

"Sorry! That's easy to say! Rebecca, we are trying to deal with everything with Da and you just… just… make things worse by…" As soon as she says Da's name her voice begins to waver.

"Sarah. Sarah don't cry. I'm sorry. I'm really, really sorry." God, it's stifling in this box. I feel the sweat on my back. I can scarcely breathe. I open the door with my foot, trying to let some air in. A lorry trundles by, its brakes squealing as it stops at the junction.

"Sorry, Sarah, what was that?" I let the door fall.

"I said, I miss him."

Her voice is scarcely above a whisper. The telephone box is filthy but I let my head drop onto the smeared pane of glass anyway.

"I know, Sarah. I know."

"Yeah, but you're not here, are you?"

"I'll make it up to you."

"Make it up? How are you going to do that exactly?"

I look into the newsagent's shop window outside the telephone box.

"I'll bring you a stick of rock and a soft toy Nessie with a tartan hat."

I can hear her snort at the other end but it is a half-laugh, despite herself.

"Silly cow," she says, and it makes me smile faintly hearing Sarah talk this way.

"How many do you think will come to the funeral?"

"Peggy reckons not more than twenty or thirty of us."

"I'll phone Blacksmith's and see if they can do sandwiches and sausage rolls after. I can do that from up here."

"I've done it," says Sarah.

"Sorry."

"When are you coming back?"

"I'll stay a day. Maybe two," I say vaguely.

"You'll make the funeral, then," she says with a dry edge that isn't like her. I nearly tell her not to be stupid but I suppose she has a right. A right to be angry.

"Shameena phoned you. I told her you were away. She said if you got in touch, to tell you to phone her."

"Did you tell her about the funeral arrangements? Is she going to sing?"

"Yes. I've arranged with Father Riley for her to sing at the end of the service, like you asked. Before the coffin is taken out."

Before the coffin is taken out. It could be any old corpse in a box we were talking about. But what else can we say?

"I'm going to see Father Riley tonight. Let him know."

"Yeah, remind him she's a Muslim singer."

"Oh shut up, Becca."

"Listen, Sarah?"

"What?"

There is a child having a tantrum outside the box. She keeps trying to sit on the pavement and her red-faced mother is hauling her up off the ground, trying to drag her along the street. I put one finger in my ear and try to choose my words carefully.

"I just want to say that I came to Inverness, well, because… you know we lived near here once and it just felt like coming closer to Da… it was spur of the moment."

There is silence. I am not sure if Sarah is crying. She is probably thinking it is a journey we could have made together some time.

After the funeral. I wait for her to speak but she says nothing.

"I'll see you later, Sarah."

"Okay," she says and I hear her sniff. The receiver is halfway down when I hear her call.

"Becca?"

"Yeah?"

"Drive carefully."

"Will do," I say. I put the phone down with relief, shove open the door and breathe deeply.

CHAPTER TWO

The hottest June in years. An oddity. A freak of nature. The sun roasts me cruelly like a stuffed pig on a spit, skin sizzling like crackling. It finds every hidden corner, bores through my eyes to the very sockets; creeps, stealthy as an intruder, through the hair on the back of my neck, leaving angry red fingerprints on soft, white, skin. And the heat that isn't absorbed into my body thuds like a dead weight onto dust-baked pavements, bounces back dully into a wall I am constantly walking into. There's a dampness over the bridge of my nose, and in the pit of my arms, and down the length of my spine, and everywhere else is sucked dry, dry as roasted sawdust.

It's a fifteen-minute stroll to cross the river and walk up through the town to the library. In this heat, even a short walk is draining. I am tired out with lack of sleep but also with hay fever. It feels like my body is using every scrap of energy to fight an intruder. One minute my eyes and my nose stream, like a tap turned on full; the next my defences slam shut, and the pipe-work round my body simply blocks. Nothing flows.

It's a relief to finally find the library, hidden off the main street, tucked in a quiet square next to the bus station. Once through the swing doors, the quiet hits, refreshing as gentle rain. The serenity makes it feel cooler in here than it really is.

I get impatient with libraries normally. The worthy, preachy, po-faced silence of them. Sarah and I used to go to the library every week as kids and she loved it, tucking her feet under her in the bean bags laid out for kids, snuggling down happily in the cocoon of silence. It made me feel like I'd been buried alive. I snatched the books and left, taking them to the park in the summer, lying on the grass with my jacket under my head, a world at my feet and another in my hands. In the winter I'd run a bubble bath and lie for hours, turning the hot tap with my toes when the water cooled, until the water was up to my neck and the book pages had the water marks of a lapping tide.

But today, the silence seems like a hiding place. I walk through to the reference library, an enclosed, old-fashioned room tucked away at the back of the building, where all the back copies of the local papers are stored. The *Highland Herald*. The *Inverness Focus*. If I started school in Glasgow, and had my fifth birthday at Auntie Peggy's shortly before that, we must have moved from Lochglas sometime during my fourth year, not long after Sarah was born. If I start there, and work my way back, I should find something.

There are hard copies of old newspapers, bound in leather, going right back to the nineteenth century, but the librarian says I have to view the ones I want on microfilm. The filing cabinet drawer slams shut as she takes out boxes of film and loads the first into the machine for me. I sit watching as each page is thrown up onto the sloped white desk, like an art easel, in front of me.

The world of twenty-five years ago is a curiosity. It is like standing on the outside and looking into the glass bubble of another world. I can hold it up to the light, examine the shape of it, and the colours of it, like a curio. But it must stay enclosed. I can knock on the window, but I cannot enter that world. Adverts for cars that look like East European imports now. Adverts for shop sales, for styles long gone: an old lady's dress with floral print, the kind Peggy would wear; a chic winter coat with fur collar and cuffs, and a full skirt. It tugs some vague cord of recognition inside me and I look at it curiously… the fur collar, perhaps. Was that like the one Mother wore, the one that trapped her perfume in the collar?

Pages and pages of local weddings. I suppose Mother smiled like that, the day she married Da. Like the world, and everything in it, was hers. Did they make their promises without the shadow of disappointment looming over them, or did she know already? Did he? Her words ring out in my head. Words from her letter to Da. *Doesn't just a little part of you wonder about for ever?*

The handle squeaks as I turn the film faster and faster to try and get to more news pages, whirling past the inconsequential screeds of advertising hype, the listings and theatre reviews, until the text blurs into solid black columns as it spins. There are stories of local feuds and small businesses and cats stuck up trees. By April, I could tell that when the story of my mother's murder hit the *Highland Herald*, it was going to hit in a big way. And it did.

Even though I am looking for it, it is still a shock. The text spins. Stop! My heart skips a beat. There she is, my mother, looking out laughingly from a picture on the front page of the paper. I wipe my clammy hands down the sides of my jeans.

It is front page, but a small story to start with. Small town, small-town view. Friday July 7th.

LOCHGLAS ELDER'S DAUGHTER MISSING.

The daughter of a well-known local businessman and Free Church Elder, Donald MacKenzie, has gone missing from her secluded Lochglas home. Kathleen Connaghan, who gave birth to her second child just six weeks ago, has not been seen for two days, after leaving her eldest child, Rebecca (4), at play group. Police confirmed the missing woman's car was found abandoned on the outskirts of Inverness...

The stories went on for months, exploding into huge headlines, shrinking into side columns as the story ebbed and flowed.

July 14th: **WHERE IS KATHLEEN?**
July 21st: **KATHLEEN COME HOME, PLEADS HUSBAND**

As the weeks went by there was speculation of every kind. Kathleen Connaghan was suffering from post-natal depression. Kathleen Connaghan was in debt. Kathleen Connaghan had stolen money from her father's shop and disappeared abroad with a new lover.

By July 28th, in the absence of juicy new angles, it was a struggle to keep the story afloat. There was a small update on an inside page but on August 7th, the story was back with a bang. **KATHLEEN CAUGHT IN LOVE TRIANGLE.** Twenty years had made a difference to newspaper coverage. It seemed gentler than today's tabloids. More formal, more restrained. But even then they liked a good sex scandal.

My eyes scoured down the story.

Missing Lochglas woman Kathleen Connaghan was having a long-running affair with local businessman James Cory and was due to meet him on the day she disappeared, her closest friend has revealed. Housewife Jackie Sandford claims the thirty-two-year-old married mother of two had secret lunchtime liaisons with the businessman who owns Inverness firm Cory Construction.

"Kathleen was ready to leave Joe for James Cory," Mrs Sandford confirmed yesterday. "She was besotted with him. The day she disappeared she told me she was meeting him to try and sort out their future."

Mrs Sandford, who also lives in Lochglas, says she's speaking out because she now fears her missing friend is dead. "Kathleen wouldn't just leave her children like this. She wouldn't stay away this long without getting in touch. I didn't want to say anything at first but now I am frightened we are never going to see her again. Somebody knows where she is. They've got to do as I am doing and speak out. We have to find out what happened to Kathleen."

In a bizarre twist, it emerged that Mrs Connaghan's husband, Joseph, an accountant with Inverness firm David Carruthers and Co., handles Cory Construction's accounts. David Carruthers and James Cory, both 35, are known to have been close friends since school days, and played together as teenagers in local band, Tin Whistle. Both are members of Inverness Golf Club.

However, Mrs Sandford says her friend did not meet James Cory as a consequence of her husband's job. They met through her father, Donald MacKenzie, who owns MacKenzie's Outfitters in Church Street, Inverness.

"Donald and his wife Marion had a dinner party at their house about a year ago and that's how James and Kathleen met," says Mrs Sandford. "Joseph was actually there at their first meeting."

The affair began shortly after. Mrs Sandford claims the missing woman had tried to end it after a few months, but Mr Cory continued to pursue her. "Kathleen told me that James Cory used to phone David Carruthers and ask him to send Joe to out-of-town firms when he wanted to see Kathleen," says Mrs Sandford.

The two lovers would meet for lunch or dinner, sometimes even at the Connaghans' Lochglas home. "James would bring Kathleen gifts, including bottles of vintage champagne. At the start she was careful to hide everything from Joe but she got careless. She was flattered by all the attention. She did love Joe, but she couldn't resist the glamour and excitement that James offered her."

Recently, Mrs Connaghan told her close friend that she wanted to leave her husband of nine years and set up home with Mr Cory. "I told her she was crazy. James hadn't even told his wife Anna about her. I think she was putting pressure on him to tell Anna, but James was never going to rock the boat and leave her for Kathleen. But Kathleen just couldn't see it. I tried to tell her, but when it came to James she was blind."

Mrs Sandford even reveals that Mrs Connaghan's three-week-old baby was not her husband's. "Kathleen and Joe's marriage was in serious trouble after the affair started because Joe guessed almost right away and Kathleen moved into the children's room. Then she got pregnant after three months of seeing James. Kathleen told me that Joe broke down in tears when he heard about the pregnancy but said if she put the affair behind her, he was willing to start again and be a family. Joe was fourteen years older than Kathleen and worshipped the ground she walked on. I know Kathleen felt really guilty and promised she would end it, but two months later she was back seeing James."

When contacted by the *Highland Herald*, James Cory refused to confirm the affair or the fact that he was due to meet the vivacious brunette the day she disappeared. "I am sorry, I can't make any comment," he said yesterday at the Inverness office of Cory Construction. Joseph Connaghan also declined to comment. Police enquiries continue.

It was only when I finished reading that I realised I had been holding my breath. I exhaled deeply and wiped a tear away. I was crying for Da, and crying for Sarah, and crying for me, and I suppose I was crying for Mother too. Poor, silly, deluded Mother. But it was Sarah that made my heart sore right now. My sister. Except she wasn't. She was my half-sister.

❦

All those years. All those years of lies. And yet I couldn't blame Da for not telling her she wasn't his. How could I blame him?

Jackie Sandford's story started a frenzy. The gloves were off and endless stories followed. Sordid details of Mother and Cory's affair. Accounts of how they "made passionate love while her innocent young children slept upstairs". Speculation from locals that she might have run off with a third man, that she was still alive. And then, in the August, other Cory mistresses came crawling out of the woodwork: **KATHLEEN NOT THE FIRST**, screamed the front page.

Two months after Mother went missing, there was another angle: **NEW POLICE CHIEF APPOINTED TO KATHLEEN MYSTERY**. In the absence of progress in the hunt for the murderer, and against a background of allegations about police incompetence, Chief Inspector Terry Simons had been appointed to lead the inquiry and give it a fresh impetus. I took out a small notebook from my bag and wrote his name down. But it was the story about the police questioning both Cory and Da that gave the papers the courage to cut right to the bone. **KATHLEEN MURDER: THE HUSBAND OR THE LOVER?**

Cory, according to the paper, was due to meet Kathleen at one o'clock that day. He left his office at ten to one. By this time, Cory

160

was giving the papers quotes, admitting he *did* meet Mother but saying he left her at quarter to two, having arranged another tryst for the following afternoon. He denied Mother was putting pressure on him to leave his wife, Anna. In the newspaper picture, Anna looked like a Tory politician's wife: attractive in an upper-crust kind of way. Neat blonde. Stiff permed curls. Pale and a bit bloodless. She circled his arm with both of hers like a human handcuff and smiled a cool, pallid smile that suggested Cory would pay for the rest of his life for her humiliation. **FRESH START**, said the headline. Not for Mother there wasn't.

But where was her body? The papers didn't say, of course. Not directly. But they made sure they mentioned Cory's big project at the time of Mother's disappearance. Made sure they mentioned his hands-on involvement in the early stages of the project, when the concrete was being poured into the foundations of the building. The implication was obvious. If Cory killed her, chances were that right now, Mother was lying under several tons of concrete in the foundations of a multi-storey car park.

Da's work schedule for that week, the reports said, showed he was working alone the afternoon she died, driving to a project out of town. According to a spokesman for the company he was visiting, he arrived an hour late for his appointment. He could have detoured. He had time to kill her. They both had.

CHAPTER THREE

I don't go looking for the church. I come out of the library and walk round and round the town in a daze until my feet are sore, ending up down by the river watching swans. Graceful, elegant swans who mate for life. I have walked by the building several times, a traditional stone-built church with a spire. Then I walk back and walk in. There are a handful of people waiting for confession before morning mass.

I sit in the confession queue, mechanically moving up a seat as each person in front of me disappears inside the confessional. I tell myself I don't really intend going in. There is time to leave. I haven't been to confession since I was fourteen.

But part of me wants to talk to a priest. The old Catholic part, that I thought was long buried, rises from the dead and tap dances inside my head. My turn next. I can skip out the side when I get to the first seat. Instead, I open the confessional door, close it, stand in the dark.

I can hear a newspaper rustle from behind the grille as I close the door. A slight movement behind the black curtain. Now there's a thing. Does the priest only stop doing the crossword if you have an interesting enough confession?

"I'm not here for confession," I say. There is a short silence, a rustle. I can hear a sniff, the kind of sniff when you are trying to breathe through a blocked nose.

"Okay," says the priest. The voice is young, nasal. I detect a note of interest, a hint of playfulness. "What shall we do instead then?"

I smile in the darkness, in spite of myself. You think your world's crashed and within a couple of hours you can smile. What is that? Resilience or shallowness?

"I'd like to talk to you if that's okay. Ask you something."

"Fire away." There is another sniff, a small gasp of breath. I know how he feels.

"You're a hay-fever sufferer," I say, kneeling down in front of the curtain like I did when I was a child. I couldn't very well stay standing at the door.

"How did you know that?"

"I'm a clairvoyant."

"You won't need me then."

"I thought confession was about the past, not the future."

"I thought you weren't here for confession."

Smart ass. I like him. Sarah says I make decisions about people too quickly but I say it's primeval instinct and some people have lost theirs. When you were standing on the savannah millions of years ago, a stranger was either friend or foe and you needed to make up your mind quick.

"So," he says, gently. "What *are* you here for?"

I stare into the curtain, my eyes growing accustomed to the dark. I can pick out a shadowy outline behind the partition.

"I've just been told… just discovered… that my father might have murdered someone." How strange those words sound together. I can hardly believe I am hearing them, saying them. "I don't know what to do."

Bet that unblocked his nasal passages. I try to imagine his face on the other side. Is he shocked? Have his eyebrows shot up, his mouth opened slightly? How often do priests hear talk of murder in confession. Once in a lifetime? Twice? Never? If I hadn't wanted to kneel in front of the grille, I could have sat on the chair that was positioned on his side for those who preferred to see the priest. I suppose I could have watched his face. But then he could have watched mine. Miss Edwards, who was into the 'new' confession at school, recommended that we girls just face the priest and "talk to him like you'd talk to God". She was barking, Miss Edwards.

"When you say you don't know what to do," says the voice behind the curtain slowly, "do you mean you don't know whether to confront your father about it? Or maybe whether to go to the police?"

"No, no, I couldn't do either of those."

"Why not?"

"Because he's dead."

"Who's dead?

"My dad."

"I see," he says, but of course he doesn't see at all.

"When did he die?"

"Last Friday."

"Oh… so recent… I'm sorry."

"The thing is, my dad might not have done it. I don't know."

"Who do you think he might have killed?"

"My mother."

I don't need to see his face to know the silence that follows is a shocked one. I tell him it all then, in the darkness, the words tumbling out in a jumble of thoughts and suspicions and ideas and fears. Da. Mother. Sarah. He says little apart from an occasional prompt, a question, a clarification. I cry but it feels good. I am

164

telling everything to a stranger who I will never have to see again. Dumping. Unloading.

Someone for whom this discussion has absolutely no consequences. That is the beauty of it.

"Priests and counsellors," I sniff eventually. "You're indispensable."

"But only one of us is free, eh?"

"Oh good. I wasn't sure."

I hear him laugh, a wheezy laugh.

"All sorts of people come into confession," he says. "Are you a Catholic?"

"Yeah, a Catholic atheist."

"Want a Polo mint?" he says.

"No, you'll see me if I come round for it."

A packet of Polo mints appears round the side of the grille.

"Here." It makes me laugh seeing the disembodied hand. It is young, white, thin, clean. Well-shaped nails. The hand of a man whose work involves brain, not brawn.

"What's your name?"

I hesitate. The beauty is anonymity. No consequences.

"Julie," I say.

"Okay." I know that he knows I am lying.

"Yours?"

"Peter."

"I call you Father Peter?"

"Just Peter. Or Pete." He breathes hard, takes a gasp of air, blows his nose. "The thing is, Julie, I'm happy to talk to you but I'm not sure your reason for telling me this and what you want from me. People normally talk to me about things they have done themselves. This is about something someone else has done. Or may not have done. You say your parents are both dead. So is your concern that if your father didn't do it, the real killer is not being brought to justice?"

"No, no, no," I say, almost fretfully. He is missing the point entirely. "No, I don't care about *him*."

"What do you care about then?"

"About Da. I worry that… *if* he did it… what might have happened to him now. Now he's dead."

"To his soul?"

"I suppose so."

"I thought you didn't believe in God?"

"Let's not split hairs," I say, bringing my teeth down on the Polo mint. Sounds like gunfire in the stillness of the confessional.

"Sorry. I'm a cruncher."

"I'm a sucker."

"Yeah? Well that's priests for you. How do you eat your After Eights?"

"If nobody's looking, in one, sideways."

I smile and wipe a tear away at the same time. .

"You?" he said.

"Nibbles, right corner first."

"Right."

Silence.

"Julie," he says, "we're having a laugh but I can tell you are actually really upset out there. Do you want to sit in the chair beside me? Just talk normally where we can see one another?"

"No thanks. I'm not being rude. It's just… easier this way." Anonymity was always easier. That's why I kept moving. Once, when I was working away, I went out with a man for six weeks and never told him my real name. I'd said it was Sue the night we met, just for a laugh, thinking we'd never see one another again. I dumped him rather than tell him the truth. I wasn't sure if I was fed up of him or fed up of Sue.

"I honestly don't know why I am here," I continue. "Except grief makes you do funny things, instinctive things, you know? Things that aren't rational and that in six months' time you won't be able to believe you've done. Like try to find out what a God you don't think you believe in may, or may not, do to your dad who may, or may not, have murdered your mother. "

"Okay," Peter says, and his voice has a sense of purpose. Like he's been presented with a problem and he is going to solve it. "Let's say – for the sake of argument – that your father committed a murder. There are two theological issues we have to consider: repentance and penance. Would your father have been sorry?"

"How can I know that?"

"I don't know if this helps," he says slowly, "but St Thomas once said, 'Considering the omnipotence and mercy of God, no one should despair of the salvation of anyone in this life.' Or something like that."

"My father was a good man."

I hear his chair creak as he sits back. "Well, you do know how he felt then. A good man who does a terrible thing feels horror and sorrow and repentance. So now ask, did he do penance for the wrong? Obviously he couldn't give your mother back her life, like a thief could give back stolen property. But do you think there were other ways in which he paid? Did he pray? Did he make sacrifices?" He paused. "Maybe that's harder to answer."

167

"Harder?" I said, "No, easier. He paid his whole life. He paid *with* his life. Everything was about me and Sa… about me and my sister. And my sister… she wasn't even his. He took another man's child and he looked after her because she was my mother's. No, he did more than that. He *loved* her because she was my mother's. And every time he looked at her, it must have been like looking at him. When he looked at me he saw my mother, and when he looked at my sister he saw her lover. I call that penance."

"So do I. He sounds… well… he doesn't sound like a man who would have committed murder easily."

"He wasn't."

"Maybe that's your answer then."

"I wasn't saying he did it."

"I know that. You were just… checking the position."

"That's it." I can smell mint in the air.

"If he had come to you and confessed, and you had given him absolution, what words would you have used?" I am curious. It's so long. I can't remember.

"The words we always use in confession." He begins to recite them softly.

God, the Father of mercies,
through the death and the resurrection of his Son
has reconciled the world to himself
and sent the Holy Spirit among us
for the forgiveness of sins;
through the ministry of the Church
may God give you pardon and peace,
and I absolve you from your sins in the name of the Father,
and of the Son and of the Holy Spirit.

"Amen," I say. Even I don't know if I am being sarcastic or not. Pardon and peace. It sounds appealing even to a sometimes atheist. I want that for Da. Maybe I can be his stand-in.

"The thing is," he says, "you are confused just now, but perhaps you believe in more than you think."

"That sounds good," I say. "What does it mean?"

"Well, right now you don't know what to believe. I can understand that. But remember, if you have certainty you wouldn't need faith. And we all need faith."

I have the feeling he is about to move in on the God bit. I can skip the hard sell. I stand up.

"You're going now?"

"I'd better. I'm sorry I've taken up so much time. There will be a big queue now."

"If you could just see your way to crying a bit when you go out, it'll help. They'll wait till Father Dunn is on because he's a soft touch."

"I'll do my best." We both know that morning mass has started out there, that there will be no further confessions just now.

"If you need to see me again, you know where I am."

"Thanks. Thanks for talking."

"Good luck, Julie. And I'm sorry… sorry about your father. I'll pray for him."

I bite my lip. *I'll pray for him.* It stirs something in me. I suppose the old Catholic who joins the drunks and goes to mass at midnight on Christmas Eve.

"'If someone said on Christmas Eve, Come see the oxen kneel…'" I say softly, quoting a Hardy poem we learned at school. But I can't remember exactly how the last bit goes. His voice cuts in.

169

"'I should go with him in the gloom, Hoping it might be so,'" he finishes.

"You missed a bit," I say, frowning, trying to remember.

"That's the important bit. Hope."

"You're going to make me cry again."

"I'm only thinking of my confession queue."

"Here, take this." I stick my hand round his side of the confessional. "It'll change your life."

"What is it?" he asks, taking it.

"Clarityn. One a day. Clears the tubes."

I hear him laugh as I close the door.

Heads swivel as I come out of the confessional, right in the middle of the Creed. My eyes must be red. I wonder what they think I am guilty of, to come out looking like this. I walk quickly down the side aisle with my head down, and out through the swing doors at the back. I look back through the window of the church door and see Father Peter appear from the confessional. Mid thirties, thin, dark hair. Nice. My type, even. But then you know my track record.

He looks around casually but I can tell he is curious; he is scanning faces looking for Julie. I walk quickly down the steps and back into town.

"So," I think, exhaling deeply. "What the hell was all that about?"

No doubt he is wondering the same.

CHAPTER FOUR

Time for facts. The small notebook in my handbag contains a few scribbled names from the cuttings in the library. Jackie Sandford. Chief Inspector Terry Simons. David Carruthers. Of all of them, Jackie Sandford is the one I really want to talk to. She was obviously my mother's confidante. There are only two Sandfords in the book, neither of them based in Lochglas. There is an answer at both numbers when I ring, but neither knows Jackie. I phone Lochglas Post Office and asked if anyone there knew a Jackie Sandford who once lived in the village. The voice at the other end sounds young.

"I'll ask," she says, and I hear her call across the shop. "Maggie, have you ever heard of a Jackie Sandford in Lochglas?"

There is an exclamation of surprise.

"Jackie Sandford! She moved away years ago." I hear the voice moving closer to the phone, as if the person is going to take over the receiver. "Who's asking?" I put the receiver down with a click – I'm not sure why – and it rocks slightly in the cradle.

The disappointment cuts me. But I have only a couple of days. I can't waste time following up leads that might go nowhere. The number for David Carruthers and Co., chartered accountants, is easy. I hesitate about whether he's worth phoning.

And he'll tip Cory off about the fact that I'm here. But then, Cory's going to know soon enough. I dial.

"Good morning, Carruthers and Co."

"Hello. Is it possible to speak to Mr Carruthers, please?"

There is a short silence. "David Carruthers?"

"Yes please."

"I am very sorry, but David Carruthers died about a year ago."

"Oh I see. I'm sorry... I..." What do I say now? I feel a momentary panic, am unable to think.

"Who's calling please? Perhaps I can redirect your call for you."

"No... Well, actually... is Mr Carruthers's wife still alive?"

I cross my fingers that Mr Carruthers had a wife.

"Yes, she is, but could I ask your name please?"

I am reluctant to give my name. I always am.

"Rebecca Connaghan. Would it be possible to get a number for Mrs Carruthers?"

"I am sorry, I can't give that information out, but I could pass on a message for you."

"Yes please. Could you tell her that Rebecca Connaghan would like to speak to her please? Ehm... If you could just say that her husband knew my mother, Kathleen Connaghan."

"Okay."

She hasn't repeated the name. Has she written it down?

"The name is very important."

"I'm sorry?"

"The name. My mother's name, Kathleen Connaghan. Can you make sure you give her the name Kathleen Connaghan?"

"And do you have a number Mrs Carruthers can reach you on?"

I give her my mobile then fish in my pocket for the landlady's card to give her. I want to make sure. I put the phone down

172

feeling dispirited. None of this is going well. I don't expect to hear from Mrs Carruthers and I don't know how useful she'd be anyway. One moved. One dead. One unavailable. Not a great hit rate. Maybe Cory is dead, too. But I don't think so. How do I know? I just do.

I go for a coffee in a posh coffee shop, buy a cake for the price of an entire lunch, and eat it without tasting it. I'll phone Terry Simons next, but I can't try and phone Mother's relatives. If I look up MacKenzie in the Highland phone book, I'll be here all day. And anyway, it's not exactly the kind of conversation you can have by phone, is it? Excuse me, do you know who killed my mother?

CHAPTER FIVE

Terry Simons is standing at the window when I see him first. Burly, solid, a strong physical presence that is just on the turn into old age. The broad shoulders are beginning to curl slightly at the edges, like stale sandwiches; the bull neck is collapsing in on itself. He moves freely enough, and yet there is that first, telltale stiffness. Without the vigour of youth, the bulk of his body is settling into flab. He wears a short-sleeved shirt, white with a thin maroon check that is picked up by a sleeveless sweater in the same colour. The sweater is pulled tight, straining over a burgeoning paunch.

Simons looks like he suffers from high blood pressure, his bruised cheeks stained the colour of port wine. His hands are tucked into his trouser pockets, as if he's rattling change in there while he looks out over his garden, out to the green fields beyond, where the construction companies are moving in to build new estates of semis. The window frames him like a glass cage.

He is waiting for me. I see the little start, the way he moves instantly to the door when he spots me. He had agreed speedily, even greedily, when I phoned and mentioned Kathleen Connaghan's name. This is no intrusion. Simons is glad to be called out of retirement, to be back on police business even for half an hour.

There is the stale smell of fish in the hallway when the door closes. Breakfast kippers maybe, or last night's cod. The trapped heat, the feeling that the smell is old – how old? – makes me feel vaguely claustrophobic. Perhaps the smell is so ingrained it is simply part of this hall now, like the peach swirled wallpaper and the spindly legged telephone table. There is a sense of a life on view in Terry Simons' house, but then, I'm looking for clues. *Who lives in a house like this?* A toddler's musical rolling toy is trapped under the radiator: a grandchild's perhaps. Or a neighbour's? Then a golf trolley with clubs. A circular coat stand with a woman's raincoat and several umbrellas in the base, one a multi-coloured golf umbrella.

"Miss Connaghan," says Simons formally, standing back and ushering me in with a wave of his hand, like he's showing a suspect into a waiting room. There is something about the gesture that irritates me. A sense of authority. Authority always puts my back up.

"Thanks for seeing me, Mr Simons."

"Not at all. Not at all," he says, indicating an armchair for me to sit in. "Glad to meet you."

We sit with the awkward tension of the just-met. The armchair is in direct sunlight, the blinding shafts streaming through the window and hitting the left side of my face mercilessly. I am too ill at ease to ask if I may move.

"You said on the phone you are retired now, Mr Simons. Are you enjoying it?"

"Oh yes," he says.

I'm not sure I believe him. He sits down, the change still jangling in his pocket, the fingers working it mechanically. A gesture of suppressed boredom that has become habit. When he sits, a roll of fat hangs over the waistband of his grey trousers, the taut jumper strapping it into place like a sausage in a skin.

"Good to have time with the family," he says.

I am unconvinced. Terry Simons wears an old man's carpet slippers on his feet, and an old man's frustration in his eyes.

"But you miss the work?"

"Sometimes. Yes, sometimes I do."

He clears his throat. I can tell from his accent that he is not a Highlander. The voice is low and slightly guttural, like mine. Hard-edged. Turns out he moved up from Glasgow for promotion.

As Simons would say, we 'proceed to business' quickly. He is full of that kind of robotic talk, speaks as if constantly giving evidence. "I was proceeding along Springburn Avenue…" That kind of thing. He can't help himself. Thirty-five years a copper. He has a police chief's confidence, the kind of certainty in his own opinions that simply doesn't entertain doubt. His homicide clear-up rate as a Chief Inspector was 92 per cent, he says. Kathleen Connaghan was one of the 8 per cent. He makes no allowance for the fact that the statistic he is discussing is my mother.

It wasn't that he didn't know who killed her, he says, scrutinising my face for a reaction. I look blankly at him, the sun still beating relentlessly on the side of my face. There's a steel in his eyes that suddenly shocks me, and a cement-like certainty carved into the crow's-feet lines. He strikes me as vaguely ridiculous, a man whose sense of himself became too ingrained, too static, in his job. It happens to people in power. Their jobs entail making judgements, and if they don't learn to trust their instincts they will be paralysed. But then they come to rely on them too much. There's no room for indecision, and no room for growth because no one questions them any more.

But if I am honest, he is not only ridiculous but frightening. He has power that is nothing to do with status. I am here to find out that Da didn't murder my mother. What if he tells me that he did?

"You knew who killed my mother at the time?"

"No doubt about it."

"So why couldn't you prove it?"

"Bad luck." He shrugs. "Sometimes it happens. But it was Joe Connaghan. I was certain of that."

A wave of nausea rises in my stomach.

"I'm sorry," he says stoutly. But he isn't. He isn't sorry in the least.

"We just never managed to make it stick. No body, you see," he says, shaking his head. "If we'd found the body, we'd have got him. We sent some divers into the loch but it was too expensive to continue for long. Two more days," he says bitterly. "That's all I asked for, but they pulled the plug. Two more days and I'd have got him. I'm sure of it. For years I waited for that body to be washed up, but he was smart enough to do the job properly. I'll give him that." He pushes back a lock of white hair that has flopped forward onto his forehead. He talks like I have no connection to Joseph Connaghan.

"James Cory…" It's all I can manage to stutter out.

"Ach…" he says impatiently, shaking his head. "James Cory! That was all nonsense. I feel sorry for the man." He puts his hand up as if to stop me speaking, but I haven't said a word. "I know, I know," he continues. "He shouldn't have been playing away from home and James knows he was in the wrong about that. But he was hounded at the time, and you know there are some people who have never let it go, even to this day. I'd like to help him if

I could, clear up the question mark that's hung over him all this time." He looks at me keenly. "Did your father ever…?"

"Why were you so sure?"

"About Connaghan?" His eyebrows shoot up. "It was obvious. The day Kathleen Connaghan disappeared, she and James Cory were seen leaving the Stables bar, three miles outside of Inverness. We had a positive sighting to back up James' timing, and then nothing. That was around one-forty. James Cory was back in his office at two. Around one-forty-five, Joe Connaghan went missing for two hours. He was late for his afternoon appointment at Brady's Garage. He never had a satisfactory explanation of where he was for that time."

"What did he say?"

"Said he drove out of Inverness alone to think."

"And…?"

Simons looks at me as if I have to be stupid not to see the truth.

"He had no alibi, no witnesses, nobody who saw him. Some coincidence. The day his wife goes missing, he does too?"

"But I read once that the last person seen publicly with a victim is nearly always the murderer…"

Simons shakes his head.

"Not this time. The timings… look at the timings."

Simons doesn't take his eyes off my face the whole time he talks. Scanning, calculating. The sun has shifted position slightly, is shining through the window like a spotlight, directly into my eyes. I lean on the arm of the chair, using my hand to shield me. It feels like Simons is closing in on me. When did I become the quarry here?

"Then Connaghan turns up in an emotional state that afternoon, an hour late for his appointment…" continues Simons.

Why does he keep calling my father by his surname and Cory by his first name?

"Who said he was in an emotional state?"

"Jim Brady at the tyre garage. Said Connaghan was shaking and agitated when he was looking at the books."

Every word of Simons is punching me in the guts, winding me. I want him to stop. There is a panic bubbling inside me; a physical bubble that makes me want to cough. A terror that Simons is going to say something that will make me know for certain Da is a murderer. What would the words be that would convince me? I don't know. I don't know what they are. But I want to run in case he says them.

Simons looked at me shrewdly. "Connaghan said the reason he was upset that afternoon was that he had gone out alone with the intention of committing suicide."

He said he knew he was losing Kathleen; it was only a matter of time. So he had gone up to the loch and fitted a pipe to the exhaust and switched on but couldn't go through with it. Said he couldn't do it to his kids. Though of course, as it turned out, one of them *wasn't* his kid.

Simons knows the impact he's having. I can see it in his eyes. He senses blood. I clench my teeth tight together to stop the trembling in my jaw. Suicide.

Oh Da.

Something on the inside of me melts, like everything solid is liquefying, running into a river of no shape, no substance. So much unknown inside my father's heart. So much I never guessed.

"I didn't believe him," says Simons, watching me still. "I think Kathleen went to meet her husband that lunchtime after she

179

left the Stables. I think she finally told him they were through, that she loved James Cory. Connaghan couldn't handle it. He suggested they take a drive somewhere quiet to talk. Then he killed her and put her body in his boot before dumping her in the loch."

His grey eyes are pinning me back in my seat, fastening me to the lump of floral cushion at my back. I look at the way he is sitting forward in his chair now, the sausage skin round his middle tighter than ever. He didn't agree to see me to help me, that's for sure. He is using me more than I am using him. I came here thinking it might solve things for me. Instead, he wants me to solve things for him. He hopes I will unwittingly say something that will help clear up the Connaghan mystery that has endured for almost twenty-five years. A final feather in his fraying old cap. And the added benefit of helping an old friend. 'James'.

Simons clasps his hands over his knees and looks intently.

"Did your father ever say anything about what happened to your mother, about the…"

"Nothing," I say flatly, not even waiting for him to finish. I am past caring if I sound rude. The smell of fish seems to have seeped in here from the hallway. It's creeping under the door, oozing through the pores of the walls. The room is hot and stale, the direct heat on my face from the sun unbearable. My left cheek feels hot and pink, like it has been slapped. I stand up.

"I have to go now."

"No, don't go yet," he says quickly. "You've only just got here. We can talk some more." He smiles benignly. "I'll make you a cup of tea. Mary will be back shortly and…"

"That's kind of you, but I really have to go. I don't have long. Time is short before I have to get back to Glasgow."

"Leave me your number," he urges. "I can keep in touch… let you know if anything…"

I pull a pen from my bag, tear a scrap of paper from a notebook, and scribble it hastily.

"Goodbye," I say quickly, holding out my hand to shake hands. As his hand stretches out, I see a glint on his finger. A gold ring with a blue background and a pattern in the centre. A capital 'G'. It seems familiar. I've seen a ring like that before. Where?

"Just one thing before I go," I say, opening the door. "What made you rule out James Cory so completely? What made you so certain?"

"There was no evidence," says Simons, and he shrugs. "And anyway, I had known James Cory for years. Golf club," he says, nodding to the buggy in the hall.

Was everyone in this bloody town in the golf club?

"You stuck up for him because he was a friend?"

Simons's face hardens. I see the shutters closing over his eyes, the flush of anger in his cheeks.

"I've been in the force a long time and I have never, ever helped a guilty man," he says. "I just didn't believe James Cory was the kind of man to do something like that. I *knew* him."

Knew him? What does he mean 'knew him'? Who knows anybody in this world? I mean really knows them. Knows what's right deep inside them; knows what colour their guts are when they are turned inside out. Did he really know Cory? Did I know Da?

"Maybe you didn't know him as well as you think," I say. "My father was not a murderer."

As I step out, a small grey-haired woman with a tired perm walks up the path, a shopping bag in each hand. She smiles at me wanly.

"James Cory did not kill Kathleen Connaghan," says Terry Simons quietly at the door. "And that's the truth." The grey-haired woman looks surprised as I walk past her without a word.

The truth? Is it? Whose truth? There are too many extra pieces in this puzzle. Bits which look as if they fit, but don't. Bits which distort the picture when you try to get a clear view. They're all there in front of me: sharp-edged, smooth-edged, regular and angular. Right now I have no ideas which bits are part of the proper picture, and which bits are simply red herrings.

☙❧

I got off with one of my hotel managers once. Little more than that. Some heavy flirting, a quick snog over the filing cabinet in his room. I suppose I was a bit flattered he picked me out, and anyway, I fancied a quiet season. It was one of the perks of being the boss's bird in a hotel. Fewer early shifts.

It didn't last long. On one of our first dates he took me out with some mate of his and his lady friend. Couldn't stand her. She was a smug little puss, delicate and dainty as a kitten when she was with her man, always preening and purring. She'd hang on his arm, and rub her leg quietly against his under the table, and smile like there was cream dripping off her whiskers. It was a different story when there were no men about.

Anyway, he was called Craig, my hotel manager, and he was unimportant, completely unimportant. But after I leave Terry Simons, a mental picture suddenly drops into place. The ring. Terry Simons' ring. That's where I remember it from. Craig used to wear one. And this long-forgotten conversation drifts back into mind.

We were in the pub, the four of us, and he and his mate started talking about some guy from a nearby town. He had done well for himself in cash and carry and had just opened up another outlet, moving into some new premises locally.

Craig's pal said he'd met him at a local Chamber of Commerce meeting. And then Craig, thinking me and the puss weren't listening, says quietly, "Is he on the square?" Oh yeah. "A regular attender," his mate says, and it was like the two of them were talking in some kind of code. I caught Craig's eye and looked at him quizzically, but he just looked a bit discomfited and changed the subject.

"What was all that about?" I asked him later.

"What?"

"That 'on the square' stuff. What does that mean?"

He shook his head dismissively, tried to sound light.

"It's nothing. It's... just an expression. It means being in the Masons."

His late father was a Freemason. In fact, the ring Craig wore was originally his dad's. And the 'G'? Stood for God, apparently.

"But you're not a Mason are you?"

"It's just a business thing," said Craig, a bit defensively I thought.

I burst out laughing. "Oooh," I said, sidling up to him on the couch and running my hand lightly along his leg. "I bet you've got the knees for the rolled-up trouser legs, brother Craig."

I don't remember what he said. But I do remember he didn't laugh back.

CHAPTER SIX

I turn on the radio as I head across the Kessock bridge toward Lochglas. There is a pop track on the radio, with a classical piano and soaring strings. I like the combination, turn up the volume as I cross the bridge. The early evening light is fantastic out across the water, the sunshine dulled with a touch of haar. I turn the volume up and up and up, the piano notes filling the small space of the car, the heavy bass thumping like a heartbeat, until it feels that there is so much energy in here it will explode, and the car will lift from the road.

Across the water, the hills and the sky and the shore are washed with a transparent grey-blue light and the effect is so eerie, so magical, that I think of Da and how much he would have loved it. I don't know what it is, but there is something in that combination of piano and strings and light that makes my heart swell, and right in this minute I think Da is everywhere here. He is in the mute grey hills, and in the drifting sea of cloud, and in the rays of sunshine that filter through the mist and streak like lightning bolts across the water. He is in the earth and in the sky and in the water. He is in the low, languorous flight of the sea bird across the surface and into the blue horizon. He still exists. He is all around me. Everywhere.

I remember them then, the words we sang in church as children about our Heavenly Father, as they called him. Words we sang sweetly but without comprehension.

And each rare moment
That I've felt His presence,
I shall remember and forever cherish.

Da.

I feel euphoric. And then suddenly the music fades and the feeling inside drifts away with the notes, ethereal as the sea haar, and its going leaves me empty. The faith, the belief, the certainty, evaporate. The blue light doesn't seem warm any longer, but thin and mean and cold. He is gone.

❧

The unbearable bit of those first days after Da died was not just the shock but the confusion. The certainty one minute that something remained of him, and the certainty the next that he was quite gone. Of thinking there was a soul and then thinking there was none. Of thinking there was a future and then being certain there was only a past. But what was it Da had said to Khadim? There is always a future whether you want it or not.

By the time I reach Lochglas, I feel subdued and tired, but driven. There are no options here, no side roads, no diversions. There is only straight on. I stop at Spar and look in. Yes, Marion is there in her pink overall, laughing with a customer. I pick up a paper and wait to pay.

"Hello again," she says. "Still here?"

"For another day or two."

"The forecast's still good. Such an amazing spell we've had."

I nod and hand over the money for the paper.

"Remember you told me about the couple who owned the house? I was wondering if the murdered woman, Kath Connaghan, still had relatives here?"

"Well her parents are both dead now but her sister, Kirstin is still here. But if it's the house you want to enquire about, I don't think Kirstin will know where Joseph Connaghan is. I don't think they're in touch."

"Probably not," I say, carelessly as I can, "but I just thought I'd ask." I smile. "It's such a fantastic place."

"Fancy being a local then?" laughs Marion. "You'd soon get fed up in the winter, a young lassie like you."

"Oh, I don't know. Where does Kirstin live? She's my only shot."

"Second house past the Post Office," says Marion, handing me the change. "But I know she's out this evening because it's WRI night. You'd maybe get her in the morning."

Bored in the winter? With WRI on offer? Maybe I'd even learn how to peel a star fruit.

❦

A bottle of vodka; an old friend. I buy it in the supermarket round the corner from the B & B. It is nearing 10 p.m. but still light, the day refusing to give way, the air still and warm and scented by hanging baskets fixed to the lampposts outside. There is an empty space next to the supermarket car park, rough waste ground with a bulldozer standing in one corner, piles of stone blocks, scaffolding. Wire fencing encircles the ground, and it is only on the way back that I realise I have passed the signs several times without noticing the words that are plastered every few yards on the fencing. 'Cory Construction' the notice says. 'A

186

Highland Council project in partnership with Cory Construction'.

Back in the room, I undress and sit in my underwear on top of the bed. Even a sheet is too much in these airless nights. I sit with the pillows propped behind me, my knees drawn up to cradle the bottle, pouring two doubles in quick succession, waiting for the alcohol to flood my system. Tonight, it feels as if I could drink the whole bottle and nothing would counteract the adrenalin. It's only when the third double is being poured that I begin to feel that familiar numbing, the soothing effects flooding into my limbs and relaxing them. It is a relief and I reach over for the lemonade bottle, humming under my breath to the music from the radio clock on the bedside table. From the depths of my handbag, which is discarded on the floor and tucked halfway under the bed, comes a muffled beep.

I glance at my watch. 11 p.m. Sarah? I lean over the edge of the bed, reaching for the bag, giggling slightly as I grab hold of the base to stop myself falling. Close! I heave myself up, chucking out items from the bag until the sheets are covered with discarded papers, a cheque book, a pen and lipstick, and then impatiently I tip the whole thing upside down until a purse and phone fall out in a flurry of crumbs and dust. A text. Withheld number. Click. I stare at the short message, frowning. 'Go home.' Who the...? Then I shrug, chucking it on the bed and reaching for the bottle.

The message comes three times in the next hour. Go home. It is only when the phone beeps a fourth time that I realise I am alert, waiting. The sound makes me jump. 'Go home, bitch.' There is only a bedside light on but I suddenly become aware that across the room, the curtains are not closed. Night has fallen now and a thin sliver of moon falls into the room. I throw a wrap over my underwear and stumble across to close the curtains, shutting out the world, the sudden malevolence that darkness has brought. I cross the room and pull the additional snib across the door, then climb back into bed and pour another measure from the rapidly dwindling bottle. From somewhere inside the rumpled duvet, another beep sounds insistently.

TUESDAY

CHAPTER ONE

Things seem different in the morning. Less threatening. They always do when the darkness is replaced with light, and as the morning sunshine streams through my bedroom windows, the strange uneasiness I felt receiving those texts in the night fades slightly. Da always accused me of being a bit foolhardy and I prove him right by suppressing any instinctive sense of danger. Lochglas is a small place and I am an outsider asking questions about a dark spot in its history. My phone calls... my questions in the Spar... it's probably all public knowledge by now. I've left my number in lots of places already. It intrigues me that all these years after my mother was murdered, someone still cares enough to text abuse to me, but there was no specific threat in the texts, just an instruction to go home and leave things alone. Small places don't like outsiders. Incomers. In a couple of days I will be gone and it is unlikely I will ever be back.

I am tired, though, and a bit hungover, and barely hear the landlady as she chats at breakfast. She suggests a nice walk along the river, a visit to what she calls the Islands. I am only half taking in what she says. Tourists like it along there, she says. I nod politely, ask a question or two, but I know I won't be walking there this morning. I will be driving to Lochglas, to the house two doors down from the Post Office.

Outside the house, I sit in the car for a few minutes, trying to compose myself. The experience with Terry Simons has unnerved me. I am scared of this woman too. Scared that she, too, could destroy the last vestiges of my faith in Da. You think you want to know things until you get to know them. If I hadn't come on this journey, if I hadn't wanted to know, I'd have a very different picture of Da and Mother right now. But I know too much now not to try to find out the rest. I can't un-know.

My aunt's house is a small whitewashed cottage with a grey slate roof and a bright green painted door with a glass panel. I can see a shape moving towards me through the glass when I ring the bell. The pressure builds in my chest as the shape looms closer. A woman in her mid fifties answers. Short, cropped dark hair. Beige trousers, lemon shirt. Small pearl earrings. She doesn't look anything like the pictures of mother, but then I don't know how mother would have looked in her mid fifties.

"Kirstin?" I say.

I, on the other hand, look so like the pictures of my mother that I think she might guess right away, but she looks at me without recognition. Funny how some people see resemblances straight off and other just don't get it.

"Hello," she says, looking enquiringly at me.

My heat beats loudly, steadily. "Look, I'm really sorry to call on you unannounced," I begin in a rush, "and I hope you don't mind me disturbing you, but my name is Rebecca Connaghan. I think we might be related…?" If I was disappointed in her initial reaction, she makes up for it now. She blanches and gives a little gasp, an awkward, inward inhalation, and says, "oh" at the same time, so the word comes out strangled and muffled. Her hand grasps for the door.

"I'm sorry. I've startled you."

"No, you're all right," she says, but she is shaken. "Come in."

She leads me into a quiet sitting room overlooking the road. Passers-by walk inches from her window and she has Venetian blinds fitted, the light coming in waves through the slats. The room has a neat, old-fashioned feel with lace antimacassars on the arms and the backs of chairs, and a vase of pink chrysanthemums sitting on the table near the window.

"Take a seat," she motions and we sit down in awkward silence.

Kirstin seems genuinely sad when I tell her about Da. She is a thin, precise woman, rather anxious. Her skin is pale, almost bloodless, except for a few tiny broken veins in her cheeks, fine as red thread.

"I'm sorry," she says. "I'm very sorry."

"Why," I ask, "did the two of you not keep in touch?"

She says nothing for a minute.

"How much do you know?" she asks finally.

I tell her about the house and the library cuttings and she listens intently.

"You know about Cory then?"

"Yeah. I know about Cory."

She hesitates.

"Do you want tea? Coffee?"

"No, I'm fine thanks."

I wait for her to speak but she doesn't. I suppose it is hard for her. I have, after all, literally turned up on her doorstep. Apart from Peggy and Charlie, she is the only relative I have ever met and my eyes are fixed on her face with a sense of curiosity. Trying to see Mother. Trying to see me, maybe. Her skin is so pale.

193

She's dyeing her hair the wrong colour, I think, the thought popping into my head from nowhere. Her hair is too dark. She should be honey, not black. Funny how, even in the face of the serious, the banal never quite backs off.

"Was there some kind of… I don't know… feud between Da and you?" I ask eventually.

She shakes her head. "When it happened, when Kath disappeared, your father and I supported each other at first. But I didn't know about Cory. Joe never told me; Kath never told me. And when that came out…" Her voice trailed away.

"What?"

She looks uncomfortable.

"I didn't know what to think. I didn't know if Joe had lost control with Kath or not."

"You mean murdered her."

"You have to understand what that time was like," she says, a little defensively. "It was the most awful, awful time of our lives. The day she disappeared I got a call from Doreen, the lassie that ran the play group. Kath hadn't turned up to pick you up. I had Sarah and I was worried right away. Kath was always running, always late, but not by an hour. Not when she was picking you up. And the hour turned to two and the two to three and then to a day… two days… a week. We were all just trying to hold it together. We weren't sleeping. We weren't eating. If her body had been found we might have been able to come to terms with it, but while she was missing it was just like living in limbo. We couldn't function. Well, I couldn't."

Kirstin reaches into a handbag, takes out a packet of cigarettes, offers me one. I shake my head.

"Every time the phone rang, I jumped. I kept thinking it was Kath. And every time I cried because it wasn't. I was crying myself to sleep at night and crying when I woke up. My husband Donald was having to force me out of bed in the morning. I'd stand in the shower and howl and he'd have to come back and turn off the water to make me get out."

"And Da…?"

"Joe was on the brink of breakdown. It was only having to look after you and Sarah that kept him sane. His sister came up from Glasgow to help him…"

"Peggy?"

"Yes, Peggy." Kirstin flicks a lighter and the flame shoots up. Her hand shakes slightly as she lights the cigarette. "But he kept in close contact with me. And as the days turned into weeks and Kath was still missing, he knew some people were beginning to suspect him." She hesitates, throwing the lighter onto a small table beside her chair. "All the talk gets to you. After a while, even I began to suspect him. Joe loved her; he loved her so much. We all knew that."

I think she was saying love was more powerful than hate. That it made you do more destructive things. She takes a tissue out of the box beside her and blows her nose.

"There was an article in the paper one day and the headline was, 'The Husband or the Lover?'"

"I saw it in the library."

She nods. "Joe came round that morning with the paper. Peggy had taken you to play group but he had Sarah with him, asleep in a carry cot. He was upset and shaking. Really, really agitated. He threw the paper down on my kitchen table and said what were people going to think? I knew he needed some support but I just couldn't give it to him. All I could think when I looked at him was, did you do it? Did you kill my sister?"

She takes a drag of her cigarette and neither of us speaks for a minute, our own thoughts floating out into the silence with Kirstin's cigarette smoke. Out in the street, there is movement. Through the Venetian blinds I can see a couple. I watch them pass by the low sitting-room window; no heads, just two waists, two pairs of jeans-clad legs, two sets of sturdy shoes.

"Did Da know what you were thinking?" I ask.

She nods. "After a minute or two ranting, he suddenly realised I wasn't saying anything. I'll never forget the look he gave me… A kind of… angry… a cold, cold look. And then he said, so quietly it frightened me, 'Some people think I murdered Kath, Kirstin. What do you think?'"

"What did you say?"

"Nothing. I said absolutely nothing. Joe stared at me and then he just shook his head and said, 'I see.' I remember he put his hands on the table and bowed his head, as if thinking what to do next. I began to panic then. It was silly. But I just… I began to think… you know… what if he *had* killed Kath."

She is talking almost as if she can still taste that moment in her mouth. I wasn't even there but all I can taste is Da's betrayal.

"Donald wasn't in. I was on my own and I really began to sweat. I'd known Joe for years but suddenly I felt as if I was locked in my kitchen with a stranger. What if he turned on me? What if he thought he had to get rid of me too? I was terrified and when he looked up I think he could see the fear. He knew what I was thinking. I said to him, 'Maybe you'd better just go now, Joe.' He didn't answer for a minute and then he said, 'Yeah, maybe I better had.' And he picked up Sarah and walked out without another word. When I heard the front door click shut I ran out and turned the lock after him."

She takes another puff of the cigarette, stubs out the rest in an ashtray though it is only half smoked. There is pity in her eyes when she looks at me.

"I'm sorry," she says gently. "This is your dad I am talking about."

"What happened when you next saw him?" I ask quietly. I feel hurt for Da listening to this. There is a tightness, a soreness in my chest. But how can I blame her for wondering what I'd wondered myself?

"I didn't," she says, and for a second I don't understand. "I never saw him again," she explains. "He took you and Sarah and he left late that night and he never came back. He packed some cases and simply left the house as it was. When I realised he was gone, I went to the police. I thought it proved he did it and certainly that was the story Cory was putting about. But the police said he'd left a forwarding address with them, that they knew where he was."

"But everyone thought it was Da, that he'd run away?"

"For a while. I let it be known that the police knew where Joe was, that he hadn't simply run off." She looks at me. "I didn't hate him," she says and her eyes appeal for understanding. "But I knew both those men. Joe Connaghan, James Cory. I knew both and I would have said neither of them was capable of murder. You know? And that shakes your judgement. Either way, you got it wrong. In the end you just don't know what to think, who to trust."

She picks up another cigarette, lights it. "I still think about her, still miss her. You never get over it." Her voice breaks completely for the first time. She reaches for another tissue. "Sure you don't want tea?"

197

I hesitate. She needs something to focus on.

"Just if you're having one."

She nods.

"Come on through."

"What was my mother like?" I ask as she leads me through to the kitchen.

Kirstin fills the kettle without taking off the lid, the water gushing in and spraying off the spout, spattering small water marks onto her pale lemon short-sleeved shirt.

"She was flighty and funny and capable of great kindness. But she was also selfish and immature and..." She flicks the switch on the kettle and sits down at the table. "And she was just my sister," she says, as if nothing else need be said. "I started out my life with a big sister and then suddenly I just didn't have one any more. When my parents died there was no one to share that with, to grieve with. For large parts of my life since she died, I have felt very alone. Of course there's Donald, and my daughter Jen but... it's hard to explain. It's just a loneliness."

"You were close then?"

"That's the strange thing. Not really. Not close the way she was to some of her friends. She didn't tell me about what was going on in her life, about Cory, but there was a tie there that couldn't be broken. We grew up together. In those days we fought and we argued and we fell out, but we also laughed and told each other secrets and backed one another up when Mum and Dad were trying to keep too tight a rein on us."

"Blood ties," I say.

"Yes, I suppose so. We were different characters. But we always knew we were sisters if we needed someone." Kirstin gets up from the table and takes two mugs from the cupboard.

"Is Sarah up here with you?"

"She doesn't know I am here."

"Are the two of you close?"

"Yes and no," I say noncommittally. "Like you and Mum, probably."

"Nothing round here was big enough for Kath whereas I... I was quite content, you know? Kath was the one who got caught smoking and sneaking out when she was meant to be doing homework. She was the one who went off with people she wasn't meant to be with, to places she wasn't meant to be going to. Boring Bertha she called me." Her laugh turns into a hard, chesty cough. She hands me a mug.

"Is that why she went for Cory?"

Kirstin nods. "Probably."

"But didn't she realise that she was just a fling to him, that he wasn't the kind of man who was going to always be around?"

"But Kath wasn't the kind of woman who was always going to be around either. Anyway, she made that fatal mistake women always make. She thought she was different. She thought she could change him." She takes a sip from her mug.

"You don't know Cory, but he was a big man round these parts. He was successful. He had money and position and power. Whereas Joe..." She smiles. "Don't get me wrong. Joe was a good-looking man when he was young. Kath wouldn't have fallen for him otherwise. She thought he was older and sophisticated and a catch. But he wasn't... he wasn't... a wordly man. No, not a worldly man," she repeats thoughtfully. "And as Kath got older he didn't seem sophisticated any more. Just... Just safe and dull..." She breaks off and looked at me with a pang. "I'm sorry, I shouldn't be talking about your dad like this."

I shake my head. "I'd rather know. Look, I have to ask you this. Do most people round here still think he did it?"

"Some said your father; some said Cory. Everyone had a theory. Nobody could prove any of them. Not even the police. But it's a long time ago… people forget. There are so many young ones and incomers in the village who don't know anything about what happened here."

I hear a key in the lock of the front door.

"That'll be Donald," she says, and she moves swiftly out into the hall. I hear their voices murmuring. Donald comes into the kitchen, his jeans and workman's boots covered in dry mud and dust.

"This is Rebecca," says Kirstin.

I stand up. He looks curiously at me, nods.

"I'll not shake hands," he says, holding up blackened, work-soiled hands. He looks at Kirstin. "I'll just go and have a bath and change." I hear his heavy footsteps disappearing upstairs.

I look out of her kitchen window at the sweep of the hill and the bay of the loch nestling below. Lochglas. The grey loch. It is so utterly tranquil. How could such ugliness have germinated here, grown and taken shape in the face of this beauty?

"Where do you think her body is?" I ask Kirstin suddenly, and she looks taken aback.

"You've heard the story about the car park?"

I nod.

"I suppose it's possible. But I've always wondered if Kath's buried out in the loch."

What she really means is, she always wondered if Da did it. If Cory did it, she was in the car park. If Da did it, she was in the loch. The grey loch.

"I hate the thought of it," she continues, "because Kath was frightened of water. She couldn't swim and I can't bear it, the thought of her lying there, trapped in seaweed, bloated and puffy with the water. I've never told anyone this but… but every morning for the last twenty years I have looked out on the loch…" Her voice begins to waver uncontrollably and I want to reach out to her, but I don't feel I know her well enough to touch her. "And I've said, 'Morning Kath.' Just in case she's there, like, you know? Morning Kath. It makes me feel better."

She sips from her mug, trying to regain control.

"What about now, Kirstin? Right now, who do you think did it?" It is almost an appeal.

"Me?" She exhales deeply, blowing her cheeks out and avoiding my eye, looking into the depths of her mug.

"I don't know," she says slowly. "That's as honest as I can be."

"I'm sorry that it's going to end like this," I say. "I'm sorry we can't know one another. But I can't ever tell Sarah… I just can't tell her."

Kirstin nods.

"I understand. I know that sometimes you have to cut people out of your life." She reaches out suddenly for my hand, following her instinct in the way I didn't, a surprise gesture that both touches and embarrasses me. "I'm sorry I had to do that to Joe… to your dad. I liked Joe when Kath first got together with him. And I know what she was like. Kath was difficult. There was no doubt about that. But there was nothing she did that could have deserved… nothing. And I'm not saying Joe did it. I'm just saying that I couldn't bear to see him and wonder. For as long as I had even the tiniest doubt, I couldn't look at him. And he knew that. I know that's wrong if he was innocent. But I couldn't… I'm sorry if I hurt him. I'm not saying it was fair. But it wasn't fair what happened to Kath. And she was my sister... You understand? She was my sister."

CHAPTER TWO

Sisters. Sister Sarah. Blood is thicker than water. But as it turned out, our blood was diluted, and where did that leave us, Sarah and me? Half-sisters. Nearly sisters. Has that been the root of the distance that has grown between us over the years? Somewhere deep inside us, have we always known?

I told Kirstin that I couldn't ever tell Sarah the truth. Telling Sarah would not be like telling Father Peter, a conversation without consequences. Sarah loved Da. Ironic that he is the only parent we have shared, and the only one we do not have in common. But she doesn't know that. How could I take him from her, tell her that the man she loved wasn't really her father? That her real father was some rich bastard who brought her mother champagne then dumped her in the foundations of a car park?

There is something else. I know it is not my information to give. I know if she were to be told, it should have been Da who told her. But he is not here. In his absence, there is a little part of me that won't be stilled, that thinks she has the right to know. To tell her would be like telling her that the life she lived never really existed. It was just a fantasy. But not to tell her is to allow her to go on living a lie. More secrets. More shadows.

You see the dilemma. It masquerades as something else, another problem altogether. For the dilemma is not just whether to tell, or not to tell. The dilemma is how to untangle the knotted threads of my own motivation. I can pick either course of action and hug it closely to my chest, warm myself with the embers of my own rectitude. I was right for this reason, for that reason. But there will also be another possibility, another reason for doing what I do.

If I stay silent, will it be because I want power that she doesn't have; the power of secret knowledge? The power of truth? Da will be all mine and she will never even know. If I tell her, will it be because somewhere deep inside I am fuelled by malice? Perfect Sarah, with her pretty blonde hair and blue eyes. If only we had peeled all those layers of love and hate back, I would know. But we are not quite there yet. The strings of puppet Sarah are in my hand. I am in control; I can cut them with a single snip.

Am I jealous of Sarah? I don't know any more. Perhaps a little. Of her perfection, her simplicity. The way she always chose order where I opted for chaos. I despised her order. But how often do you despise what you cannot have? I know that now I feel a sense of loss. It would be different had I always known; the trauma comes from unexpected revelation. I want her, my little sister, now that she no longer *is* my sister. I want her back.

But don't get me wrong. I don't want to be Sarah. Don't want her life, her job. Don't want Des. Definitely don't want Des. Da always said he thought Des had a good enough heart. Da didn't know about the washing-machine night. I never forgave Des for that.

Sarah and I were doing the crossword in the sitting room when he came in.

"Your father," he said as he closed the door, and he shook his head with a silly, rueful little smile.

"What's he up to now?" asked Sarah.

"I went into the kitchen and he's sitting there on top of the washing machine, not doing anything, just looking at the floor," said Des, wide eyed. "On top of the bloody washing machine! I said, 'All right Joe?' And he said, 'Fine thanks Des.'"

Des rolled his eyes. "Do you think his mind's going? That's the way my mother went when the dementia started."

Des's mum died last year, and the fact that he looked after her is the reason he says he isn't married yet. I think there's a rather more fundamental reason. With apologies to Sarah, no woman in her right mind would have him. I was mad with him for suggesting Da was losing his mind. Typical, snotty Des. Da could be off-beat, even eccentric, at times but that's because he had an interesting mind. Des is so stolid he couldn't see Da was smarter than him. "I'd find Mum wandering in the garden at midnight or walking to the shops in her slippers," continued Des.

I could have wrapped his diamond-patterned tie round his thick, stupid neck. And I probably would have if Da hadn't come in just then and gone into his tool box for something. Probably something to fix the machine. I expect he was just having thinking time, sitting there on top of it. Sarah hurriedly picked up the paper.

"Here's a clue, everyone," she said self-consciously, her face flushed. "Win the argument and say Amen to that. Four words… four, three, four and four.

"Any letters?" asked Des.

"First word starts with H.

"Now," said Des. "If we just think about…"

"Have the last word," Da said absently, and wandered out again.

He was good at working out clues, Da. Better than me. I have all these pieces assembling in front of me that I don't know how to make sense of. There are two pictures on the jigsaw box and I don't know which one I have the pieces for. There we all are, in fragments in front of me: Da, Mother, Cory, Peggy and Charlie, sister Sarah, and me. But how do we all fit together?

∞

The next piece is easy. I have kept this one till last because I know it fits in the picture somewhere. I head into town, ask directions to his offices. He has come a long way since my mother's time. The offices are two storeys high with an exterior of gleaming glass and polished chrome. A national company. He has an office in Glasgow, another in Yorkshire. I stand across the road at a bus stop and watch. I can see the reception through the swing doors. Fresh flowers. Exotic green pot plants in corners. Women who look like they are auditioning for an American soap with gleaming hair and tight skirts and kitten heels. I can see their mouths move in conversation. They talk, smile, walk, sit, oblivious to the fact that someone stands outside and watches them.

But it is not them I am waiting for. I keep moving into the shadows, away from the direct sunlight, watching. I wait for over an hour just to catch a glimpse of him. I know it is him as soon as he appears. I stiffen when he comes into view; watch him. Even all these years after those newspaper photographs were taken, he is still recognisable. But I have the feeling that in some instinctive place I would know him anyway.

He walks right up to the desk at the window of the first floor. You can tell he is important just by the way he walks. The cut of

206

the suit. The proprietorial way he puts his arm round the secretary's shoulder when she stands up. She fetches him some papers. He smiles. He sits on her desk. I watch every last movement. The way his hand goes to his hair every so often and smooths it back; the way he tilts his head when he listens. Yes, I know him.

After five minutes he goes back to his office. I have seen him, really seen him. I feel high with it, pumped up, ferocious. I half walk, half run back towards town to pick up my car. My cheeks are red with the heat and the exertion, my heart pumping just enough that I am aware of its rhythm in my chest. The gears crunch as I move the car. My legs shake on the pedals and I let the clutch up too quickly, the car jerking to a stalled halt. I turn the key again impatiently, rev the engine, kangaroo hop forward. Back to Cory Construction, round the back to the car park and wait in a side street across the road opposite the entrance. He leaves early, at quarter past five, and I watch him get into a flash convertible. A young man's car that only an old man could afford.

Nothing in the mirror. The car indicator ticks as I signal left, follow him out through the town. He goes through the traffic lights and it turns to amber as I approach. I put my foot down on the accelerator, sail through as it turns red. It is me who is in charge, in control. I am watching him; he is not watching me. I am the pursuer; he the pursued. It gives me such a feeling of power, like he is an animal and I am tracking him. Sniffing him out. Left. Right. Right again. Round the town centre, out into the open road.

A few miles out of town he slows, turns left, drives up a hill lined with pink rhododendron bushes. There is a small, exclusive development of maybe four or five houses at the top, with spectacular views out across the hills. It is a cul de sac. He turns into his driveway and I see him glance at my old battered car as I drive past and on to the end of the road to turn.

The driveway has two stone lion gate heads at the entranceway. I slow going past, see the extensive front lawn with a sprinkling fountain, catch just a glimpse through the trees of a detached house. An extensive, red-roofed house with a sun deck at one end and a conservatory at the other. I can hardly bear the thought of it. Twenty-five years of luxury while my mother turned to dust under a ton of earth and concrete. We have things to talk about, James Cory and I. But not yet. Not quite yet.

CHAPTER THREE

This whole thing has become like a scab that I can't stop picking. There are times, like in Terry Simons' house, when it gets too sore to continue and I vow to leave the wound alone, let it heal. But as soon as the immediate pain dies down, the compulsion creeps back and I can't keep my fingers away. I know that when I lift the crust of the scab, chances are I am going to remove more than dead skin. I'm going to pull new, fragile skin with it and draw blood. But even then, I just can't seem to stop. I can't stop pick, pick, picking.

Terry Simons is bothering me. The ring. On the square. *On the square.* The phrase goes round and round inside my head and I don't know why. It leads me back to the library, a half hunch, but what am I looking for? Masons. Masons. *An Inside Story: The Secret World of Freemasonry*, it says in the library catalogue. The book is there on the shelves when I look, a dark red cover with bold black writing on the spine. Inside, there's a whole section on the police, a separate one on the judiciary. I flip over the pages, my eyes lighting on an extract from a newspaper cutting about the controversial memoirs of a senior policeman. 1969. David Thomas, Head of Monmouthshire CID. "The insidious effect of Freemasonry among the police has to be experienced to be believed."

A serving police officer's testimony. "We all knew it happened. If two men were up for promotion and one belonged to the lodge, well all other things being equal... The boss said it was the same with any kind of club. If you knew a man through the golf club, it was going to make you closer. You were going to get to know them better over a round of golf. It wasn't corruption, it was human nature, he said. In the end I decided to join. It was just a club, and a club that you were better in than out of."

Scandals. The collapse of Scotland Yard, 1877. And then a hundred years later, history repeating itself.

The major impetus for challenging corruption in the Metropolitan Police came with the appointment of Sir Robert Mark in 1972. The notorious 'Porn Squad Trials' of the 1970's involved wholesale corruption in an entire section of the capital's CID police force. Officers in the Porn Squad were found to have turned a blind eye to the activities of Soho pornography dealers in return for substantial payments. It was subsequently discovered that some of the dealers and officers belonged to the same Masonic lodges.

A senior officer of the Porn Squad, Detective Chief Inspector Bill Moody, was jailed for twelve years in 1977. It was, however, difficult to obtain evidence even from Masonic officers who were not involved in the corruption. Those who were 'on the level' or 'on the square', in other words members of the Lodge, saw it as their duty to protect their Masonic brothers.....

That was London. What was happening 600 miles away in Inverness? I close the book. It's a strong word, corruption. A tiger of a word. But sometimes corruption is quieter than a tiger. Sometimes it's a worm. It's slow burrowing, goes so deep you scarcely know it's there any more. Is Terry Simons corrupt or merely misguided in defending Cory? I push down the alternative – that Cory really is innocent. I can't know about Simons until I know what influences him.

And sometimes you don't even know what influences yourself.

A quote from my mother's letter that I found in the bureau comes back to me. 'The Masonic mafia' she had written flippantly. It was clear from what she wrote that David Carruthers had been a Mason. Was Cory? Probably. But did that mean Terry Simons automatically felt a duty to him, either consciously or subconsciously? Because corruption... well, it seems to me it isn't always deliberate, straightforward, black and white. You know what it is? It's *see you in the club... why don't you join us... one of us*. Papes. Prods. Muslims. Jews. Little boxes, little boxes. Masons. Opus Dei. The Tribe of Angels. Black boxes, white boxes. Boxes like Tariq and I would have ended up in.

Maybe it does matter if Cory was a Mason and maybe it doesn't. Maybe it's simpler than Masons and non-Masons. Maybe it's just about insiders and outsiders. Some of us are always going to be outsiders. It's what we know and what we expect. Da was an outsider. But James Cory? He was an insider. I *know* you, James Cory. One of us. Not guilty.

CHAPTER FOUR

Back in the B & B room, an opened packet of supermarket sandwiches lies on the table by the window, a bite out of one sandwich. They irritate me too much to eat them. At twenty-eight, I still live like a broke nineteen-year-old student. I would have stretched to something better than a sandwich but I wanted to buy a bottle of wine. So they sit there, the egg and cress and the half-drunk bottle of cheapo red, like a silent reproof. A symbol of my failure to amount to anything. I want to tell them to fuck off but I can't. I might need them. Bloody life all over.

A phone rings in the distance, somewhere down the hall, then a tap comes at my door. Nobody has the B & B number except Mrs Carruthers. But when I answer, it's a man's voice.

"Hello?"

"Hello, Rebecca Connaghan?"

"Speaking."

"This is David Carruthers."

My heart quickens, then slows to a thumping, staccato beat.

"David Carruthers? I thought… I'm sorry I didn't… I was told David Carruthers was dead."

"I'm his son. My father died just over a year ago."

"I'm sorry…"

"I'm told you were looking for my mother," he continues over me. I get the feeling he is uninterested in social niceties. His voice is clipped, formal.

"Yes, I thought, well, I hope… that she might be able to help me."

"I doubt it."

The dry tone stiffens my hackles.

"I'm Kathleen Connaghan's daughter."

"Yes, your message said."

"I'm up from Glasgow. I'm trying… trying to find out what happened to her."

"Well there's nothing my mother can tell you. I must ask you to leave her in peace."

"What happened to Kathleen Connaghan had nothing to do with my mother or anyone else in my family. As you can imagine, she is still coming to terms with losing my father. She's not well and I really don't want her upset at the moment."

"I'm sorry to hear she's not well. I really don't want to upset her. I could just speak to her briefly, I won't…"

"I'm sorry, she can't help you."

"But I…"

"You're not listening to what I am saying. My mother can't help you. She is already upset by your call and she just doesn't want any of this stuff resurfacing again. It had absolutely nothing to do with her or my dad."

"Perhaps I could meet with you first and explain everything and then you could…"

But he interrupts again. "What on earth could I tell you? I was so young when all this happened."

"Just ten minutes…"

"You really don't seem to understand." He sounds impatient

now, his words little explosions of irritation. But I refuse to do the polite thing. I surf his anger, use the momentum of it to keep me upright.

"I'll meet any time that's convenient for you."

"Look," he says. "I'm really busy and I don't see…"

"I've just lost my dad."

The words catch in my throat, trembling there before emerging from my mouth, taking even me by surprise. On the wall where the phone hangs there is a pin board with cards stuck at every angle. Taxi numbers, cinema listings, a pizza delivery number. My fingers pick at a green drawing pin stuck tightly in the cork, working it loose.

"I'm sorry," he says finally.

"Thanks."

"I know how hard that is." His voice is softened, but has not been robbed of its purpose. "But… sorry… I can't help you."

I don't speak because I can't. My finger works at the pin, the skin red and temporarily indented, until the pin suddenly skites uncontrollably from the board. A taxi card flutters down, landing propped against the skirting board.

He says nothing but the silence is disconcerting him. I can sense uncertainty ravelling round him like a cord, choking his certainty.

"Are you on your own?"

"Yes."

He is weakening. Even in my distress I can detach myself, recognise the main chance. A picture flashes into my mind. Father Dangerous, in the hotel room, lying beside me. I hear his voice. So many ghosts these days, but none the one I am looking for. "God, you're hard, Rebecca," says the ghost.

"Please meet me," I say quietly, resting my head against the pinboard.

David Carruthers hesitates.

"Please."

"Ten minutes is all I can manage."

"When?"

"Now. Let's get this done."

We meet in a town-centre bar with purple, marbled-effect wallpaper and dim, conical lights that hang low over wooden tables. Tea lights flicker in purple glass jars in the centre of the table. I know David Carruthers when he enters because of the way he hesitates, his eyes flicking round the room, searching. I try to catch his eye but he doesn't see me, tucked as I am in the corner by the window. I like corners. They hold you in tight, like a womb.

He's dressed in jeans and a t-shirt, a soft, expensive-looking, black leather jacket on top. I can tell he's vain. It's far too hot for a jacket. He smells of money.

It's not just in his clothes but in his confidence, in the way he stands sure-footed in the centre of that room. I see it in the hotels I work in. Rich people walk differently.

They talk like someone ought to listen. They hold themselves differently. The way David Carruthers holds himself now.

I watch him turning, slowly, slowly. Eyes flicking but no haste, no scurrying need to move from the centre stage. He is a little older than me; I'd guess in his early thirties. He has a strong nose. Not a boxer's nose; it is too fine and chiselled for that, but irregular. Delicately arched, almost feminine lips. His skin is olive, and a faint dark stubble is beginning to shadow his chin. I must say I like a man with dark hair. I move from the table.

215

"David Carruthers?" I say from behind him.

He turns, unsmiling. His eyes hold mine a little curiously as he holds out a hand.

"Hello." Grip firm, but brief. Long piano-player's fingers.

"I'm over here," I say, nodding at the table where my bag is hung over the back of my chair. "Can I get you a drink?"

"I'll get them," he says. It's more statement than offer. I let him. Why should I argue with a rich man?

"What is it you want to know?" he asks, putting a large glass of wine down on the table in front of me.

"I want to know if your father ever talked to you about my mother."

He shrugs carelessly. The gesture gets under my skin.

"Once." He takes a sip of beer. "Not until a few years ago. We went on a trip to London together."

"What did he say?"

"Not much."

"My father worked for him."

"Yes I know."

"He used to send my father out of town when James Cory wanted to see my mother."

"Hmm." It is a neutral sound. I don't know what it means.

"I want to know if James Cory killed my mother."

"You mean you want to know if your father did."

It is the truth. I bite my lip.

"I'm sorry," he says. "That was harsh."

A waitress comes to remove empty glasses from the next table. We watch her, saying nothing, as she wipes a cloth over the surface. The glasses clink as she fits four into one hand between her fingers.

"Did your father think Cory was capable…" The waitress turns back, an afterthought, lifts the ashtray. I stop talking until she has left again. "Did your father think Cory was capable of murder?"

"Absolutely not."

The white wine in my glass is chilled. It hits my stomach, and the lake of supermarket red, with the sudden force of a swallowed ice cube. It feels good.

"Why was he so sure?"

"He was with James when James got the call that your mother was missing. A friend of your mother's called him wanting to know if he knew where she was."

"Karen Sandford?"

"Could have been."

"You don't know Karen Sandford? Know where she, is I mean?"

"No."

"And?"

"My father said James went ashen. He was standing when he took the call but dad said he remembered him grabbing hold of the back of the chair."

"Why would he do that? He didn't know she was dead, did he?"

"I'm only telling you what he said. I wasn't there," he retorts brusquely. "But if someone goes missing when they are meant to be picking up their child, it's not looking good, is it?"

I take another drink. A dull ache has been spreading through my skull for the last half-hour, I guess from lack of food. One cream cake. One bite of egg and cress.

"Did your father really *never* doubt Cory?"

I notice that just for a second, David Carruthers avoids my eye. Just long enough for me to wonder.

"He really thought my father did it?"

"He liked your dad."

"But he supported Cory."

"They went back a long way."

"You didn't answer my question."

"What?"

"Did your father have any doubts?"

"I don't think he could believe James was capable of murder."

Still he does not answer the question directly.

"Or he didn't want to believe…"

"Maybe."

"And he didn't want to get involved."

"Can you blame him?"

"Yeah, I can actually. He helped screw up my dad's fucking life."

My anger is like a sudden surge on an accelerator pedal. Instantly, instinct makes my foot slacken and the anger dies. I take a slug of wine. Carruthers seems startled. I feel tired suddenly, emotionally tired, like tiredness is a great big mouth that is just slowly sucking me in and swallowing me up without even bothering to chew. I lean my elbows on the table and put my head in my hands. Carruthers watches silently.

"Your dad just went back to normal and got his life back. It was easy for him. Like it was obviously easy for you," I say bitterly. I reach for my glass, swallow the rest in one.

He says nothing but catches the eye of the waitress, points to my glass.

"Another large white wine please."

That's the confidence of the rich. They don't ask; they just do.

"How do you know I want one?"

"Don't you?"

"Yeah."

His eyebrows shoot up, then he half laughs, shakes his head. He lifts his glass.

"You're talking shite, you know."

"What?"

"About things being easy. Sometimes what's easy is seeing people the way you want to see them, rather than the way they are."

The dull ache in my head is becoming a throb, a distant drumbeat in my head.

"What's wrong? Did your toy train break when you threw it out of the pram?"

His hand freezes, the glass halfway to his mouth.

"My God you're arrogant!"

It's my turn to shrug.

"Listen," he says, "I'm not going to try and pretend my life has been like yours. I had my mother and my father around and I'm grateful for it. But I'm not going to apologise for it. Maybe my father shouldn't have got involved, but whatever happened – and you don't know what happened any more than I do – it wasn't his fault."

What does he mean, get involved? The thought is only a passing one. Carruthers leans forward over the table and his voice is low and urgent.

"The police crawled all over our house when she disappeared. My father was taken in for questioning along with James. At one point, they were even trying to say that he had helped James dispose of the body. They took his car away and had it stripped right down, looking for blood stains or hairs.

And every time they went away, he was never sure when they were coming back, what the next theory would be. My mother was convinced Dad was going to be locked up for something he had no part in… It was your mother who had the affair," he says, stabbing a finger at me. "But it was my mother who spent years on antidepressants."

Carruthers slumps back into the chair.

"She became ill?"

"She's always been… a bit fragile. She's been bothered with depression off and on for years. I'm not saying it wouldn't have happened anyway because Mum, well…" He changes his mind about what he is going to say. "But it certainly started around that time. It didn't help. Look, that's why I don't want you to meet with her. I really don't want her upset and there's nothing she could tell you, I know that. Honestly. I want you to promise not to try and contact her again."

"Why did the police think your father was involved?"

"Because they were close friends. Because they worked together. Because my father's car was seen parked outside James's house the night before your mother disappeared. As if that was something strange. They were always in and out of each other's houses. And Dad said he had some complicated tax stuff to sort out that he needed to speak to James about. But according to some ludicrous local theory, they were sitting round having supper and a bottle of wine while they discussed how to bump off James's bloody mistress." He grimaces. "Christ I'm sorry… I didn't mean…"

I shake my head, dismissing him with a wave of my hand. The wine is biting, making me feel light-headed.

"The police left him alone eventually, though?"

"Eventually. When Terry Simons took over. He was the police chief who was sent in to take over the case."

"I know. We've met," I say dryly.

Carruthers looks surprised.

"Anyway, my dad wasn't involved. I think Simons realised that pretty early on. And I mean, if James was going to commit murder, there's no way he'd sit and discuss it. He's a loner."

"If? I thought you said there was no way?"

Exasperation shadows Carruthers' face as he stares into his glass.

"Was James Cory a Mason?"

He looks puzzled.

"He and Dad both were. Why? What's that got to do with anything?"

"I just wondered….Were you close to your dad?"

"Yeah. But closer to my mum." He is looking at me suspiciously.

"Only child?"

He nods. "You?"

"One sister."

The word feels strange now. It doesn't fit right any more. Music pumps out of a jukebox by the bar, a distant rhythm in my head, like a vibration from another room. Strange bar, strange town, strange guy. What am I doing here?

As if echoing the thought, Carruthers says, "What made you come here so soon after your dad died?"

I don't know how to answer. The more I tell people, the less sure I become.

"I…" I stop, unable to say anything. The thump of the music is a step out of time with the thump in my head, one a discordant echo of the other. *Thump*, thump… *Thump*, thump… It is too hard to put the words together. Carruthers is staring at me. "I…"

He lays his hand on my arm for a moment, an instinctive gesture. He seems embarrassed then, lifts it back awkwardly.

"Were you close to your dad?"

"I loved him," I say simply. What else is there to say? "And then I came here and found out… found out… she was murdered."

His face freezes.

"Shit," he says. "You didn't know before you came up here? That's not why you came? You didn't know your mother was murdered?"

I shake my head. We sit together then for a while, silently. I watch the light fading outside, darkening swiftly now, an orange moon rising.

"I didn't want to meet you tonight," he says suddenly. "I just didn't want to get involved. And now I wish I hadn't."

"Why?"

"Because I *feel* involved. But there's nothing I can do. I'd like to help you and I can't. Nobody can. You need to go home, Rebecca. There's nothing anyone can do here. I'm sorry."

"You feel sorry for me?"

"Yes," he says softly, kindly even. "I do."

"Save it." I drain my glass. The room spins slowly. "I don't want your pity."

I have offended him. He sits back from the table in a rush, his arms thrown back against the seat. Half irritated, half hurt.

"One last thing." I have to go now. I need to get out of the smoke and the heat and the noise, out into the evening where I can hide in the darkness. "Would James Cory ever have left his wife for my mother?"

222

It's hard to think straight now. Hard to select precisely the right word.

Somewhere in the alcohol-induced confusion inside my head, I think this question will prove everything. If he would really have left his wife, he wouldn't have killed my mother. If he would have left his wife, he must have loved my mother. And if he really loved her, why would he kill her?

"I… I don't think so. Not from what I heard," Carruthers sounds hesitant.

"Why not?"

"From what I heard…" He stalls by taking another drink from his glass. "I think your mother… I don't think James felt… she wasn't…."

"You mean she was the kind of woman you took to bed but didn't marry?"

"I didn't say that."

"No."

He thought it, though. I always know when men think that stuff.

He frowns. "James's wife, Anna… she came from a wealthy family. In the early days of Cory Construction, it was basically her father who was financing it. There was no way he was going to leave Anna. And he was right. Look at it now."

Money had to come into it somewhere, I suppose. Money always comes into it somewhere.

"I don't have a bloody clue why I am telling you all this." He looks at the table and shakes his head, then glances up at me slyly. "Because you've got nice eyes, probably."

Flirt. What's he thinking? Like mother, like daughter? I can play it though. I can play that game.

"And you," I say, stabbing my finger into his shoulder, "have a nice… leather jacket."

He laughs into his glass.

"Is that the best you can do?"

I hold his eyes for a moment. "No."

He's really quite attractive, David Carruthers, I think. Really quite attractive.

I stand up. Too sudden. I grab the table and he catches my arm.

"I'll walk you back. It's by the river isn't it?"

"It's okay," I say, shaking off his arm gently. "I can manage."

"I'll walk you back."

I shrug, a 'please yourself' shrug. It is too complicated to argue. Too complicated for words.

Outside, there are groups of youths hanging about at the chip shop on the corner. Shouts, squeals of female laughter, some kind of carry-on. I need to concentrate on walking.

"*Watch* it, Gary," shouts a girl, and Gary grabs her round the waist and propels her, screaming, across the pavement. It is me who stumbles into her path rather than the other way round. Carruthers catches me.

"It's okay," I mutter. My mouth feels dry, dehydrated. "I'm not drunk."

"I think you're more emotional than drunk," he says. "When you're feeling that way a couple of drinks is enough."

"Yeah, well, I had a couple before we met."

"Figures," he says.

He puts his arm lightly round my shoulder, guiding me across the road. We walk silently for a while, up to the traffic lights at the bridge before turning down by the river. The lights from the street lamps shine in the water, the reflections quivering in the blackness.

Above, the moon riding high now in a pink streaked, velvet sky. A couple walks towards us, the girl with her arm through her partner's for support, teetering on stilettos that ring sharp and steely on the pavement. It is only five minutes to the B & B, which sits back in the road, facing the river. We stand on the pavement opposite, next to the water. The downstairs light is off but the exterior porch light has been left on. 'No vacancies' says the sign beneath.

Now I am here, I don't want to go into the dead of the darkness, feel the door close behind me. My eyes are smarting. I feel dishevelled.

"Thanks for walking me."

"Will you be okay?"

I nod.

"You don't look it."

I am inches from him. I can smell him, the smell of heat and aftershave, sweet and musky and comforting. The smell I associate with being wanted. I should go now, walk across the road and up the path. I don't move.

"I hope your mother… you know…" What's the word I'm looking for?

He nods. And then he gives me one of those looks that changes things. That look where suddenly you stop looking at a stranger and start to see something else.

Possibilities, maybe.

"I don't like to think of you on your own."

"I don't like to think of me on my own either."

He reaches out, tucks a stray strand of hair behind my ears.

"You don't need to stay here tonight," he says softly. "Not if you don't want. If you want company."

In the stillness that follows, I look out at the water, flowing, flowing, steadily down to the bridge. Rippled, mirrored with light, its pace all its own. Unalterable. I think about it, his offer. Think of drifting with the flow, letting it sweep me down where it will. I am tempted. No chance to think, to talk to the dead in the coffin of my room. Just the touch of the living, the heat of the moment, the comfort of no tomorrow. There are people who belong to right now and Carruthers is one. And until now, he is everything that I have ever needed, sweet and impermanent, the smell of him gone by daybreak, leaving only the promise of a blank new day.

But maybe it's time now. Time to stop drifting with the tide. Make the river flow the way I want it, instead of casting myself like flotsam on the top. I shake my head. "I need to go," I say softly.

We stand close still, and I put out my hand.

"Thanks for meeting with me."

We shake hands and when our arms drop, I hesitate. He leans forward then, gives a brief, awkward hug. I wrap my arms round the soft leather jacket. For a few seconds, I feel the comfort of being touched and almost change my mind.

"Take care, Rebecca," he says. "And please, do yourself a favour. Go home. Don't try to open this all up."

I don't look back until I reach the porch. I turn then, see him standing with his back to me. He is leaning, with his forearms on the railings and his hands clasped, lost in thought, looking out across the dappled water that dances silver with reflected light.

CHAPTER FIVE

Spirit Daddy. Where. Are. You? Why can't I find you? Why don't you answer? Tonight I am not going to get angry. I am going to drink another glass of wine and chat. Because you have to answer sometime, don't you, Da? You have to answer sometime.

So much to talk about today. So many people. They remain in my head in little tableaux. Terry Simons looking out of his window. Kirstin sitting in one of her lace-trimmed armchairs. David Carruthers, leaning against the railings down by the river. David Carruthers. Shame about David Carruthers. And then they begin to move, the characters, like little clips from a film. Scenes from someone else's life.

The one who is always there is Cory, a silent presence who squats like a massive Buddha in every scene. I haven't heard him speak yet. Not yet. It's gone, the adrenaline, the pumping, thumping, craziness that seeing him for the first time provoked. I'm swinging from one extreme to another now. Up one minute, down the next. Maybe I'm crazy. Do you think I could be crazy? Of course, you won't say either way, will you? You won't say anything at all.

I've had a little wine tonight, Da. A lot of wine. Help me sleep. But I'm wide awake with a furred tongue and a furred mind. I saw Kirstin today. Of course, I told you that already. You know that. Maybe you knew it before I told you. You know everything now, Mr Spirit Daddy. Do you know it even before it happens now you are dead? Or do you have to wait until it unfolds, like the rest of us?

I hurt for you when I heard Kirstin doubted you. And then I felt ashamed because I've been doubting you too. Now I'm a bit angry. With Kirstin. With Mother. Even with you for going. And for not talking back to me. I always get angry with everyone else when it's myself I'm really angry at. That's why Sarah cops it so much.

I cannot imagine what it took for you to love Sarah. Were you aware, always aware in everything we did together, that she was another man's child? Did you see the shadow of her father in her eyes; did you feel him in the weight of her when you picked her up? She was already a few months old when Mother died. I guess at the start you learned to love her because it was the only way you could stay with Mother. But when Mother died, what then? What links to Sarah were you left with? I guess you started off loving her for Mother's sake and ended up loving her for her own. She is worthy of love, I know that.

You shed your old life like a snakeskin for me and for Sarah. You simply left the detritus behind and grew a new skin, scale by scale. You know, I think I understand about the accountancy and the bus driving now. You wanted to leave everything that was past, in the past: the house by the loch and the yellow and white crockery and the furniture and the job and the people. You didn't even want the money for the house. You took what was worth taking, and that was Sarah and me.

I remember you talking about Grandpa leaving Donegal once and you said he never completely moved on, that he left a bit of himself there on that rocky old hill. You must have done the same in the Highlands. I am curious about how much of you was missing in the Da that we knew. Which bits of you got left behind in that bay at Lochglas, stranded like the little boats on the sand when the tide goes out?

I am surprised to hear myself say it, but I think I understand why you didn't want us to know about Mother. I'm not sure you were right, but I do understand. I have the same dilemma myself now, with Sarah. It is not so easy. I see what happens. You make a decision in a crisis and there is no going back. No changing minds.

Two years after your decision, you couldn't suddenly decide you'd tell us about Mother after all. Or five years later, or ten. You had to go on going on. You wanted us to believe in the new life. You wanted us to believe in you. Never have that belief tarnished by the kind of lingering doubt that eats up your soul. Peggy was right after all. She did destroy you, didn't she?

Listen to the wine, the comforting glug, glug, glug of it as it pours into the glass. Cheers, Da. Here's to old friends. Have you met Mother again wherever you are? They say when you die that you go down a long tunnel of light. That there's always someone familiar there to meet you. Who met you? Was it Mother? Did you see her? Did you love her still? Maybe Mother can love you in death more completely than she loved you in life. Maybe that would even be worth dying for.

Am I making sense? It's cheap, this wine. We liked a good red, you and I, but you wouldn't think much of this. It's thin and bitter. And you know what I keep thinking? I keep thinking I am drinking blood. Too much talk of murder. Too much Catholicism. Blood of Christ. Bathe me in your wounds. You know, I expect Father Riley would say the wine in heaven is so much richer, so much more mellow, than here on earth. I should bloody hope so. I wish we could swap glasses.

229

What can I tell you now? No response, eh? Did I tell you Shameena will sing for us at the funeral? Sing for you. Dear Shameena. Remember when she sang after Tariq died? Answer me Da, for God's sake. Do you remember?

Oh all right, don't answer. I'll just keep talking anyway. If you want to join in at any time, please do. Walk around in my mind, why don't you? Oh. My phone is buzzing. Ha! Is it you? Clever old you! What's the O_2 reception like in heaven? Well, well. Another text. 'Go home.' Not very friendly round here, are they, Da? Not like Glasgow.

So, what were we talking about? Yes, the night Shameena sang. The night of the benefit concert for the Heart Foundation. It was her idea, of course, to raise funds for the charity, for Tariq. But I think maybe she also thought this would be Tariq's way of helping her get into opera. If Khadim and Nazima could just hear her sing publicly...

What you won't remember is that Tariq visited that night. You won't remember because I never told you. That's right. Dead Tariq visited. This is not the wine talking, Da. Well maybe it is, partly. Loosens my tongue. We all have little secrets, don't we? I just didn't realise until the last few days how many. I find myself talking to you in my head and saying, "You never knew because..." or, "I never told you because..."

Shameena had worked so hard to put that concert on. She wrote to the council herself to ask for permission to use the local school hall. Her own music teacher, Miss Macintosh, agreed to accompany her but Shameena practised and practised on her own for weeks before. Sometimes, I would go round and listen to her rehearse, just to encourage her. She sang for Tariq. She sang for love. I'm sorry. Was that sentimental? I always get maudlin with alcohol. Excuse me while I pour another.

Do you remember I left you in the audience and went backstage to see her and wish her luck that night? That's when it happened. The chairs were laid out in the hall, the legs scraping along the wooden floor, the hum of chatter growing gradually louder. I just meant to pop my head around the door but Shameena was sitting in an easy chair with tears streaming down her face.

"Shameena?"

She didn't answer.

"Shameena," I repeated, coming in and closing the door. "What's wrong?"

"Becca, he's been here. He's been here."

"Who's been here?" I knelt down beside her chair.

"Tariq."

I didn't want to hear. I was frightened by what she was saying, by the way she looked. And because I was frightened, I was sharp. You know how sharp I can be, Da.

"Shameena, what are you talking about?"

She wiped her eyes with the heel of her hand.

"I was warming up." She stood up and walked to the table. "I was standing here with my music. And I felt someone enter the room."

"You felt them?"

"Yes, but when I turned around" – she swirled around to show me – "there was no one there." She looked at me expectantly.

"Shameena, it's natural you're thinking about Tariq. Tonight is all about him, about his memory. It's not surprising that you feel… maybe feel close to him… and…"

She shook her head.

"It was him."

"Tariq's dead, Shameena."

231

"I don't care what you say. I know what happened. I know Tariq was here. The room suddenly went so cold. I could feel a tingle on my skin. I knew it was Tariq. I just knew it was. And then I felt him pass through me." She began to cry. *"He passed right through me. I could feel the pressure of him. He wanted to wish me luck. It was his way of holding me."*

"Don't be frightened," I said, though it was me who was frightened.

"Frightened?" she said, as if she didn't understand. *"I'm not frightened! It's just so... so emotional, so good, having him back. Even for a little while..."* She looked at me. *"You think I'm mad but I don't care. It happened. There is nothing you can ever tell me, Becca, that will convince me Tariq wasn't here. I know what I felt. I know it was him. He was real."*

She slipped off the heavy gold bracelet she wore round her right wrist, and held it up to me. It had been her grandmother's. I knew it was her favourite piece of jewellery.

"Real as that. You might as well tell me this bracelet doesn't exist." She was beginning to get agitated.

"Okay, okay," I said.

I remember the look Shameena gave me then, like she could see right inside me. It made me uneasy.

"You loved him, Rebecca, didn't you?"

I stared at her, unable to say a word.

"I think he loved you too."

"Did he say?" I asked instantly.

She hesitated and I knew he hadn't.

"He didn't have to say. I knew."

And this is the bit, Da, where it gets really odd. I felt something then at my back, and I turned around and Shameena whispered

232

delightedly, "He's back. He's back, isn't he, Becca? You can feel him." And suddenly the room temperature plummeted. I felt a weight, the pressure of a weight forcing its way through my body. I looked at Shameena. There were tears streaming down her face and I could feel tears streaming down mine, and then within seconds the feeling had gone and Shameena and I clung together in the centre of the room. But it was so quick, Da, all so quick that even though I was there, even though I felt it, I wasn't sure later what had happened. It happened to me and I'm still not sure I believe it happened. Maybe it was the power of her suggestion. Nothing like that has ever happened to me again.

Do you know how that makes me feel, Da? When I think of Shameena and how certain she was, I think of you, and I wonder why you won't talk to me. Why you won't come. If you are really out there, give me a sign. Other people get signs. Is it that I didn't love you enough? That you didn't love me enough? Am I not worth it? Did Tariq love Shameena more than you love me? Or is it that there really is nothing of you out there? You're gone. Spent. Finished.

I'm not going to séances to find you, Da. Glasses and Ouija boards and darkened rooms and fraud. Is there anybody there? I'd never be sure that way, would I? I'd never be sure it was really you. I don't want to involve anyone else in this. If you want to give me a message, you don't need anyone else as medium. If you want to, you'll find a way. How do spirits communicate? I don't know. I'm hoping I'm going to find out. But no one else needs to be involved. This is between me and you, Da. Me and you alone.

The night Tariq visited, Shameena sang for her audience like it was her last ever song, like it was her death song. I always hated that opera stuff you played on Saturday mornings when you

233

weren't working, Da. Bizet and Verdi and God knows what. All that screeching coming from your old tinny stereo.

Shameena's voice wasn't fully trained yet, of course. But there was a beauty about the freshness of it, the possibility of it. She sang arias from Madame Butterfly and Carmen as well as the Puccini. But it was the unknown song at the finale that left me in bits. Do you remember it, Da? It was an old Pakistani song that she said the Melody Queen used to sing. It was about a girl whose brother went riding off to war on a black steed and never returned. The Goddess of War said her brother would be returned to her if she sang a song so beautiful that it silenced the nightingale. The girl ran to the forest and she sang and she sang, but always the trill of the nightingale accompanied her. Until she realised she must sing with her heart instead of her voice, and at her first notes the nightingale stopped. But it was too late. A second past midnight. Her brother never returned.

Shameena would have silenced the nightingale that night. She sang with her heart. For the first time, I listened with mine. In the dark, next to you, Da. The rustling stopped in the audience. Maybe it had such an effect because nearly everyone who was there knew about Tariq, but there was a stillness that bound all of us. There was a great lump in my throat, the size of a cricket ball, and I couldn't swallow.

There was silence when she finished, for at least four seconds. Four seconds is a long time after someone has sung. One. Two. Three. Four. Then the clapping started, and the cheering. It was just a dusty old school hall with no atmosphere, but people got to their feet and whistled and Shameena smiled. She looked different. Like she was really alive. Like every hair on her head and every nail on her finger and every muscle and every cell of her was living and breathing and pulsating.

Someone told me once that taking LSD was like that. You could see the life force in everything, every tiny little thing. In an orange skin or a flower petal or even on a pen on the desk. Everything in the world was alive and everything was good and everything was connected. I was envious of Shameena right then but glad for her too. She didn't need LSD. She had her singing.

I looked among the crowd to find Khadim and Nazima. They weren't on their feet, but Khadim was clapping stiffly and I could see the muscles in his face quivering. Nazima had her dopatta over her eyes and her head bowed.

I want Shameena to silence the nightingale for me on Friday. I am relying on her. Though I am relying on this wine first to get me through another night. Just one more glass. Maybe I'll sing myself then. I wish I could sing, Da. I wish I could sing to you. But you'll know when Shameena sings, it's my song really. My song to you.

CHAPTER SIX

A neighbour has been to my door, asking me to turn down Shameena's CD. I was very apologetic. I had not realised how late it had got, how absorbed I had become in the past, in writing down my memories. How far I had travelled from the present. It has been like walking through the wardrobe door into Narnia, like falling down the rabbit hole into Wonderland. Eventually, the visited world becomes so real that you forget where you have come from. Until the knocking and ringing starts at the door. Until the polite apologies spill from your mouth. Those apologies make me smile wryly to myself as I close the door. Five years ago, I might just as easily have told the neighbour to fuck off.

Flicking back through what I have just written about Shameena's concert, I can see that you might have questions about Tariq. Perhaps you wonder why he is in my mind so much, why I dreamt of him during this time. (And, I may say, still do.) What does he have to do with my story? There is only one word I can use in answer: everything.

Tariq helped form what I thought love was, helped form me. He shaped my life, just as Da did by his presence and Mother did by her absence. Everything I did after he died was an expression of my hopelessness, just as everything Da did after Mother died was an expression of his. What was that idiotic period with Father Dangerous but an expression of my grief, my defiance, my resentment? My self-destructive need for things to go wrong? I see that now. When I set off for Inverness, my whole identity was in question. Tariq was part of that identity.

Even now, more than fifteen years after he died, I think of Tariq. Yes, I was young and inexperienced. And yes, I admit it, it might have come to nothing. Perhaps my feelings are wrapped up in the nostalgia of teenage infatuation, when every emotion feels so intense and unique to you alone. But I still think Tariq was meant to be the love of my life. I think some of the anger I carry inside me, have always carried, is because people I love always leave me sooner or later. Or perhaps I've just been to too many psychology classes in the last five years.

The attraction Tariq and I experienced transcended everything that stood in its way. Our skin colour, our religions, our differing cultures and experiences. There was something that was stronger than all of that. I regret almost every man who followed him but the only thing I regret about Tariq is that we did not get to prove what we could have been.

Love shapes you, moulds you, influences your behaviour, whether that is for good or ill. Da discovered that and I discovered it too. We were both doomed that way. Do you understand where I am going with this? You see, if you think this story is about murder, you are wrong. You are wrong. It may not be a love story exactly, but it is certainly a story about love.

WEDNESDAY

CHAPTER ONE

Shameena's voice is a mere whisper now as I write, but I keep the CD on repeat. I feel a strange superstition that the memories will stop if the music does. Not that I remember much of that drunken night in the B & B, though I certainly remember waking up in the morning.

Sunlight through closed curtains. It filters through the dense jungle ferns of the fabric, washing the room in an underwater light, grey and green and rippled with shadow. A breeze finds the crack of open window, slithers through to blow gently on the hem of the curtain, a tiny wave of movement spreading across the mottled carpet. Squinting through half-shut eyes, I watch the waves lap gently on the shore of the wardrobe and then, it seems, the whole room begins to move, undulating softly on a calm sea.

Where is this? Swathed in leafy green fabrics, clean as mint. Rough pine and polished glass and hand-picked daisies in a pottery vase. The room tilts disconcertingly, the bed a boat cast adrift in unknown waters. Where? An empty bottle stands by the bedside, and a glass, with a mouthful of red wine abandoned in the bottom. Oh God. I remember. I try to lift myself from the pillows but my head is pounding and I feel sick. I sink back down slowly, glad of the softness that moulds around me. Lying flat, the movement continues but the nausea partially subsides.

I raise my wrist without shifting my head, looking for my watch. The light is brokered by the closed curtains, but it is a light that has grown strong, not the soft, tentative light of a breaking dawn. Nine o'clock! I had meant to be outside the offices of Cory Construction by eight o'clock, waiting for James Cory to arrive.

I have played out the scene in my mind a hundred times since standing outside his office yesterday. How he'll look. What I'll say. How he'll reply. I always get the script's best lines, obviously. Cory walks towards the offices and I step out of a doorway and stand in front of him. He is shocked when I introduce myself, on the back foot. My questions destroy him. He crumbles in front of me physically, morally, disintegrating into the dust of his own lies. He is nothing.

In reality, it is going to be me on the back foot. Now I have to get through receptionists and appointment diaries and office protocol. Shit. I sit, then lie across the bed, moving my legs without raising my head, shuffling to the edge, feet feeling for the rough, sack-like surface of carpet beneath. In the bathroom, I put the toilet lid down and sit tentatively, leaning against the cool, white tiles of the wall, reaching for the sink awkwardly, running water into a glass. I force myself to drink glass after glass. A dull thump beats in the centre of my head.

My phone beeps. A text. 'Go home. Please.' Oh fuck off, I think wearily throwing it on the bed. Whoever it is has turned polite. No more 'bitch'. Even says please. Nutter.

Later, in the dining room, my landlady brings food to fellow guests at the next table. A large white dinner plate with breakfast cast adrift in the middle: a single slice of white edged bacon; an egg that glistens with fat like well-oiled flesh in sun cream; a sausage burst in the middle and arched like a bow; an undercooked half tomato. I smile weakly at her.

"Just orange juice and toast this morning, thanks."

She clears the other tables while I scrape a little sweet lime marmalade on dry, brittle toast. Her fifteen-year-old daughter wants to be an actress; I get a blow-by-blow account of her performance as Sandy in the school production of *Grease*. The details float outwards, upwards; light and inconsequential as dandelion chaff. Inside, I am with James Cory watching him shrivel. Shrivel over and over and over again. The landlady chats on. She doesn't know. There is nothing about me that tells her. Infidelity. Betrayal. Murder. Secrecy. We are strangers, all of us.

CHAPTER TWO

I don't get to Cory Construction as planned. I lie on the bed after breakfast, waiting for the waves of nausea to recede. When my phone rings, my heart skips a beat and I glance nervously at the screen. Number withheld. This continual phone intrusion is unsettling, as if the cold breath of a stalker blows the hairs on my neck with his whispering, yet I cannot see him. A flash of anger erupts inside me that someone thinks they can scare me in this way, but still my fingers tremble slightly as I press 'Accept call'. I say nothing, waiting for the caller to speak first.

"Rebecca?" An older woman's voice. For a moment I think it is Peggy and am torn between relief and a wish that I had not answered.

"Rebecca Connaghan?"

The voice is too frail to be Peggy.

"Yes?" My voice is sharp, almost hostile with unease.

"This is Jackie Sandford."

The surprise makes me unable to process an answer. I become aware of the television playing softly in the background and run my hand over the rumpled duvet looking for the remote control.

"I got your number from my brother, James Sandford."

"I… I don't know your brother." I sit down on the edge of the bed, switching off the television. "Do I?"

"You phoned him looking for me."

The memory comes back of the Highland telephone directory and the two Sandfords listed: Angus and James.

"But he said you weren't connected."

She ignores this.

"I don't want you to tell anyone you have spoken to me."

Her voice sounds a little weak, but determined. There is something else mixed in. Anxiety, perhaps even fear. Her age… the idea that she should still feel fear… it makes my back prickle.

"Where are you? Can I come to see you?"

"No. I live a long way away."

"Where?"

She senses the urgency, my eagerness, and retreats suddenly.

"I can't tell you that."

Everything has been so strange the last few days, so unnerving, that I suddenly wonder for a minute if this is a trick. Is it really Jackie Sandford? I wait for her to speak again, unwilling to frighten her off with persistent questions.

"Rebecca…" She says the name fondly, with a hint of nostalgia. "I wish I could meet you but…" Her voice falters. I am listening acutely to every signal. "Your mum and I… We were close… for a while."

That phrase 'for a while' alerts me but I cannot hold on to the thought long enough to work it out.

"I remember you as a little girl," she is saying now. "I looked after you." She does not laugh and yet I sense amusement. "You were a thrawn wee thing."

An unexpected rush of emotion. Memories of days of which I have no recollection prompt a yearning I had no idea I even felt. A yearning for a kind of innocence before the ugliness. I

245

want the world restored, made whole again.

"Do you know what happened to my mother?"

"You haven't promised yet."

"Promised what?"

"That you won't say you have spoken to me. I can't risk it."

"Why not?"

"That will become obvious. But you have to promise me."

"I don't have any choice then."

"I'm sorry."

Her voice holds genuine regret.

"How do you know I will even keep my promise?"

"I don't." She sounds suddenly exhausted. "I have to trust you. For Kath's sake."

My mother's name is almost a whisper.

"I promise."

"Thank you."

There is a slightly awkward silence before I plunge in.

"I read the old newspapers… the stuff you said about my mother having an affair with James Cory."

"Yes. James was furious with me…"

"You said she was going to talk to him about their future the day she disappeared. Are you certain about that?"

"Yes. I tried to talk her out of it. I told her not to take things to the brink because he would never leave his wife. She was risking everything."

"How did you know? That Cory would never leave his wife, I mean."

There is silence, and for a moment I think we have lost connection.

"Jackie?"

"Because I…" She stops. I know she is distressed even though I cannot see her. I can feel it. "I just… I just knew him."

"You sounded like you were going to say something else there."

"Did I?"

"How did you know?"

She does not answer.

"How did you know?" I coax, more softly.

"Because I had an affair with him too."

In the silence I cross to the window. The light is pure and bright and penetrating. I think of Lochglas, the small village across the bridge. A tiny, godforsaken backwater. Peaceful, you'd think. But that beautiful little spot, where the sun's rays hit the sheltered bay like bands of polished gold, has the same tarnished ugliness as everywhere else. People are people and wherever they gather there is love and jealousy and betrayal and confusion. And turning from the window, putting my back to the spotlight, I know I must include myself in that.

My mother never knew, she tells me. And Jackie wasn't seeing Cory at the same time. In fact, he dumped her for my mother.

"I thought, stupidly, that I was the one. I wasn't married at the time and I thought he would leave Anna for me. But the truth was…" Her voice trails away. "The truth was what it always is in these matters," she concludes quietly.

It fascinates me, that little shard of bitterness in her voice. All these years later. The rejection of it still hurts.

My mother had fallen into the same trap.

"She thought, just as I had, that he was going to leave Anna for her. She told me that she was going to speak to him the day they met for lunch, the day she went missing."

247

"But maybe she didn't speak to him. We'll never know."

"But we do know. I spoke to her."

"When?"

"After lunch."

My heart skips a beat at her words and I cross back over to the bed and sit on the edge before my legs give way. She spoke to my mother after lunch. My mother and Cory were seen leaving the restaurant together, but the call to Jackie Sandford proves Cory did actually leave her. Kath was still alive when he went and she called Jackie Sandford shortly after. Cory was back in his office at 2 p.m. It couldn't have been him.

CHAPTER THREE

My voice sounds alien even to me as I stumble out questions. High and strained.

"What time? What time did she phone you?"

"About five minutes after James left her. She was on a high about what had happened over lunch and wanted to talk. There was only me. She was sort of laughing but I could tell by her voice she was shaking a bit, you know that way you get when you are sort of excited but sort of scared at the same time. She said James had been angry at first but everything had ended well."

"Angry? What was he angry about?"

"Kath had talked to him about when he was going to leave Anna and he was making the usual excuses. She pushed things a bit and in the end he agreed."

"What do you mean she pushed things?"

Jackie Sandford sounds tired.

"It's complicated."

"I have time," I say, but she doesn't reply. "If you do?" I add.

"I'm not very well," she says.

Oh God, don't let her hang up.

"Please."

"I can only talk to you this once. I can't do this again."

"You won't have to. I promise."

"Wait a minute."

I hear a door creak as it opens and she says something in a low voice. There is the sound of water running. A glass being filled? A muttered thanks. I can hear a voice, high, concerned. Don't get upset, the voice is saying, then it becomes too muffled to hear before rising again in pitch. Mum, sit down! Yes, yes. Just a little longer. A shuffling. Another creak of the door before it closes firmly. The receiver knocks against a table.

"Are you still there?"

"Yes, I'm here, Jackie."

"Like I said, it's complicated…"

Jackie tells me Cory's business had been doing well at the time. Maybe too well. He had picked up a lot of council contracts and people were talking. Cory was a Mason – and so were the chief executive and the chief planning officer at the council. My mother had told Cory she knew enough about the contracts to create a stink and drop him in it.

I close my eyes momentarily. What the hell had my mother been playing at?

"Why did she want someone who had to be blackmailed into being with her?" I ask.

"She didn't see it like that. She said she was just persuading him to do what he really wanted anyway," says Jackie. "She was giving him a reason to keep her sweet. She kept laughing. I'm not sure how much she'd had to drink that lunchtime. But she said men like Cory were fascinated by her. They liked her manipulations. It excited them, she said. But she really got James wrong because *he* was the one who always had to be in control. I told her she was being silly but she wouldn't listen. She said she was going to phone Joe right there and then to tell him that she'd made up her mind."

"Did she?"

"I don't know. I never spoke to her again."

"You never said this in the papers."

"No."

"Why not?"

"I told you, James was furious when I told a journalist about their affair."

"And why did you? Tell them, I mean."

"Because nothing was happening. The police were interviewing the same people over and over and getting nowhere. I knew there had to be more publicity, another twist to the story to keep the pressure on..."

"On who?"

She doesn't answer the question directly.

"On whoever killed Kath. So I gave a little bit more of the story each time, hoping that it would prompt something, some kind of new lead."

That was true. I had noticed in the library that Jackie Sandford's story had unfolded over the course of several articles.

"Why did you stop?"

"I moved."

"Because of what happened?"

"James..."

She stops abruptly.

"What? What did he do?"

"It was hard to prove."

I wait. There is the sound of a glass being placed back on a table.

"When I first spoke," she continues, "he got in touch and told me to keep my mouth shut because I wasn't helping to find Kath's killer. All I was doing was ruining his reputation."

"But you ignored him?"

"At first. But then everything started going wrong."

"What do you mean?"

"The Masons, Rebecca… How much do you know about them?"

"Very little."

"About as much as most Masons know, then," she mutters.

Every so often there is an acerbity to Jackie Sandford's tone that moves her out of the linen-and-lavender, old-lady category. Maybe that's what my mother liked about her. From what I've heard about her, I doubt Kath would have turned into linen and lavender either.

Jackie suggests I do some research online. Masonic secrecy and corruption is well documented now. The fact that in those days, senior Masons who reached the 'top' third layer had no idea there were another thirty-three secret layers above. But most Masons, she says, thought they were buying into a benign organisation that had brotherhood at its core. If a Mason died, for instance, brother Masons would sometimes secretly ensure – through a Masonic bank manager – that his debts were paid off for his family.

"A kind of Christianity?" I ask.

"A kind of mafia," she retorts. "Oh, the values it expounded sounded decent. Look after your brothers, all that. But any organisation that looks after its own at the expense of others runs the risk of corruption."

"But what did that have to do with you moving away?"

"They're everywhere."

"Who?"

"The Masons!" she snaps, irritation breaking through the fatigue in her voice. "Sorry," she mutters. "I'm in a bit of pain."

Before I can ask what's wrong with her she has launched

into an explanation of the power of the Masons as a national network. Bank managers, judges, chief executives, senior policemen, the major utilities... It's the most powerful secret society on earth, she says. And if a group of Masons come together and unite against an individual, they can make that person's life hell.

The first thing that happened was her electricity going off. She didn't realise what was going on to begin with. The electricity board said it was a recurring fault they couldn't locate. Then they claimed her bill hadn't been paid, before suddenly 'finding' the paperwork. Next her bank refused to honour a cheque, saying she was overdrawn. It got sorted out but it was never fully explained.

It all sounds so implausible that I begin to wonder about Jackie Sandford and how reliable she is. But she has story after story. A top judge who reached the pinnacles of British Freemasonry then decided it was incompatible with his Christianity and spilled the beans. A businessman who had a dispute with a Mason and found himself taken in by a Masonic police chief to be questioned on charges of pornography.

"What happened to him?"

"He committed suicide."

"Oh God..."

"And I can understand why. The pressure gets to you. It was bad enough for me at the start but after the second newspaper interview, all hell broke loose. It wasn't just constant interruptions to my electricity and water supplies, which would be off for days and miraculously come back on again an hour or two before workmen arrived. It was the police. They continually stopped me when I was out in my car to run checks on the registration, or to check the insurance, or to examine the tyres. It was harassment. I had to disconnect the phone because it would ring constantly but there would be nobody there when I answered. Then there was a break-in at my house. I was a nervous wreck in the end. I couldn't take any more."

I know what she means. The anonymous texts to me in the last few days have been nothing compared to what she endured but the effect has been insidious, creeping through me in the way cold seeps into you unnoticed, until suddenly you are freezing and unable to get warm. The first text barely touched me. But then it built up. A gradual sense of fear when the phone buzzed. A weakening of control. An uncharacteristic helplessness. You get gradually worn away, the way the surface of rock gets eroded under the relentless crash of waves. So yes, I understand Jackie Sandford's eventual breakdown. But there was one thing I didn't understand.

"Why would sane people go to those lengths to support Cory?" I ask.

I don't understand about organisations. Rules. Authority. I couldn't join an army or wear a uniform. It's all I can do to smile when the police stop me for routine checks when I'm driving. Instinctively, I want to tell them to piss off. That's what uniforms do to me. But even I can sort of see why an army or a police force might be necessary. But a secret society? What for?

"I've had plenty of years to look into it, Rebecca. Plenty of time to reflect. There's a bit in the Masonic handbook that says you have to conceal all the crimes of your brother Masons. And should you be summoned as a witness against him, you must always be sure to shield him."

"So what charges were Cory's 'brothers' trying to shield him from – corruption or murder?"

"That's the question. That's what I was trying to find out at the time. But the truth is I got so scared I had to get out. I didn't dare say any more. I married, changed my name, and moved away."

"But all these years later… surely…"

"My family…"

"Are you frightened still?"

"Not of that," she says softly. "Not of him. But my family… It's simpler just to make sure."

"Jackie. Did…?"

Suddenly I cannot get the words out. They are stuck in my throat. Da. My Da.

"I know what you are going to ask." She is suddenly gentle, compassionate.

"I don't know, Rebecca. I can't pretend to know. But I know your father was a good man."

"You said she phoned you after lunch." Despair fills me. "She was alive when he left. How could Cory have killed her?"

Jackie is quiet for some time.

"But we don't know what happened after that. Nor before it," she adds cryptically.

"Before it? What do you mean?"

"Maybe James had it all planned. And if he did… well, he wouldn't get his hands dirty."

I don't understand what she means at first.

"James didn't cut the electricity supply personally," Jackie says. "He didn't interfere with my water. He didn't break into the bank and temporarily change my account details. James doesn't do things himself. He hires people to do it for him. Just like he hires a gardener."

Oh my God.

"You mean he hired someone to kill her? A hit man? Round here?"

"Don't get taken in by the picture-postcard landscape, Rebecca. People are people. You know when you turn over a rock and all sorts of insects scuttle around underneath? When you have money, you know which rock to turn over."

A voice in the background. A woman. Come on, Mum, she's saying. This isn't doing you any good.

"Just a moment…"

The receiver is taken from her.

"Hello?" The voice is firm.

"Yes."

"This is Jackie's daughter. I'm sorry, but she really has to go now. She's getting exhausted. She's not well, you know."

Her voice is accusing, as if I should know better.

"I'm sorry," I say. "I didn't know…"

"She has cancer."

"Oh… I'm sorry… I hope she… she… Please give her my thanks. For speaking to me, I mean. I am grateful. I am very grateful…"

"I'll tell her." The voice softens. "I'm sorry. She told me about your mum. She wanted to speak to you. Insisted, in fact. But she's not up to this."

"I understand."

I put the phone down. The room is full of sunlight but I feel enveloped by darkness. The way Da used to get. Surrounded by shadows. Sucked of energy. I understand now. I lie down again on top of the bed. How long does Jackie Sandford have left? It saddens me to think of an adult lifetime lived – all those years my mother has been lying cold in the earth. Her generation is dying out. How long before the truth dies too?

For the first time, I find myself imagining what my mother felt at her killer's hands. Perhaps she is becoming more real to me in an odd kind of way. Strange questions invade my mind. What was she wearing when she died? Had she dressed up for her lunch with Cory? Lipstick? What colour? Pink? Plum? Red? Orange? What colour?

When I was a little girl, I used to sit at Peggy's dressing table with a pot of old discarded makeup she gave me to play with and draw a shaky Cupid's bow of lipstick round my mouth, smudged, artless, a tangerine kiss that exploded outside its edges. But what was my mother's colour? And why does it matter? It doesn't and yet it does. Like the paint colour in Da's dingy old hall. My mother would not have known her preparations that day were final. Is it less cruel, I wonder, to die at the hands of a stranger than someone you thought you loved?

❧

The information from Jackie Sandford settles into my brain slowly. My frustration builds. Her call took me by surprise. I had no planning, no time to think. The unasked questions seem so obvious now, with the benefit of hindsight. But there is one thing I can check myself. In the afternoon I go back to the library to look at the local papers again. At one point, she had mentioned an investigation into allegations of council corruption in the awarding of contracts. If I can find mention of that, it will not only confirm she is telling the truth, it will tell me what happened in that investigation.

The search does not take long. It was, as you might imagine, front-page news. **COUNCIL CHIEFS CLEARED OF CORRUP-**

TION ALLEGATIONS. I skim the story quickly. There is no mention of Masonic links as the reason for the allegations. And of course people were under no official obligation to declare themselves Masons. As I run down the story, my eyes catch sight of a familiar name and I backtrack to a quote.

"Allegations that the chief executive and chief planning officer of the council were involved in irregular procedures with regard to the awarding of council building contracts are entirely without foundation," said the man heading the investigation. My head sinks into my arms. His name? Chief Superintendent Terry Simons.

CHAPTER FOUR

Moonlight is falling through the B & B window, lighting the room. In my head I can hear the haunting opening notes of one of Da's favourite pieces of music, Beethoven's *Moonlight Sonata*. Softly, softly it fills the space in my head, the darkness in my heart, as delicately as the shaft of light fills the room through the window. My throat tightens, as if there is too narrow a space to swallow. Each note sounds inside my head as clearly as if the piano is in this room.

I slip my feet into my shoes and lift a cardigan. It is the early hours but I know it will be a long time before I can sleep. Tiptoeing to the front door, I close it soundlessly behind me and walk along the river towards the bridge. There are plenty of people still, distant shouts from dark streets, laughter from pub doorways. Benign. Safe compared to Glasgow, I think. It is so picturesque by the river that it seems almost kitsch to a city dweller like me, the bridges lit by twinkling necklaces of light that glitter lightly in the black skirt of water below. I walk towards the main bridge across town, following the road onwards past the restaurant lights and hotels, down towards the town's theatre. I think this is where the Ness Islands are, the riverside walk the landlady mentioned. There are little bridges, apparently, crossing from the road to the miniature islands in the middle of the river.

The road gets gradually quieter as I walk towards the Islands but I can see a bridge in the distance. The walk has helped calm me. The sound of the water running in the darkness is soothing. I will not cross to the Islands, of course – I'll leave that for daylight – but I will walk to the bridge before turning back. There are no houses here and the streetlamps have ended but it is close to the bustle of town still.

The feeling of unease is gradual, hard to define. An instinct. A sudden awareness. I stop. Listen. Take a few steps forward. Listen again. I turn my head, staring into the black night. A crackle, like a twig being snapped. Or was it? Silence. My phone beeps and makes me physically jump. My hand shakes as I grab it out of my bag. A text: 'I can see you.' I look round, though I can see little in the darkness, scanning the shadows for movement.

I turn sharply to go back the way I have come, then hesitate. Where is he? What if he is not further on into the blackness ahead but behind me, somewhere in the belt of darkness between me and the town lights? He. Surely it must be a he? What if I walk straight back into him before I reach the town again? I start one way, then turn the other, but I cannot go on into the darkness where there is no light. I look all round, heart thumping. There is only straight on, or back. I turn sharply back and walk quickly, stifling the urge to run.

Beep. Beep. Beep. I almost drop the phone as it vibrates in my hand. I don't stop, keep moving, my trembling fingers opening the text as I walk. 'Race you?' I start to run, not fast but a steady trot. Is this how my mother felt? This overwhelming fear? The trapdoor closing. Who is it? Has Terry Simon alerted the brethren? The Masonic mafia who drove Jackie Sandford out? Has

Cory hired another hitman? Are they just trying to scare me? Or am I to meet the same fate as my mother?

My breath is coming in short gasps. Beep. Beep. Beep. I glance down at the screen. 'Run. But you can't win.' I run fast now, run towards the distant light, until my lungs are bursting. The phone beeps constantly but I no longer read it. Can't turn round. Can't look back. Where is he? The lights of the first hotel are coming closer, the lit windows of a seafood restaurant burning brightly. The road curves and I run, run, run, but before I can reach the light, it's over. I run slap into him in the darkness. I open my mouth and scream with the passion of a woman who suddenly knows how much she wants to live. Hands in the darkness grabbing my arms. I flail out at him.

"Jesus!" says a voice. "It's okay!"

I continue to scream; the only thing filtering into my consciousness is that the voice is male. I do not hear the words.

"It's okay!"

Jumping back, I am about to turn the other way, run again, when I realise there are actually two shapes, two men. Two men walking home from the pub.

"Are you okay?"

I am shaking, unable to answer.

"What's happened? Has somebody hurt you?"

"Sorry," I mutter. "Sorry. I was startled… I…" I back off, head down, then move sharply past them without looking either of them in the eye. "Sorry…" I repeat.

"Fuck's sake, what was that about?" one of them says as I shoot off.

"She gave me a bloody heart attack," says the other. "Drama queen!"

261

My legs can barely carry me as I walk back across the main bridge towards the B & B. The streets are busy again, people milling outside fast-food shops, a few drunken screeches.

"Want a chip, darlin'?" someone says drunkenly as I pass.

I'd normally have a barbed quip but I don't even look up.

"Don't be shy!" he shouts at my retreating figure.

At the guest house, my trembling fingers can barely get the key in the lock. I close the door behind me and snib it. Then snib my own bedroom door and block the moonlight with the curtains. Beep. Beep. Beep. Another text. I take a deep breath and try to make my fingers function sufficiently to press read. 'I let you win. This time.'

CHAPTER FIVE

For a few minutes tonight, I thought I was going to join you, Da. I thought the secrets of the grave were about to be shown to me. What is it the Bible says about mysteries being revealed to mere children? I felt like a child out there, stumbling in the darkness, overcome by fear and helplessness. Death does that to you. No, that's not quite right. Life does that to you. Life is just a long process of wandering in the night, looking for daylight, waiting in vain for dawn. Occasionally, you get to admire a sunset.

Am I any closer to the truth, Da? Am I? I no longer think I am going to uncover it completely. If tonight taught me anything, it is that I have to leave this place. I will be glad to go because the truth is, I am too frightened to stay. We all have our limits. My limbs tremble still, and my hands shake as if they have a life of their own, separate from me. Worse, my resolve is broken. My cowardice disappoints me, but I learnt out there that I want to live. I cannot die for old, undiscovered secrets. Especially old secrets that, once they are uncovered, might destroy me.

You did the right thing in leaving your old life. I understand now the need you had to simply walk away from here and take nothing with you. This place, with its pretty façade and ugly underbelly, it invades you, seeps through your pores until you turn from it in disgust. Who is it who wants me gone? Do I know too much? And if I know too much, what do I know too much about?

263

The corruption? The Masons? The murder?

Who texts me? Who follows me? Cory must know I am here by now. Or is there some other anonymous enemy that I don't even recognise yet? Can I trust Jackie Sandford and what she told me? Or David Carruthers? Or even my aunt Kirstin? I no longer know what is real and what is not, who is friend and who is foe. And what of you, Da? Are you in a place where you know it all, or a place where all has ended?

I want to go home, Da. Tomorrow. I am even fighting the urge to go now, to jump in the car and go right this minute. Go spontaneously, the way I came. I want to feel safe. I want to see Sarah and Peggy and Charlie. But I have to wait until morning because there are two more things I have to do. If I don't, I will live with regrets. Two more things. One small thing for Mother. One big one for you.

THURSDAY

CHAPTER ONE

"Did you get to the Islands yet?" the landlady asks as she puts a pot of coffee down in front of me on the breakfast table.

"What?"

I look up sharply. Why is she asking that? What does she know?

"The Islands," she says. She is busying herself lifting dirty dishes from the next table but her hands have stilled and she looks up in surprise at my tone. "The walk I mentioned down at the river?"

"Oh, yes. No. Well… yes, I went part of the way. I didn't cross the bridge."

I reach for the coffee pot to busy myself, using one hand to steady the nervous tremor in the other. I feel embarrassed: I can tell she has clocked the tremble.

"Well," she says, glancing away deliberately and busying herself wiping the table clean, "there's not really that much to see. They're tiny, but visitors find them quaint and like using them to cross to the other side of the river."

I slowly stir a spoonful of sugar into my coffee cup. So whoever was texting might not have followed me back to town. He might have escaped across the bridge and then over to the other side of the river. I look at the landlady speculatively. How do you know who to trust in life? For all I know, she's part of it. Maybe her husband's a Mason in this town.

"Some toast?" she says kindly.

"Please."

I try to keep it casual but even to me, my next question sounds odd.

"Does your husband help you with the business?"

"My husband?"

"Yes." I smile thinly. "I was just thinking… in the summer… all the breakfasts. It's a lot."

"Oh, I have someone come in to help when we're busy but mostly I can manage myself. Paul works shifts so he's not always around."

"Shifts?"

"Aye. He's a policeman."

Shit. Does he know Terry Simons?

"I hope I didn't disturb you last night."

"Last night?"

"I couldn't sleep. I went for a walk late on. I hope I didn't disturb you coming back in."

The landlady pauses a moment, resting the dirty plates she has gathered on the back of a chair.

"Oh, don't worry about that. You come and go as you please." She laughs lightly. "There's not much can wake Paul – and not much that wakes me apart from Paul snoring!" She looks keenly at me. "It's so hot even late on, isn't it? Hard to sleep. And it's bonny down by the river at night."

"Yes," I say. "Yes it is."

I smile at her, more naturally this time. I am being ridiculous. This whole thing is making me crazy, making me imagine conspiracies and twisted motivations. But places like this… they seem a reasonable size until you spend some time in them. And then they just keep on getting smaller and smaller and smaller.

CHAPTER TWO

"Can I help you?" The doors of Cory Construction have barely closed behind me before the receptionist leaps on me like an underfed guard dog. She takes off a pair of poncy-looking glasses, looking upwards through a flutter of mascara-heavy eyelashes.

"I'd like to see Mr Cory, please."

Her smile is fixed. She catches a strand of loose hair with a pink polished nail and tucks it smoothly behind her ear.

"Do you have an appointment?"

She knows I don't, silly cow.

"No, but if you tell him Rebecca Connaghan is in reception I'm sure he'll see me." Confidence confuses people. I say it authoritatively but there is sweat on my back.

"I'm sorry," she begins, "Mr Cory has a full diary this morning."

I don't bother waiting for the rest. I don't have time. I see a door across the reception that has a name tag on it and I head for it. If it isn't his, I am in trouble. I'll be thrown out before I find the right one. The receptionist jumps from behind her desk.

"I'm sorry, you can't go in there," she says, almost running across the offices. She moves so quickly, she twists suddenly on her high heel. I knock briefly on the door but don't wait for an answer. She comes running in behind me.

"I'm sorry, Mr Cory," she says, "This woman refused to wait."

James Cory looks up in surprise when his door bursts open but it is the second look that passes through his eyes that really registers shock. Kirstin might not have recognised me but Cory certainly does. I know what he is thinking. I've seen that look before. That haunted look. I saw it in Pa's eyes, the night I wore my green dress to Peggy's.

"Rebecca Connaghan," I say, holding out my hand to shake hands. He says nothing, does not stand to take my proffered hand. He simply stares.

"What's the matter? Seen a ghost?"

He recovers quickly, I'll give him that.

"It's all right Shellie," he says, looking at his receptionist and smiling. "I'll give Miss Connaghan a couple of minutes. I heard she was in town."

I could have been a rep on a sales call, the unflustered way he spoke.

Cory must be pushing sixty by now but I'd have placed him younger, maybe early fifties. Whatever burden he's carried over the years, it isn't showing. You expect it to show. Like grief showed on Nazima. But there is nothing to suggest James Cory's sins worm inside him.

Even sitting at a desk, I can see he's tall. His hair is well cut and still quite dark, though sprinkled with silver at the temples. He is wearing a white shirt and blue patterned tie, small, tightly packed royal blue diamonds against a navy background. The jacket of his navy suit hangs on a coat stand beside his desk. It has not been dumped over the stand. The hoop on the jacket collar has been placed over the iron curl. Just so.

When I think of James Cory in future it will not be one solid presence that I remember, but a series of flashing impressions, of

270

inconsequential details that I drink in now as I look. Golf-club tie pin, gold cuff links, gold signet ring on his wedding finger, expensive black leather shoes with a gleaming buckle at the side. Flashes of light sparkling on gold. Tiny gap in his front teeth. Brown eyes. I can see why she went for him. He is handsome in the way Sarah's Des is handsome. Broad shoulders, trim frame with maybe just a slight thickening round the executive middle. Smooth bastard. Hate whiplashes inside me like the sudden flick of a fish fin. I wondered how I would feel and now I know. Smooth, smooth bastard.

"Miss Connaghan," he says. "I heard you were in town."

As I thought, there is little that is not passed on in this town.

"What can I do for you?" he says, and I can see immediately the way he wants to play it. Conflict avoidance. Talk like he is simply a stranger, a man who knows nothing about me. Not like the man who screwed my mother while she was married to my father. Not like the prime suspect in her murder.

"You knew my mother, Kathleen."

"A long time ago."

"I want to know what happened to her."

He gives a hint of a laugh as if I've said something ridiculously childish. He pulls his chair in closer to his desk.

"A lot of people would like to know what happened to her."

"Including you?"

"Including me."

He doesn't ask me to sit down but I sit anyway, looking him in the eye across the desk.

"You were the last to see her alive."

"I don't think you'll find you can prove that. Always assuming she's dead, of course."

271

"What?" I look at him incredulously.

"Always assuming she didn't take herself off to some exotic place and build a new life for herself."

I despise him for that.

"Twenty-three years and no postcard?"

I look at his tanned skin and wonder how many sunshine holidays he's been on in the last twenty-three years. Skin gently warmed by shafts of sunshine, the cold trickle of guilt warmed to blood temperature. How many years did it take for the thoughts to stop, the intrusion to end, his head to come back under his own control? Mother's bones in the stiffening earth.

A pulse beats in Cory's neck.

"You don't believe she's alive. You don't believe that."

He shrugs. "Some people did."

"The police treated it as a murder inquiry. It has never been closed."

"Yes, but they never found a body, did they?"

"No, very difficult to have a prosecution if you don't have a body."

He tilts his head to one side, like he's considering an object: a painting perhaps, or a vase.

"You are very like her," he says suddenly and smiles. Cold affability, bleak as winter moorland.

"I know. My father told me."

"How is Joe?" he says smoothly.

"Less well than you. Dead."

He looks startled. "I didn't… When?"

"Last Friday."

"I see." I think he knows better than to say he is sorry. He sits very, very still. It is hard to fathom what is going on inside his head but I guess he is relieved. "You haven't said you're sorry yet. About my father. "

"I don't think I can win in this conversation, do you?"

I shrug. "Seems to me you make a habit of winning in everything."

He was alive wasn't he? On that score alone he was winning. Da never even got his three score and ten. And as for Mother...

The phone on his desk rings. He glances at it with irritation before picking it up.

"No calls just now please, Shellie." He breaks off, listens. "I see. Yes, put him through." I lean forward to his desk, pick up a photograph. His two daughters, I assume. His eyes catch mine. A warning.

"Nice," I say, the sarcasm a thin filling in a thick sandwich of sincerity.

"Hello, David," he says. His eyes flick away. "Yes, I know. She's here."

David Carruthers? Bastard. He believed in me last night. I know he did. But some time after he left me, when I was no longer there to remind him of who I was, he stopped believing and now he's warning Cory. Who did he *know* – Rebecca Connaghan or James Cory? He *knew* James Cory. The corruption of familiarity. Well, it doesn't matter. None of it matters.

"Okay, I will. Thank you David. Regards to your mother. Yes. Yes. Bye."

"Son of an old friend," he says pointedly.

"Important to have friends you can trust, people in your life who you know are *on the level*."

A blink, a slight hesitation, but no verbal response.

"My father was never very good at all that networking stuff.

273

But he was a friend of yours wasn't he, Mr Cory?"

Cory shifts slightly in his seat.

"He was an employee of a friend of mine."

"But you socialised sometimes."

"The odd occasion. I didn't know him well."

"No, I don't suppose you did. You were too busy getting to know his wife."

"Look," he says politely, without the slightest hint of anger, "is there something specific I can help you with? If not, I really do have a lot to do. I have an appointment in just a few minutes."

"Did you kill my mother?" The question hangs unanswered in the air for a second. I hold my breath. His eyes barely flicker.

"No," he says, "of course I didn't."

"Where's she buried?"

He says nothing.

"If she was murdered, who would your money be on?"

"I'm not a betting man."

"My father?"

He shrugs.

"Your father's dead. It's not for me…" He looks at me shrewdly. "But I'd say he had rather more motive than me, wouldn't you? It wasn't me your mother was leaving."

"No, but you didn't want her to leave him, did you? You just wanted to carry on with a bit on the side and not rock your cosy life. What did you talk about that last day?"

"It's a long time ago."

"Don't tell me you don't remember!"

"We talked about the future."

He must have been over this territory a hundred times with the police. But not for many years. Not with the daughter of his mistress. It doesn't seem to matter. James Cory looks completely in control.

"So what was the future?"

"We hadn't resolved it. We didn't know."

"You mean you didn't know. She was making it difficult for you, wasn't she?" I say, leaning across his desk. I cannot get to him, cannot get inside his head. Instead I want to physically enter his space now, invade his comfort zone. "Suddenly your bit on the side was getting complicated because she wanted more. Your wife didn't know about my mother, did she? You didn't want her to know."

"I don't think that's any of your business." He runs a finger softly round the inside of his shirt collar. But his voice betrays nothing.

"Did you love my mother?"

He ignores the question.

"Did you love her?"

He sighs impatiently. "I cared about her. I wished things could have been different. But that was a long time ago. Now, I really am sorry to hear about your father and I know that you must be upset… But I don't think I can be of any further help to you."

"Do you wish it was Sarah who had come to see you?"

"Who?" he says. He looks genuinely puzzled. The bastard really has forgotten her name.

"My sister."

He sits back in his chair, trying to stare me out, but I meet his gaze.

"I'm sure your sister is charming," he says, "but I cannot see what possible interest she can be of to me. Now, as I said, I don't think I can help you any more." He stands up, walks to the door and opens it.

I swing round in my chair and look at him. I am in no hurry. I will not be hurried. Cory waits. I look at him and suddenly I cannot believe it. I cannot believe how easily my faith was shaken. How can I explain this moment to you, the significance of it, the way everything changed afterwards. It was an epiphany. It was St Paul on the road to Damascus, an upsurge of faith, of belief, in the absence of any tangible proof that I can hand to others. You will accept me or dismiss me as you will.

When I look at Cory I realise that I do not know this man, and yet in some primitive place I know every signal he sends to me. Just like I knew every signal of Da's. I knew things about Da in my heart that I couldn't see with my eyes. But that doesn't mean they weren't real things. Did I know the colour of Da's guts when they spilled out? I think I did. It's just that I did what David Carruthers did. I forgot that I knew.

I knew his dark and his light. His simplicity and his complexity. The only thing I am not sure I knew was his dreams. Perhaps a daughter can never fully know her father's dreams. I think now that Mother took them with her when she died. I'm not surprised about the days he spent enveloped in that grey mist inside his own head; I'm surprised that there weren't more of them.

I walk up to Cory slowly, and things feel clearer than they have since Da left. I put my face right next to his, the way I'd watched the neds on the bus do to Khadim.

Instinctively he moves back but I move forward again, bringing my face to within an inch of his. I can smell his expensive aftershave; it masks nothing for me. I know the real stench of him. I see the bead of sweat on his top lip. There is a picture in my head of the saliva trickling down Khadim's face, and I can't help thinking how it's the wrong people who get spat on in life.

And then I smile at him, and I whisper so close to him that he must feel my breath on his face like the gentlest summer breeze. "I *know*," I whisper softly.

Triumph. It does not matter that it is won and lost in a blink. The momentary flicker of fear that flits across his eyes in that fraction of a second is more satisfying than any gobful of saliva trickling down his smooth bastard face.

CHAPTER THREE

One last visit. The tiny chemist shop in Lochglas is dark and old fashioned and smells vaguely of lavender soap and TCP. I knew they'd stock Yardley. They have an entire shelf. Soaps and talcs and perfume and thick, creamy hand lotions fragranced with lavender and sandalwood and violet and geranium. Smells of yesterday. I can only buy English Roses in a gift pack of perfume and hand lotion. I take it to the counter. An elderly lady with white, permed hair and an overall smiles at me and takes the box, carefully removing the price.

"That's a nice one," she says, "isn't it? Twelve pounds ninety-five, please."

It is cheaper than a bouquet. I take the perfume out and put it in my bag and throw the rest of the box into the back seat of the car. I drive back towards Inverness. I go past the bay but do not stop, do not glance towards the loch or wonder if Mother is in there. An act of faith.

I head for a little-used car park on the outskirts of town. The car park Cory Construction were working on when my mother was murdered. It was to be part of a shopping centre that never materialised, my landlady had told me. Phase one for a non-existent phase two. The shopping centre was moved elsewhere. Public money gone to waste. There were whispers of corruption, jobs for the boys. It stands, not a white elephant so much as a grey concrete one, dumped in the mire of its own dirt and excrement. With the shopping centre being built in a different area, the car park stands away from the heart of the city and is little used. It is only two storeys high and spray-painted graffiti, red as blood, stains one side. I park on the second storey and lock the car. Is she really buried here, encased in hundreds of tons of rubble and concrete? My mother?

I walk down a flight of stairs, lit by a flickering fluorescent strip light. The stairs are filthy, a collection of cigarette butts and crisp packets and flattened beer cans that echo in the stairwell when kicked. It is no place to die. No place to end up. I try thinking of her, not having a conversation the way I do with Da, but just thinking of her, trying to feel her round me. Despite everything, the memories that have come back over the last few days about Da, there has been nothing more about Mother. She isn't Mum or Ma or Mummy; she is just Mother. In my head, there is still only the feel of a fur collar and the vague scent of roses. I couldn't say I love her. I don't know her well enough to love her, though I certainly know some of her weaknesses. But I feel a vague… tenderness, maybe. The beginning of a love, or the end of one.

A door bangs and there are footsteps on the stairs above. I stand to the wall to let a man pass me. I hear him whistling as he reaches the bottom and another door bangs. I go right to the basement, as close to the foundations of the place as I can. It stinks. There is an empty whisky bottle on the ground and beer cans and dark patches of liquid gunge on the floor. I take out the perfume bottle from my bag and click open the top. I put my finger on the spray and walk quickly through the basement and out into the stairwell again, spraying till the mechanism chokes and the bottle is empty. Somewhere inside me, I say goodbye without using the word. It is finished. Then I throw the bottle into the corner with the whisky bottle and the cans and leave, the sickly sweet scent of roses mingling with the acrid stench of old beer and stale piss.

⚭

Crisps in the car, no time for lunch. Licking the tang of salt from my fingers, the faint, damp smear of fat on the steering wheel. Da's car, tinny with the vibration of speed.

It's a race against time to reach home, to be there for Pa's body being brought into the church. The shell of him. The *remains*, as Father Riley would say. I am not sure if I bring his spirit with me or leave it behind in the bay of Lochglas, blowing through the deserted house, whistling through the gaps in the jagged glass.

Sarah and Peggy are waiting. The anger hidden in a smile, a tear, a pained embrace. Three women, a triumvirate of grief. For the moment, the rest waits. The rapprochement breaks weakly, the watery light of a false dawn.

CHAPTER FOUR

I was shaking, Da. I hated being that close to him. I was so close I could smell him. I could see his Adam's apple. I could almost hear him swallow. But I couldn't let him know I was frightened. And I shook him, I think I really shook him. I saw it in his eyes. The funny thing is, I wasn't lying when I said I knew. I did know.

Do you know that feeling when you've lost something and you keep looking and looking for it but still you can't see it? You check the same places over and over. You get angry and frustrated and you think it's never going to turn up and you can't even think of anywhere to look any more. And then you look in one of the places you looked first and suddenly, miraculously, the thing you've lost is there after all. Right under your nose. And you can't quite believe it because you looked there, you really did. That's the way I feel now, Da. I was looking for something that I had all along, something that was never really lost.

You know what I like? I like the fact that I can never prove you didn't do it. It is almost religious, my faith, a belief in something I can't see, something I can't prove. The truth is that it is not impossible that you killed Mother. Terry Simons says you did it. James Cory, naturally, says you did it. Kirstin never said, but she thinks you did it. She thinks Mother is in the loch. And you know, even for me, it would not be so difficult to comprehend the leap from love to hate. They are intimate friends, love and hate. At first, you

281

think how could a man ever make love to, and murder, the same woman? But then you see that perhaps it can be part of the same process, the same outpouring, the same passion. Love and hate and jealousy and possessiveness. It is in those tragic photographs that appear in newspapers: husband and wife, murderer and victim. Here at a child's birthday party, there at a family wedding. They smile in those photographs, smile like they are the happiest families on earth.

So it is not impossible. But if you ask me what I believe, rather than what is possible, I cannot believe you killed Mother. I do not believe it of you for the same reason Terry Simons won't believe it of Cory. He knew Cory, he said. Well, I know you. But my knowing is sharper, wiser, truer, than theirs. I have to believe it.

I can't prove it. How can you prove someone didn't do something until you prove someone else did? And I won't waste a second of my life proving anything about Cory. People have tried for over twenty years to prove who did it. And he's not having twenty years of my life. He's had enough of what is mine already. When I looked at him today, I knew one thing for certain. If you had killed anyone, you would have killed him.

You know, Da, when you hear a song that you really like and you play it over and over and you play it just once too often? That last time you play it, you don't enjoy it, and the next time you hear it, it has begun to get on your nerves. And then finally you hear it and you wonder why you ever liked such a song. The lyrics are clichéd and the tune's trite and it might have dazzled you for a while with its clever catchiness but really, the whole thing is worthless. That's the way I feel about the idea that you killed Mother. How could I ever have seriously thought it, considered it? I'm sorry. I'm sorry I doubted you.

But there's something more, Da. It is not just that I do not believe you killed her. It's that even if you had, I cannot believe your whole life would be defined by it. Do I believe in God? I don't know. But I believe in redemption. These last few days, I've tried to imagine how I would feel if you killed her. I've rolled the idea round in my mouth, trying to taste it, like wine. Da killed Mother. Then I spat it out and waited to see what taste was left. It has taken a few days, but it is not as I expected; there is no bitterness, no rancid residue.

Murder is evil, I know that. But I've tried to think about evil, about what it is. Is it one, solitary action? If you had killed her, you would have done an evil thing. But it wouldn't have made you an evil man. There's a difference. You wouldn't be a mass murderer, a man set on doing evil all his life, a man who took pleasure in it.

What about Cory? Is he a normal person who did one evil thing, and then simply went back to normality? One thing's for sure: he certainly did go back to normality. He held onto everything in his life. He didn't pay. His marriage, his business, his position: nothing changed. You shed your life and he kept his. Burrowed deeper into his success. That's the way money works. People see nice white fingernails and they think you couldn't have done anything dirty with fingernails like those. What was it Father Peter said... repentance and penance? Cory? I don't think so.

CHAPTER FIVE

I was prepared to do a little repentance and penance with Sarah and Peggy. I dreaded talking to them. I parked around the corner for five minutes and breathed deeply before I went in. I had concocted a cover story on the long journey south, just to tide me over until I decide what to do about Sarah. But I didn't have to use it. There were no questions. I think the two of them had got together and decided all this nonsense was just my way of dealing with grief, and I don't suppose they were wrong there. Anyway, they must have discussed how to play it, because both of them just hugged me and said they were glad I was back. I was grateful for that.

Sarah and I went together to see Da at the funeral parlour. She had already been while I was in Lochglas, but she came again. I can still feel a tremor inside me, thinking about it. I was terrified of seeing him. Terrified. Sarah was calm. The parlour had that awful dimmed-light feeling the minute we walked through the door, that reverential hush that makes you crave the comfort of noise. There was a huge vase of pinks on the front reception, just browning slightly at the edges, like they had been singed with a match flame.

"We're here to see Joseph Connaghan," Sarah said quietly.

The way she said it, it sounded like we were in a hospital at visiting time, that we'd see Da sitting up in bed when we went in the room. I said nothing.

The woman in the dark suit smiled kindly and said to just wait one moment. She went to check one of the side rooms and, I guess, switch the lights on. Not much point in wasting electricity on the dead. She held the door open and motioned us to come through and Sarah squeezed my hand briefly. And then we were in there.

◦◊◦

You looked lovely, Da. Do you remember we used to joke about the Irish and the way they sit around at wakes and say ah, so and so was a beautiful corpse? You had me in stitches one night talking about some old timer who lost his wife. Remember that story? He was in the pub, chatting, and he said, "Ah sure now, Josephine was a lovely corpse," and another old timer said sure she was, but the nicest corpse he ever did see was his Anna. The fists were flying in minutes, like something out of that old John Wayne film, The Quiet Man, *that we watched on television one Christmas. My dead body is better than your dead body. But I'm not being Irish, Da: you really did look lovely.*

There was pink in your cheeks and a faint smile on your lips and your hands were clasped over your tummy. And I knew it was all fakery, the skill of the mortician, that peaceful smile and flush of pink, but I wanted to pretend it wasn't. I wanted to pretend there was something spiritual that made your body look like that, that there was some significance to it other than the undertaker's skill with blusher.

"He looks so peaceful, doesn't he?" whispered Sarah, and we held hands beside you, Da. I tried to imagine if you could see us.

I wanted to hold you; I so wanted to hold you. It was the fear stopped me, because all I could think about was the old you, the

285

softness of you and the smell of you and the warm, pumping blood in your veins, and I knew if I held you now it wouldn't be like that. Then Sarah put her head on your chest and she cuddled you, actually cuddled you, and I felt bad that she could do it and I couldn't.

"What does he feel like?" I whispered and she said softly that you were fine, that it wasn't frightening, it was just Da. There were more things to be frightened of than your own dad when he's dead, she said, and I knew it was true.

So I reached out a hand and I put my fingers on your hand. Not bravely, but tentatively, like I was touching a trap that might snap on my fingers any moment. And I felt the coldness, the feeling of hard, cold marble beneath my fingers and I gasped with it, with the sheer, awful horror of it. It was more than a gasp, like a squeal, and Sarah caught hold of me and held me up because my legs simply gave way beneath me, and I leant on the arms she placed under my oxters and let her take the weight of me because I could do nothing else. I didn't cry, I bawled with sheer fright, my mouth open, the howl silent.

"It's okay, Becca," Sarah whispered, "It's okay, it's okay, it's okay." She kept repeating it in my ear, whispering, soothing like a mother to a baby. My little sister. "It's okay, Becca. It's okay. It's okay. It's still Da, it's just Da… just Da… just Da, Becca. Ssh, ssh, ssh." She wrapped her arms round me then, not hesitantly, as she had when Tariq died, but with the confidence of a childhood left behind, of maturity. "It's just Da."

But it wasn't, Da. It wasn't you. You had looked so real somehow lying there, so much like you had when you were alive, but there was nothing human about the feel of your hand. You were cold as a slab of stone. I might as well have been touching one of those statues guarding you in the church that night.

I left then, Sarah holding me still, and we walked past reception where a woman was changing the pinks for fresh white lilies. Out into the streets where there was noise and talk and laughter and there was comfort in all of it. I didn't see the point in staying in there. You weren't there. I feel closer to you now, lying talking to you in the dark, than I did standing over your body.

What does that mean? I have no idea. Maybe tomorrow's whole process will be hocus pocus too. I don't know what to believe in. Except in you. I'm not sure I believe in a heavenly Father but I believe in my earthly one. I went looking for you both – and at least I found one of you. I have put my hands in your wounds and I believe. I know what I know. You were a good man, Da. All your life you were a good man. We came first, Sarah and I. Everything else was sacrificed.

Maybe you loved Mother too much to find another partner. But how could you anyway, with all that history, all that baggage, with everything that had to be kept secret? Easier to stay alone. Remember Betty, the widow who lived a few doors along from us? Sarah and I used to tease you that she had her eye on you, and in all honesty I think she probably did. She was a smart-looking woman, younger than you. But I stopped teasing you about her because it wasn't a comfortable joke. It just didn't seem funny. When we met her in the street, and she engaged you in conversation, I remember you spoke politely because your manners were always impeccable. But there was a distance there, an emotional distance, that I never saw any woman ever bridge. I wonder how it felt when you were alone at night. I wonder about the ache then.

It wouldn't have been possible really, would it? Not even if you'd wanted it. All those secrets. A whole other life to hide. If you'd met someone else, if you'd told them, would you have seen fear

287

in their eyes at every tiff? Would they have told me and Sarah? I can understand why none of it seemed worth it. Why you simply made do and got on. How could you find someone else who knew you well enough to know, really know, that you hadn't done it? To know the colour of your guts when they spilled inside out. Like I know now.

We brought your body to the church that night, a short ceremony in preparation for the requiem mass tomorrow. I keep thinking of you now, lying in that box in the still church with the lights out. I don't like to think of you there, abandoned amongst all the statues and shadows; the candles and the altar curtains; the coldness of stone walls. No one with you. It is a cold place to lie. I haven't abandoned you, Da. I carry you in a warmer place.

I dread tomorrow. I cannot imagine, I just cannot imagine, laying your body in the cold earth. Throwing dust on your coffin. Putting flowers on your grave. It hurts. Part of me doesn't want to stop hurting because it's the only live thing I have left, the only connection straight from me to you, an umbilical cord of pain. Once that goes, what's left?

Except love, I suppose. When I think about it, the only thing that's left from your life is your love and maybe that's the only thing worth keeping from a life anyway. I suppose I am part of your love. All these nights looking for something that endures from you and I was it all along. What lasts after you have gone? I do.

And Sarah. Because love isn't just about blood, is it? I am sorry. I've just realised that in all these conversations I've never once told you the obvious. I loved you, Da. Unconditionally. I love you still. Whatever you have or have not done.

CHAPTER SIX

Shameena brought me back from the land of the dead when she came north for the funeral. I could feel it almost immediately, the first tiny move outward from inner obsession. It was so good to see her. I did not tell her about Da, about Mother. But it was good to talk to her, to listen to her voice in response. So many of my conversations in the last few days had been monologues to Da. There were bonds between the living and the dead that had been forged and they cannot ever be broken.

I know now that time was special as well as terrible. It would stand alone like a small island in my life, one that is hard to reach again. But even back then, I knew a dead man could not be my only confidant.

⊙†⊚

Shameena made it to the church for Da's body being brought in. Khadim was there too, and Shameena said it was the first time she had seen him in eight years. Eight years! I cannot believe that level of obstinacy. They sat apart. She wouldn't come back to the house in case Khadim did. I told her not to be silly, but she said tonight and tomorrow were about Da and me, about Sarah and Peggy and Charlie, and not about her and Khadim. She wasn't going to risk any scenes. She needn't have worried. Khadim didn't come back either.

I know that she had found it hard to live without Khadim and Nazima. But she could not live without her dreams. It is the hardest thing in the world to live without dreams. She tried to do what Khadim wanted and spent a year studying accountancy, but she was dying inside. She always knew she was trying to take Tariq's place, that sooner or later she would have to live for herself. When she finally decided to leave, we planned it for weeks and weeks. Shameena was so methodical, much more so than me. She walked the music college audition, of course. It was the practicalities that took more time.

She said Khadim would chuck her out when he found out, so she had to get herself a room in a flat. I'm not sure he would have had it in him when it came down to it. Shameena lived in a tiny grotty room in Brixton, with peeling floral wallpaper and beige paint and taps that spat water with a deep-seated rumble. I visited her from time to time when I was working away, particularly the year I did a summer season in Kent. I used to go up to her place in London and buy her takeaway Chinese and we'd talk until the early hours of the morning.

Shameena was like a trapped bird that had been set free, but you know what happens to birds when you release them. They go mad, fluttering their wings wildly and battering them against every obstacle in their path until they realise they don't have to struggle. The most serious obstacle was Malik, a sharp-suited political researcher she met at a Labour Party meeting. Malik was funny and vibrant and used to tell us about being a teenager and climbing out of his bedroom window and down the drainpipe to meet girls his parents didn't approve of – which meant all girls who weren't "his kind". I was dead impressed by Malik. I thought he had broken through all the cultural restrictions imposed on him.

I was wrong, but as I've come to understand, how do you know anyone really? Malik attended lectures in his spare time on the feminist perspective of Marxism. Then he and Shameena became unofficially engaged and he suddenly turned into Khadim and started giving her a hard time about her clothes and her career, and talked about her giving up her music to have his babies. Shameena said what happened to the feminist perspective and he said he wasn't marrying a feminist perspective, was he?

Shameena was upset when it finished but she didn't need marriage. She didn't need anybody. She was happier than almost anyone else I knew. The only time she got upset was talking about Khadim and Nazima. She wrote to them once. Shameena told them she would be in Glasgow one Saturday and named a restaurant and a time. Only Nazima showed. Silent Nazima who never went anywhere alone. She told Shameena that she and Khadim never spoke about the letter. Nazima knew Khadim wouldn't go. And Khadim knew Nazima would.

On the Saturday, Nazima went and got her coat. Khadim said nothing. Shameena reckoned that if he had acknowledged where Nazima was going he would have had to forbid her, and he knew Nazima would have had to defy him, and then where would they be? So they both pretended. Khadim read a newspaper while she got her coat and her bag, as if it was every day that she went out walking on her own. But Nazima told Shameena that when she turned the corner of the street, she saw a figure at the upstairs window.

Nazima spent all lunch gripping Shameena's hand and not letting go. She had lost her son first, and now she had lost her daughter too. It was obstinacy, stupid obstinacy. She was nothing without her children. When it was time to go, she cried and cried and Shameena had to take her back home in a taxi. Nazima clung to her in the cab, and Shameena wiped her tears and promised she would write and they could meet again, but Nazima just shook her head and sobbed. She knew. Shameena said it broke her heart when the taxi drove off, leaving her on the pavement. As the cab turned, she stared at the house that had been her home, thinking of old times and wishing they were back. Wishing Tariq was back. The curtains upstairs moved slightly. She knew Khadim was watching.

Shameena said Khadim was too stubborn to ever make peace. I told her she should turn up on their doorstep and see what happened. I couldn't imagine him closing the door. She said she didn't want to embarrass him, that he had taken a stand and she could not compromise her father's dignity. I said stuff his dignity. Save dignity for the grave. But Shameena is almost as stubborn as him.

As we gathered to receive my father's body into the church, I wondered what each of them was thinking. Shameena was already successful, but I knew that one day she would be a star. When that happened, Khadim would have been proved wrong in his ambitions for her. And his pride would be a bigger obstacle than ever in their relationship. Death makes you acutely aware of seizing opportunities and I wanted them to seize theirs. You get a sense of urgency in the week after a death that is hard to hold onto. While it was still with me, I warned Shameena not to leave it much longer. Time runs out, I said. Time runs out before the right things are said and done.

CHAPTER SEVEN

Tariq comes to me in the night. In the darkness, when the pain is at its height. I am lying awake, thinking about the morning's funeral when I hear the click of the door, the creak as it opens gently. I turn then, see him standing in the light from the hall. He smiles at me but says nothing. He is slender still, but strong, a visible pulse beating in his bare chest. The hunched gauntness of him is gone; his shoulders filled out with the soft curve of muscle, the bruised blue lips now full and pink. Tariq, triumphant, the way I always imagined him.

I whisper his name and he holds out his arms to me. I do not raise myself from the bed to go to him. Tariq is strong, but I fear the vision is fragile. If I move, perhaps he will disappear. His arms remain open as he walks towards me but I lie still. His embrace is simply warmth, the slow spread of gentle heat through my body.

Then I feel his lips on my neck as he holds me to him, the gentleness hardening to need, and at last I move to grasp him, turn my lips to find his. Before I do, he is gone. It is not instant; the warmth simply dissolves until there is nothing left but an afterglow. The sadness that follows his going is blunted by a sense of wonder that Tariq came to me, that for a little while we touched. Afterwards, I drift almost instantly into sleep, as if he had administered a drug. A comforting sleep, the deepest since Da died.

A dream? I suppose it was. And yet it seemed so real. Dreams, reality… I'm not sure I know the difference any more.

⚬✦⚬

Five years on, I still do not know what I make of that 'visit' from Tariq. As soon as I wrote it down, I felt tempted to erase it, to pretend it did not happen. I know what people think when you say that stuff. You see it in their eyes: the polite enquiry that masks a certain sneer. A tiny rise of a cynical eyebrow. I know. I used to do it.

And yet, I cannot censor my own story. I have to assemble everything that happened. Give the evidence. Hope that one day, somehow, a reliable verdict will be possible.

FRIDAY

CHAPTER ONE

The weather breaks during the night before Da's funeral, the lazy heat replaced by air with a lemon-zest tang to it. There will be showers before morning is out. I went to sleep last night covered only by a sheet but I wake chilled in the early morning. Strangest of nights. The duvet is in a heap at the bottom of the bed and I pull it up round my neck and lie still; listening for the sounds of the living, waiting to bury the dead.

Funeral day. Grey skies and grey heart, dead as charred ash smouldering in the grate. I feel the same strange mixture of dread and acceptance I had when I cradled Da's head in my lap and simply waited for the end.

Footsteps on the stairs. Outside the door, the floorboards creak. Sarah. We decided we both wanted to leave for the funeral from Da's, from the family house that has been so much a part of our lives.

"Are you awake, Becca?"

Her voice is low.

"Yeah, come in."

The door creaks. Sarah sits on the end of the bed tucking her feet under her.

"Here." I move over in the narrow bed and lift the duvet back so she can sit in beside me. "Bloody hell! Your feet are like ice."

"Sorry." She smiles faintly. "I went down to the kitchen to put the kettle on and the floor is cold."

We sit side by side, leaning against the headboard.

"Want some tea?"

"If you're making it."

Through the thin, unlined curtains, clouds swirl in a fast-moving sky.

"Peggy's coming early this morning," says Sarah. "She said she'd be here at eight."

"Hours yet."

"And then hours until the church. It's going to seem like for ever."

I look up at the ceiling, at a black, damp patch on the white paper. A pipe had burst years ago and we'd never repainted it. Da never finished decorating jobs, which was why the house was always a mess. He would get out the plumb lines and the measuring tape and the sugar soap and I'd always end up leaving in exasperation. "Preparation is everything," he'd say. He spent so long on the preparation he never got to the job itself.

"I don't know how to get through this morning," says Sarah, so intensely that I feel guilty. For the last few days, while I have been off dealing with things inside myself, Sarah has been left dealing with everything else. Yet despite her practicality, I am far more ready for today than she is.

"I know," I say and squeeze her hand. I have felt a tenderness for Sarah since I found out, the tenderness of loss and regret. I am waiting to find out what else there is when that tenderness goes, what really binds us.

"Try and think only about the first five minutes, about surviving the first five minutes," I tell her. "Then the next five and the next and the next. One step at a time."

"Da really loved you," she says suddenly and I sense a hurt, a terrible deep hurt in her.

"He loved us both."

"I know. But I always felt…"

"What?"

She shrugs unable to speak. Her lips tremble. "You'd go off and work and I'd stay. Always. And yet, I felt he came alive a bit more when you came home."

There is silence. Grief is a terrible thing for making everyone take their gloves off, for revealing the dirty nails beneath the neat, kid leather.

"If you'd gone and I'd stayed," I point out, "it would have happened the other way round. It's just the prodigal son thing. Prodigal daughter."

"Maybe."

"Sarah, Da was really, really proud of you. Remember your graduation day? When he talked to me that day about you, I thought he was going to burst. His girl. A lawyer."

She smiles, a watery smile.

"Really?" she says, with a neediness that I've never heard in her before.

"I was jealous."

"You!" Sarah looks at me incredulously. "Why?"

"I never gave him that. I never made him proud in that way. I bummed around and made him worry. He always used to shake his head and say what was going to happen to me when he wasn't around. He said I'd end up an old bag lady on the streets without a home or a pension."

"What did you say?"

"I said it was okay, I'd have a rich bitch lawyer sister."

She smiles.

"Are you going to stay with Des?"

"Yeah," she says a little uneasily, smile fading. She thinks I am going to have a go at her. Instead, I nod.

"Do you love him?"

"Yeah," she says. "I do."

"Does he love you?"

"Think so. Hope so."

"Marry him, then," I say. She looks suspicious, like she thinks I'm being sarcastic, but I mean it. Life is short. Happiness is short. Take it while it's yours. "I thought you weren't keen." Her voice is curious. "You're always horrible to him."

"I am not!"

"Even last night…"

"That was just a joke!"

Des had been for a haircut so he would look smart for the funeral. Shorter at the sides but still full on top. Looked like he had a Mr Whippy on top of his head. "Nice haircut, Des," I'd said. "Do you want raspberry with that?"

"You don't exactly hide the fact that you don't like him."

"I don't *dis*like him. Not really. And anyway, what do I know? I'm heading for thirty without a proper job, without even a sniff of Mr Right. What do I know?" I repeat.

It is true. I know nothing. I always thought Des was dull, that he was old, that he wanted a trophy wife. Pretty little Sarah, ten years younger to serve up at corporate dinners. But you can't tell about others people's love, can you? You can't know, can't judge. Nobody knows what goes on between two people. Not ever.

"He's good to me, Becca," she says.

"Marry him then, and have lots of little lawyer children." I prop my pillow further up against the headboard. "Remember that advert that Ronnie Corbett used to be in when we were kids? Some car or other. And this little troop of kids, who looked exactly like him, all piled out of the back seat with their thick black glasses, just like his." I look at her sideways. "Your kids can be a little row of Cornettos."

She gives a little snort, a half-laugh in spite of herself.

"With Des, I feel like… for the first time in my life… I come first," she says hesitantly, looking to see if I am going to slap her down. "Like I'm not the second most important person, or the third most important. I'm the first. And that I don't have to prove myself, or try to make myself more interesting."

"Why on earth would you have to do that?"

"You were always more interesting than me."

"What? Don't be daft, Sarah. I have always been the one everyone sniffs disapprovingly at. The disruptive one. The ill-disciplined one. You were Saint Sarah."

She smiles.

"And you were Peggy's favourite," I add.

"I wasn't! I just did what she told me."

"That's a bad habit of yours."

Sarah laughs. "What about you? Is there anyone?"

I make a face, don't reply.

"Tariq?" she asks tentatively. "Was he…?"

"Who knows."

I say it more dismissively than I mean to but I can't talk about Tariq. Not today. Maybe not ever. Sarah flushes slightly.

"Maybe," I add, more softly, and she looks gratefully at me. She smiles comfortingly like she understands. I think maybe she does.

Is it emotionally stunted to say someone you knew at sixteen, someone you kissed only once, might be the best there is? I can't ever know what Tariq would have been, and that is both burden and comfort. What was there was unfulfilled, and that makes it perfect, brimming with possibilities, not spoiled by twenty years of disappointment, of expectations that never materialised. And yet, somehow I believe that there was more. That love is strange and unpredictable and timeless.

In the silence, I lift Sarah's hand from the duvet and squeeze it gently. She looks surprised.

"It's going to be awful today but we will get through it all together," I say.

She nods. "Want the first shower?"

"No, you go on. I'll make the tea."

I watch her as she goes out, with her honey hair and almond shaped eyes, her peaches-and-cream skin. She is slender and perfect, fragile as a china doll. I could smash her in pieces. I know it, and I don't know what to do. I really don't.

CHAPTER TWO

I should have known that Peggy putting her arms round me and saying, "Glad you're back dear," wasn't the end of it. That was for show. For Sarah.

She arrives at seven, not eight, while Sarah is in the shower. Charlie is with her, looking tense and uneasy. He has on the dark suit he used to wear for the office, and a white shirt with a black tie, but he's put on a few more pounds since retirement and it all looks tight and uncomfortable. The jacket barely meets round his ample middle and his face is pink, like his tie is tied too tight around his collar. Peggy walks right by me and into the living room, but Charlie hugs me. He doesn't say anything but he pats my shoulder. I look at him and he raises his eyes in Peggy's direction. He's very expressive, Charlie, without ever actually saying anything. I sometimes wonder if you added up all the words he's ever spoken, how many pages he'd fill.

Peggy is looking out the window when I walk into the sitting room, her shoulders hunched and tense. Her body has developed that wizened look of old age, some time when I wasn't looking.

"Want some tea, Peggy?" I ask.

She doesn't sit but she turns from the window.

"Where did you go when you went north, Becca?"

Silence. Charlie sits down heavily in the armchair, his eyes darting unhappily from one of us to the other.

"Inverness."

"Nowhere else?"

I nearly say no but suddenly I've had enough of secrets.

"Lochglas."

Peggy looks stricken, like someone fired a bullet straight into her belly. She looks at Charlie and he nods his head, motioning to her with his hands to calm down.

"Sit down, Peg," he says quietly. "Come on now."

"You know?" Peggy says, looking straight at me.

I nod. She falls into the sofa, like her legs can't support her own body any more. She has lost weight in the last few days, and her face seems angular and fox-like and I feel a surge of affection for her. Peggy had been short and sharp and nervous all through our lives, but she is tender too, and I have loved her for that. But I have never loved her more than now, because now I understand the extent of her loyalty to Da in all those years.

"What are you going to do?" she asks. "We have to talk quickly before Sarah…"

"I don't know," I say honestly, and her face crumples. She is too old for this, I think. I sit beside her on the sofa and take her hand.

"How did you know to go to Lochglas?"

"The bureau."

"I knew it, Charlie," she says, looking accusingly at him.

"Peggy," I say softly, but she can't look at me.

"He tried so hard to protect you," she says.

"I know."

"He didn't want you to know. He didn't want you to carry this in your life. It was such a terrible burden for him, trying to keep it secret."

"A terrible burden for you both."

I stroke her hand. It is so thin and fragile. I can feel the raised veins on the surface. They spread hard and blue like a skinny little bird's claws under the skin.

"Joe, oh Joe," she whispers, rocking back and forward in her seat. "Joe…"

I hold her now while she rocks. "Peggy, please don't get upset," I murmur against her head.

"He deserved so much more. Joe was worth more. I warned him from the start about Kath. I saw what she was. We all saw what she was. But not Joe. He just couldn't see it. She had him on a string and she dangled him this way and that. He was a fool where Kath was concerned."

"Peggy," says Charlie warningly.

"She was a tramp."

"She was Becca's mother," says Charlie firmly.

"Didn't she love him at all?" I ask. The question isn't anything to do with Mother. I just want to be reassured that Da knew love, however briefly.

"She loved herself," says Peggy.

"Peg, that's not fair," protests Charlie. "She did love him in her own way."

"Sure, for five minutes."

Charlie sighs and loosens the tie round his neck, undoing the top button of his shirt.

"What was Da like when… How did he cope when she, you know… disappeared?" I ask.

Peggy's eyes shoot from her lap up to my face.

"Your dad didn't lay a finger on her, Becca."

"No, I just mean, what happened that day?"

"She just never came home. Joe phoned me around half seven that night. I remember because Charlie had worked late and we had just finished the dinner and were sitting down to watch *Coronation Street*. Weren't we, Charlie?" she says, and Charlie half smiles.

"Then the phone rang," she continues. "It was Joe but I couldn't make out a word he was saying. Poor Joe." She shakes her head. "He was in a terrible state. Sarah was bawling in the background and he was trying to mix formula milk. He was crying and saying Kath hadn't come home. He didn't know what he was doing."

"Did you know about Cory then?"

"Oh, I knew all right. I had gone up there when he first found out about Cory and… and the baby. Kath had gone off into a fancy hotel for a week and I came to help with you. Cory paid for the hotel, of course. Said she needed some time to think, but I thought he wanted to get her on her own and convince her to have an abortion. Joe told her to have the baby and he would be a father to it. He would clean up her mess as usual." She shakes her head bitterly.

"I told Joe, I told him not to take her back. I said he was being a fool and she would end up leaving him but he wouldn't listen. He was mad for her. Always had been. She drove him crazy with that separate bed stuff when the affair with Cory took off. It was her way of controlling him, of dangling him on a string."

I feel my cheeks flush. Charlie glances apologetically at me. Peggy is talking almost to herself.

"There was no question about who the baby's father was. Joe hadn't slept with her for months. Hadn't been allowed to. But

306

he held on, thinking the affair would fizzle out, that Kath would come back to him. And when she got pregnant, Joe said he could learn to love the baby even though it wasn't his, because it was Kath's. But she had to choose between them. He was thrilled when she said they could make another go of it. But she did exactly what I told him she would do. Went back to Cory."

"When he phoned you that night, what did he think had happened to her?"

"He thought she'd gone off with Cory. He phoned Cory's house but Cory claimed he had no idea where she was. I told Joe I'd be up on the first train the next morning. Charlie dropped me at the station on the way to work. I stayed up there for the rest of July and the first week of August. Charlie used to come up at weekends. It was an awful time. It just went on and on and on. More and more stories and less and less news. Your father was taken in for questioning by the police fifteen times over those two months. I suppose Cory was too. And David Carruthers. The police knew about Cory long before the papers did. But they just couldn't get the lead they needed. Eventually we left and came back to Glasgow but I went back later on that month. Then Joe left for good."

"On the twenty-fifth of August," I say. Peggy has her handkerchief half to her nose but she freezes in surprise. "How did you know that?"

"There was an article in the library. And I spoke to Kirstin."

"To Kirstin!" Peggy's body stiffens. "She's still there? What did she say?"

"She told me what happened. How she doubted Da. She said she was sorry."

"Bit bloody late for that."

307

"She lost her sister," says Charlie unexpectedly. Peggy and I both swivel round to him. He'd been quiet so long, we'd almost forgotten he was there.

"She lost her sister," he repeats gently, looking at Peggy.

"And I lost my brother," says Peggy. "You saw him, Charlie. You were there." Her voice begins to shake. "Though you weren't there the night we came back to Glasgow. I'll never forget how Joe was that night as long as I live. The state of him."

They had driven down from Glasgow late at night, the day Da spoke to Kirstin. He couldn't bear to be there a minute longer, according to Peggy. She tried to persuade him to stay a few days and pack up the house properly but he wouldn't. He said the house felt dirty and he wanted none of it. He didn't ever want to see it again and he didn't want anything from it, or Lochglas, or Kath's family. He threw some things in a couple of suitcases, put me and Sarah in our pyjamas and lifted us into the car in the dark.

They drove in silence, Peggy says. Until somewhere round Aviemore a song came on the radio. Percy Sledge. It was 'their' song – my parents' song when they were dating. How strange for me to hear that. Da pulled into a lay-by and simply broke. Peggy tried to calm him down but he was inconsolable. Eight years, he kept saying. That's all he had got out of a lifetime.

"I said he still had a lifetime but he wouldn't hear of it," says Peggy. "Not without Kath, he kept saying. It was over. He got a bit hysterical then and stumbled away, over to the bushes. I tried to stop him, but he shook me off, and I saw him leaning against a tree and heard him retching."

I don't cry, listening to Peggy. The pain is deep and tearless. It is hard trying to picture Da, controlled, quiet Da, in that state. I try to imagine what he was feeling. The darkness. The fear. The fear, not just of losing Mother but of being blamed. Of being constantly interrogated by the police. Of being father to two children on his own for the rest of his life. And maybe worst of all, the fear of knowing that he had been given his life's share of love already. It was over.

"You woke up," Peggy says. "In the back of the car. Your dad could hear you crying and he came back. He was white and shivering, though it wasn't cold. I hadn't realised how thin he'd got. He lost two stone that summer. I said to him, 'Joe, in the back of that car are the women you're going to have to love now.'"

"What did Da say?"

"He just lifted you up and comforted you, and then he started up the engine and you went back to sleep with the noise of it, the movement." Peggy sits back on the sofa, puts her head back against the cushion.

"We talked then. About what he was going to do. I tried to persuade him to get an accountancy job in Glasgow but for some reason he didn't want to know. I couldn't understand it. What was the point of that? I told him he had two kids to support and he'd be better paid in his own profession, but he said money was nothing to him. It was a new life he wanted. A new start. He didn't want anything from the old life. He didn't ever want to talk about it. I said well, he would have to talk about it because what was he going to tell you and Sarah when you were older? And Joe said, 'Nothing.' He was going to tell you nothing."

She takes my hand this time, and we sit side by side on the sofa, fingers entwined.

"And he never did. He wanted you and Sarah to be happy, Becca. He didn't want you to carry this. It was bad enough that you would be growing up without a mother. We knew what that was like, me and Joe. Joe loved Mammy. We both did but Joe…" She stops again, unable to speak for a moment. "On Mammy's funeral day, he lay on her coffin and told Daddy he wanted to go with her. He was so intense, Joe."

Her thumb is rubbing little circles on my hand.

"He knew there was going to be pain for you both but he wanted to minimise it, to make it only the pain of not having a mother. Not the pain of having a mother who was murdered. Or the pain of having a father who had never been able to prove he didn't kill her. I promised him that I'd help. That you would never know from me."

"But Sarah?" I say.

"He was hers," she says vehemently, and for a second I am confused and think, illogically, that she means Sarah was biologically Da's child. "He loved her like she was his."

"Did he ever think about not taking Sarah with him? Leaving her to Cory or to Kirstin?"

"Cory?" spits Peggy. "You think Cory would have claimed her? And if he had, you think your dad would have left her with him? A man like that?" She shakes her head. "Joe felt that Sarah was Kath's, not Corey's. He loved Kath and he would love Sarah. Simple as that."

It isn't simple, I think, as I look out the window at the trees swaying in the growing breeze. It isn't simple at all.

Peggy squeezes my hand tight. "Becca, you can't tell Sarah… Please…"

"I don't want to tell her, Peggy," I say. I am confused, unable to think clearly. "But doesn't she have a right to…?"

"What would be the point?" demands Peggy. She shakes my

hand agitatedly. "What would be the point of telling her that the man she loved, that she's grieving for, was not her dad really? What's the point?"

"But it's about who she is, Peggy, it's her right…"

"You can't," she interrupts.

"People have the right to know where they come from."

"You *can't*," repeats Peggy, and her voice is squeaky with emotion. "Don't you see? It would be like your father's whole life was for nothing. All the sacrifices. All the pain. Trying to protect you. It would be for nothing. For *nothing*."

Her voice is getting louder. I can hear Sarah moving about in the room above us. Charlie stands up from the armchair and goes over to the sofa.

"Peg," he says, and he lifts her to her feet. He puts her head against his chest and she doesn't resist. Charlie wraps his arms right round her and she disappears into him, crying softly. "Shhh, now," he says gently. "Shhh. You've done what you can, Peg. You've done your best. Always done your best. Becca will have to do what she thinks best now. She'll do what she thinks is right." For Charlie, it is a long speech.

Sarah comes in the room. She begins to say something, then sees Peggy crying against Charlie's chest and stops.

"Come on, " I say, and pull Sarah gently from the room. "Let's go and make Peggy and Charlie some breakfast."

CHAPTER THREE

The roar of the hairdryer is irritating yet also strangely comforting. Da is to be buried this morning and nothing should feel comfortable. The noise assaults me, leaving my senses jangling. Then a lighter tone. I switch off. My phone. I scramble for my bag, emptying it out onto the duvet. A call, not a text. I think it's going to stop ringing before I manage to get to it.

"Hello?"

There is a silence, just long enough to be unnerving, then a voice that is vaguely familiar says, "Rebecca?"

"Yes?"

"It's David."

My brain does not move immediately into gear.

"David Carruthers."

"Hello David." My voice registers my surprise.

"You got back home safely."

He sounds strangely subdued.

"The funeral is today."

"I'm sorry. I… I shouldn't be phoning but…"

"It's okay." I feel alarmed and I don't know why.

"Rebecca, it was me."

I sit down suddenly on the edge of the bed, my mind making an illogical leap. For one stupid moment, I think he means it was he who murdered my mother but of course, that doesn't make sense.

"What was you?" My voice is sharp, rising more aggressively than I mean it to.

"The texts. The Islands."

"What?

"I'm sorry."

But…" I turn towards the dressing-table mirror, suddenly catching sight of my own, unguarded reflection, incredulity etched into my face. None of this seems to fit.

"But I got the first text before I met you."

"You phoned the office. My mother got the message and I knew I had to do something, the state of her… Rebecca she's ill. I wanted you to just go away and not ask questions so I sent a text hoping it would unnerve you. Then I phoned you at the guest house to make sure. I didn't plan to meet you, but…"

He means it. It was him. Fury sweeps over me as the reality sinks in.

"You bastard."

He says nothing.

"You fucking terrified me at those Islands."

"Rebecca, I wouldn't have touched you. You weren't in any real danger, I promise you. I liked you."

"You liked me? You *liked* me, you little fucker!" I jump up from the bed, unable to keep still. I am shaking with anger, my hand trembling so much that the phone knocks lightly against the metal of my hooped earring. I am aware of the noise but somehow can't think what to do to stop it.

"Listen…"

"I should get the police to you."

"Please don't. Please… I know I shouldn't have phoned but…"

"So why did you phone? To be forgiven? Fucking forget it!"

"Rebecca, I phoned to explain but also to warn you."

Something inside me goes cold. I stop suddenly, in the middle of the room, listening.

"James Cory," he says.

"What about him?"

"He… I think you…" I hear him sigh in frustration. "Look, I need to tell you this from the start. Please just listen. *Please*."

"You'd better be quick." I look at my watch. "You might have forgotten, but I've got a funeral to go to."

He ignores my hostility.

"When you phoned the office looking for my father, I did really want you to leave because my mother was so upset about the whole thing being raised again. It had been a terrible episode in my parents' lives, and she does suffer from mental illness, so she really was in a state that this was all going to be dragged up again. That bit was absolutely true."

I say nothing. I don't feel the need to give him any verbal encouragement because I'm still furious.

"My father… I told you that he once spoke to me about the whole thing."

The rain pattering gently against the bedroom window suddenly intensifies and I look over at the patterns of raindrops against the glass. So welcome after the heat.

"Rebecca, are you still there?"

"Yes."

"There was one thing I didn't tell you."

"What?"

"It might be nothing."

"*What*?"

"The week before your mother's murder, James was in the

process of setting up his office in Glasgow. He and my father had a business trip together round the same time." He hesitates. "My father said it might be completely irrelevant but... well, they were away three days and had gone to the hotel bar each night. On the final night, James said he was having an early night because of the journey next day. My father agreed but found he was a bit restless and decided, on a whim, to go out for half an hour to a small bar near the hotel. He saw James there."

"So...?"

"It might be nothing, really..."

"David, what are you trying to tell me?

"James was sitting at a table, deep in conversation with a man."

"Who?"

"My dad didn't know. It wasn't anyone he recognised. He said there was something about the way they were talking that seemed a bit odd."

"Why odd?"

"Nothing he could put his finger on. Just a general impression. The way they were sitting. The body language."

"Helpful."

He sighs.

"So what happened?"

"James put his hand in his inside pocket as if he was looking for something but at that point, the barman asked Dad if he wanted a drink and he got distracted."

"So he never saw what Cory took out of the pocket?"

"No – if he took anything out. Anyway, when Dad looked back, James caught sight of him. He had the distinct impression James wasn't pleased to see him. The striking thing was how quickly James got up and left the guy when he saw Dad. It was clear he didn't want to introduce him."

"And…?"

"That's it really. I told you it might be nothing."

It was hard to make sense of this.

"How did Cory explain the fact that he wasn't having an early night?"

"He said that he'd had an unexpected call from a business associate – something to do with the new office – so he'd agreed to meet this man late on because they were leaving early in the morning to drive back to Inverness. It sounded perfectly plausible and my father didn't think any more about it. He and James walked back to the hotel together, then had a nightcap in the hotel bar after all, before heading for bed. It was only later, after your mother died, that Dad found himself wondering again about who the man was."

I don't even know why he's telling me this. Then a bell begins to ring in my head. A newspaper story I read about a man who arranged to have his business partner killed. The attempt was botched but he was later charged with attempted murder. The basis of the prosecution was that he was filmed the week before on a hotel's CCTV, handing over money in a bar. A hitman. A clean way of killing. A way you get no blood under the fingernails, just as Jackie Sandford suspected. But of course, there was no CCTV back then to capture James Cory's actions.

"Rebecca?"

It was the final piece of the jigsaw.

"I'm thinking."

"Anyway, my father never said anything to the police."

"Why not?"

"Because it could have been exactly what James claimed. And because James was his friend and he didn't want to complicate his position by mentioning something that might have been completely irrelevant."

"And might not…"

"And might not," Carruthers agrees, his voice subdued. "Anyway, before I met you…"

"That's the bit I don't get," I say belligerently. "You actually met me… We talked… We walked by the river… Christ, I nearly…"

"That was real."

"How can it have been real when the next night you terrified the life out of me?"

"Rebecca, listen! I did that for a reason. Please try to… Before I met you, I contacted James and told him you were in town. We were old family friends and I thought you were just some nuisance who was going to open old wounds and stir up something that our families were glad to put behind us. I just wanted you to go away. But there was something about James's reaction that… well, it unnerved me."

"What?"

"I don't know. Just an instinct. There was something not right. That's all I can say, Rebecca. Something that combined in my head with the story my father told me. I know that my father wondered about that incident, in his later years especially. And then I met you and I began to think, what if James had been involved? What would he do to you? I wanted you to go home, but I knew you wouldn't. You're not the type to back off. I could tell that."

"For fuck's sake, David! What did you think Cory was going to do to me?"

317

But even asking the question makes me shiver suddenly. The silence that follows scares me.

"I needed you to go home," David says eventually.

I sit back down on the edge of the bed. We both know what James Cory is capable of. David Carruthers had told me he didn't believe Cory was capable of murder. But his actions suggest otherwise. When the chips were down, he followed his instinct. "Rebecca…?"

"What?"

"I said, can you forgive me?"

There is action, and there is motivation, and sometimes one is wrong and sometimes both are wrong. But, however wrong David Carruthers got the action, he has taken a huge emotional risk in phoning me, a risk that shows that he believes in me more than Cory. That moment at the river… Perhaps it had been real after all.

"Why did you phone today? Why did you tell me all this?"

"Because… because I didn't like the idea that I had frightened you and that you might think you were still under threat. I wanted you to know you weren't in real danger, that there wouldn't be any more texts, and that nobody would follow you home."

Shit. That hadn't even occurred to me. "But I also want to make sure you leave this now, that you don't go near James again. And yes, I admit that's partly for my mother's sake." He pauses. "But it's for yours too."

"Is Cory… Do you think he…?"

"No. I think he thinks that you've gone and that it's over. It *is* over, isn't it?" There is an appeal in his voice.

I suppose it is, but I don't answer.

"Another thing," he says.

"There's more, David? I'm not sure I can handle it." Sarcasm is my default setting. I can't help it.

"When I phoned and you were in James's office…"

"Yes."

"I had only called again to tell him I'd met you, that I didn't think you would be sticking around. I wanted him to think you were just a grieving daughter up here on a passing whim. I didn't want him near you. I told him you'd seen Terry Simons and were beginning to see that your father was most likely the guilty one."

"What did he say?"

"That he was glad you had realised the truth."

I smile grimly.

"Oh, I realised the truth all right."

"I told him you were going home, tried to make out you were no threat."

"And was I? A threat?"

"Yes, I think you probably were," he says slowly. "Did you find anything else out after we met?"

He sounds curious. But can I trust him? Maybe this is all a ruse. Maybe Cory is making him phone to find out what I know.

"I found out what I already knew. My father did not kill my mother."

"That's good, Rebecca. You have peace then. But you can't prove it, so please leave it now. Let it lie. Don't come back here."

"Not very friendly of you, David," I say mockingly.

"I want you to be safe."

I feel weary suddenly. The early rise. All the emotional tension. The ordeal still ahead. I let myself fall backwards onto the bed and stare at the ceiling.

"I wish…" he says.

319

"What?"

"I wish things could be different. That I could see you again."

For a moment, I realise how easy it would be in other circumstances to build something in the north. The little threads that might amount to strong connections. My aunt Kirstin and her family. David Carruthers. The possibility of another life. But he is right. It can't be pursued.

"Yes," I agree vaguely. It is tempting, but maybe I have finally learned some sense. I don't add an invitation to contact me when he is next in Glasgow.

I glance at my watch and sit up again.

"I have to go."

"Good luck," he says. "And I'm sorry. Really."

"Goodbye, David," I say.

For a moment after I hang up, I lie still on top of the bed, listening to the rain. There is something about David Carruthers that reminds me of Father Dangerous. He liked me enough to take a serious emotional risk. But not quite enough to be truly courageous.

❦

The memories are rolling to an end. The song Shameena sang at the funeral is coming up again on the CD, and this time I will finally switch off when it finishes. I do not know how many times I have listened in the last few weeks, but I know it will be some time before I listen again.

I would love to tie this up neatly now. Present it in a gift-wrapped box. I would love to say that I tracked down that mystery man in the hotel. I would love to say that I confronted him, that he crumbled and confessed to killing my mother. But life isn't like that, is it? The mystery man is probably dead, for a start. But there is something important to remember. Just because you can't prove something, doesn't mean it's not true.

Here's my truth. My mother thought she was being daring when she met James Cory for lunch. Bet she dressed really nicely that day, took extra care with her makeup. Bet she was skittish with it all, the way she was going to manipulate him, get what she wanted, pressurise him to leave his wife. I keep thinking of Jackie Sandford saying she was laughing with nerves and excitement afterwards. She knew she'd pushed it. But the truth was, it didn't matter what she'd said. Her fate had already been sealed the week before. She just didn't know it yet. They talked over lunch. Cory got angry. He didn't like someone else taking control. He didn't like what she was saying about corruption and the council contracts and the Masons. But he tried to placate her. He agreed to leave his wife because he knew he'd never actually have to do it. Then he left her to her fate, knowing he would never see her again. What did he think about as he walked back to his office? What did he feel? Doubt? Guilt? Or just relief? Does a psychopath get normal emotions mixed in with the madness? Meanwhile, my mother phoned Jackie Sandford. Then she phoned my father, who fell apart and drove to the loch to end his life. But he couldn't. And while he was doing that, the man in the bar, the nameless, faceless assassin, did the work he was paid to do.

I wish I knew exactly where… how… but those details are not mine to know. Life has unanswered mysteries. Her car was abandoned, so my guess is that she was bundled into another vehicle. Her life probably ended as my father drove to terminate his. But we stopped him, me and Sarah. I know we did. He thought of us.

Proof? I can't prove it. I can't produce a body, though I know

321

it's in the foundations of an Inverness car park. I can't produce DNA from the murderer, though I know the real murderer is Cory. But what I tell you, I believe to be true. I knew Da and you didn't. You have to decide for yourself whether you believe what I tell you. Whether you believe in him. Sometimes in life, we are forced to take things on faith.

CHAPTER FOUR

The church is cold when we arrive at 9.30, half an hour before the service. Father Riley says he has switched the heating on, and after a while the water begins to rumble through the old radiators. More noise than heat. They are barely warm, even when the rumbling stops and the heat is supposedly through.

Some wreaths have been delivered and left in the porch at the back of the church and we read the messages, murmuring amongst ourselves in low voices, though there is no one else here to hear. We bring them down to the front of the church and place them on the coffin. I want to hug that polished wooden box in the way I wasn't able to hug Da in the funeral parlour. I think of Da as a little boy, lying across his mother's coffin. I understand that need. But of course, I don't do anything. I lay the flowers on the top and let my hand linger there when no one is watching.

Sarah and I have sent one with deep red roses and white lilies and sprays of fragile white gypsophila. Baby's breath, the florist said it was called. Sarah and I liked that. I used the deposit for the holiday Da and I were supposed to be going on to pay my half. I wanted flowers everywhere.

You can smell the sweetness of them as soon as you walk through the door. Beautiful tall white lilies, with creamy heads and flashes of lime green in the elegant petals that blend perfectly with simple fern. Classy. It had to be something classy, I had told Sarah. Da came from nowhere, from a peasant crop of rocky land, but he was the classiest man I ever knew.

I always think of Tariq when I see lilies. The slenderness of them, the beauty. When Tariq went, it was like losing the possibility that life could be special. The vibrancy of a favourite colour; the crispness of fresh cotton sheets; the heartbeat of excitement; the explosion of a favourite taste in the mouth. Losing Tariq was like losing the colour of a painting. But losing Da is like losing the outline, the bit that holds everything up. His going is incomprehensible. He has simply always been.

Khadim is first to arrive, twenty minutes early. From the church door, I see him walk across the grounds, rolling slightly as he walks and puffing with the exertion. Khadim is getting older too. I feel a surge of tenderness for him. It isn't the coffin or the flowers or even the painful emotion of talking to Peggy that makes the first, hot tears of the day sting in my eyes. It is the sight of Khadim's best suit and his big domed tummy encased in a waistcoat and a gold chain. It is the respect for Da that I see reflected in the inky blackness of his shiny shoes, so carefully polished.

He looks sad, as the elderly do when they attend funerals, when they begin to feel like they are among the last people of their generation alive. But he is anxious too.

He doesn't know what to do in the church, he whispers to me. He doesn't know what to do during the service. Just watch me, I tell him softly. Stand when I stand, and sit when I sit, and you'll be fine. I squeeze his arm and say thank you for coming, Da would have been so pleased, and he gives me a little awkward hug and clears his throat noisily.

There is a steady trickle after that and then a little rush at five to ten and we acknowledge everyone at the back as they arrive.

324

There aren't many words, just 'I'm so sorry', over and over again, and I feel sorry for them having to talk to us when there is nothing to be said. Shameena is among the last. I hug her when she arrives.

"Thank you," I whisper, and she says nothing but leans her head against mine and holds me.

"I wore my salwar kameez," she says as we hug, "instead of black. Your dad loved colour."

"Perfect," I say, looking at the rich, deep, electric blue, edged with gold. And it is.

I watch her walk down the church, hesitate at the pew where Khadim sits. He glances up and I hold my breath. His body moves, almost imperceptibly, making room for her, and I am glad.

Sarah and I sit together, with Peggy beside Sarah, and Charlie beside me. We rise and fall like puppets on strings, without thought, without meaning. We kneel. We pray. We sing. We stand. We sit. We listen.

"Joseph Connaghan was a fine Catholic man," says Father Riley, "beloved father of Rebecca and Sarah. It is with Joseph's family that our thoughts are today." It means nothing. My eyes are drawn continually to the wooden box on the stand at my side. I keep thinking of the shell in there, the shell without the spirit. Where is his spirit? But even if the shell is all that remains, I refuse to believe that all of Da is destroyed. There is something of him in me, even in Sarah. Something that is nothing to do with blood.

Sarah and I don't look at one another as we stand side by side. But I can feel her. I can feel the stiffness of her in the moments when she struggles to hold everything together. I can feel her love for him. A tear falls from where she stands, dripping onto the hymn book in her hand, and I squash my arm up against hers and take a tissue from my pocket with a tiny movement and hand it to her, and with a tiny movement she takes it and I feel the pressure of her shoulder back.

I look at our wreath of roses on his coffin, Sarah's and mine, and the closed circle of flowers. Sarah and me, a whole circle. Roses and lilies; different but complementary. It's the moment when I know we are stripped: the thick varnish gone, the underlying layers removed. The thud of the bottom of the barrel. Peggy was right. He was her father. He was her father in everything but blood and cells and DNA. And what was that when it came to love? Cory had blood and cells and DNA to match Sarah's. What he had was nothing to what Da had.

The offertory. A slow procession carrying bread and wine to the altar as the small parish choir sings.

"Love one another, I have loved you, and I have shown you how to be free."

It could be Da talking, and perhaps it is. Things will never be the same again, but I know who I am, where I came from. I am free to be whoever I am going to be. But Sarah? How do I love her? How do I free her? By telling her the truth or by telling her nothing? Sarah is my sister but she isn't me. I needed to know the truth. She didn't. Da knew that. He loved us both in different ways and he wanted different things for us. Maybe he has been talking to me all along. Leading me to Lochglas, giving me answers. I just didn't hear him because I didn't know how to listen to the dead, how they talked. I was talking to him inside my head and maybe he was answering in there too.

326

"Heavenly Father," Father Riley is saying, "give us, today, the strength..." The words become a distant drone, like the drone of bees on a summer's day as you drift off to sleep on a garden chair.

The summer rain begins again, a faint pattering on the church roof. A shuffled queue for communion, silently filing past the coffin. I turn and see Khadim. He is wiping his eyes with a cloth handkerchief, and I turn my head back. The queue is gone, seats resumed. Father Riley takes his seat on the altar and waits, and I nod to Shameena. She walks to the front of the church in that glorious blue and gives a tiny bow, not to the altar, but to Pa's coffin. A nod of respect.

In just a few minutes the flowers will be lifted from the wood. The pall bearers will raise Da to their shoulders and we will take him to the earth. The petals on the wreaths will drip with rain, the ink on the messages running to a blur. But I hope he is listening, wherever he is, that he will hear my message clearly, my song, for him. Shameena stands at the altar and nods to the organist and the first notes of Puccini fill the church. I know she will silence the nightingale. I wonder if she sings for Khadim as much as she sings for Da. Her voice soars halfway to heaven, up, up to the rafters. It is clear and sweet and true and it pierces my heart.

"*O mio babbino caro,*" she sings. "Oh My Beloved Father."

ACKNOWLEDGEMENTS

With sincere thanks to Ben Yarde-Buller for good advice, good cheer, and great support over the years. It has all been so much appreciated.